STAGESTRUCK

A SADDLE CREEK BOOK

STAGE

STRUCK

A SADDLE CREEK BOOK

Shelley Peterson

Illustrations by Marybeth Drake

KEY PORTER BOOKS

TO MY MOTHER, JOYCE DRAKE MATTHEWS,
WHO IMPARTED TO ME HER GREAT LOVE OF LITERATURE
AND INSPIRED THE CHARACTER OF JOY FEATHERSTONE.

TO MY DECEASED GRANDMOTHER, MARY SNODGRASS DRAKE,
WHO HAD A DRAMATIC HEART AND ENCOURAGED
MY EVERY STEP UPON THE STAGE.

National Library of Canada Cataloguing in Publication Data

Peterson, Shelley, 1952–
    Stagestruck / Shelley Peterson

ISBN 978-1-55470-323-4

I. Title.

PS8581.E8417S73 2010   jC813'.54   C2010-901893-1

ONTARIO ARTS COUNCIL
CONSEIL DES ARTS DE L'ONTARIO

The publisher gratefully acknowledges the support of the Canada Council for the Arts and the Ontario Arts Council for its publishing program. We acknowledge the support of the Government of Ontario through the Ontario Media Development Corporation's Ontario Book Initiative.

We acknowledge the financial support of the Government of Canada through the Book Publishing Industry Development Program (BPIDP) for our publishing activities.

Key Porter Books Limited
Six Adelaide Street East, Tenth Floor
Toronto, Ontario
Canada M5C 1H6
www.keyporter.com

Text design and electronic formatting: Martin Gould
Printed and bound in Canada
10 11 12 13 14 5 4 3 2 1

Mixed Sources
Product group from well-managed forests, controlled sources and recycled wood or fiber
www.fsc.org Cert no. SW-COC-002358
© 1996 Forest Stewardship Council

ANCIENT FOREST ™
FRIENDLY

DAUPHIN: . . . When I bestride him, I soar, I am a hawk: he trots the air; the earth sings when he touches it; the basest horn of his hoof is more musical than the pipe of Hermes. . . .his neigh is like the bidding of a monarch, and his countenance enforces homage.

—*Henry V,* Act III, Scene vii

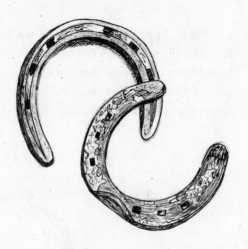

If you stand high on the cliffs behind Saddle Creek Farm, the shape of the river below forms the outline of a saddle. The water twists and winds its way through the rocky, dramatic landscape of the Niagara Escarpment in Caledon, connecting all who cross its well-worn path.

Wild animals—deer, raccoons, squirrels, porcupines, coyotes, and fox—come to drink. Hawks and owls compete for field mice, and song-birds trill in the treetops. Beavers dam off sections to build their homes, and fish are plentiful in the cold, deep pools.

If you were to paddle a canoe down the creek from the Grange to King Road, you'd pass Owen Enterprises, Merry Fields, the Malones, Hogscroft, Bradley Stables, and, of course, Saddle Creek Farm. It is a tightly knit community—a place where people care deeply for one another, and for the land around them. It is also a community that is passionate about its horses.

And what horses! Those in the area are famed for their talent and strength: the legendary Dancer; Sundancer; Moonlight Sonata. All were foaled within walking distance of Saddle Creek, and all have carried themselves and their riders to victory—both in the ring, and beyond. Some wonder what secret the area holds, to bring forth such amazing creatures. Some say it's in the water.

STAGESTRUCK

PROLOGUE

DANCER

DANCER WANTED ACTION. He paced back and forth along the fence in the field behind Hogscroft. There was sweet spring grass, a new blue salt lick, and a full water trough, but the once-mighty chestnut stallion was restless. Dancer filled his lungs with moist air, then snorted aloud. Tossing his magnificent head proudly, he swept his tangled mane over his arched neck. He bucked and bucked again, kicking high and punching out his back legs savagely. Pawing the ground with his front right hoof, he shook his head in frustration.

Dancer yearned for something more than these peaceful surroundings. He remembered the days when his mistress exercised him daily, practised challenging courses of jumps, and hacked him for miles down the roads to keep him fit.

She didn't come to ride him anymore.

Up Dancer reared, thrusting and jabbing with his front legs, hopping on his powerful rear legs. Angry and agitated, he let out a deep and resonant bellow that echoed through the Caledon hills. Down he dropped with a heavy thud. He tore off at full speed, tail high and head down, bucking like a rodeo bronco.

Christine James watched anxiously from the barn, where she'd been cleaning tack. The leather on the saddles and bridles was turning green from disuse. The slim, attractive, fifty-year-old woman held her breath as Dancer raced toward the highest part of the stone wall that separated the fields. It measured almost five feet tall and he was going far too fast on rocky ground. Christine could hardly watch. She was sure that she was about to witness the last action of her daughter's charismatic jumping star, and there was nothing she could do.

On Dancer sped, raging and reckless. At the last possible second, he lifted, legs tucked, neck stretched, muddy chestnut coat dull in the pale April sun. He soared high over the wall and landed lightly in a patch of weeds, rocks, and thistles.

Christine let out her breath in a rush and unclenched her hands. She ran her fingers through her dark, chin-length hair. *What a daredevil*, she thought. Christine spoke aloud. "This can't go on. I must call Mousie."

1

THE OLD THEATRE

ABBY MALONE RODE her elegant bay mare, Moonlight Sonata, to the top of the ridge. She looked down at Saddle Creek, and observed that the grey water, as it rushed over the rocks, mirrored the turbulence of the darkening skies.

At sixteen years of age, Abby was pretty and long-legged. Her silky blond hair was pulled into a low ponytail under her old black riding cap, and her cheeks were ruddy with health and energy. Her shape was fast becoming that of a woman, but her attitude remained unabashedly tomboyish.

Moonlight Sonata lowered her head to nibble the tender spring grass under the winter-coarsened weeds. Abby patted her sleek dark neck and studied the wild beauty of the scene below. The wind was coming up. Treetops swayed and tall reeds waved. She inhaled deeply and savoured the smells of water, earth, and pine. The air around her tingled with edgy energy, signalling the onset of an electrical storm.

"There's quite a storm coming, Moonie," she said to her trusted companion.

Suddenly, a two-year-old filly raced up the rise at full speed.

"Whoa there, Leggy!" Abby yelled authoritatively. The filly stopped inches from the edge of the ridge, reared up, then stamped her front hoof impatiently.

"You little brat," seethed Abby. "You scared me!"

Abby reached for the rope that dangled from the filly's halter and grabbed it firmly. "That's the last time I'm taking you with us, no matter how much of a fuss you make." As an act of kindness, Abby had decided to bring the anxious Leggy along for the ride, but no sooner were they off the road than she'd bolted in search of her own excitement. Now the scheming look in the young horse's eyes made Abby glare back at her in exasperation.

Moonie had given birth to this beautiful creature two years earlier, and Abby had proudly named her Moon Dancer. The youngster was already taller than her mother and still growing rapidly. The exceptional length of her legs had given her the stable name of "Leggy," and it had stuck. Her glossy chestnut coat was the exact shade of her father's, and her spirit was rebellious. "You're your father's daughter, all right," Abby observed aloud.

Leggy's sire was Dancer, the local legend. He and his owner, Hilary "Mousie" James, had won countless jumping competitions. They'd been an unbeatable team until the cruel and savage attack five years earlier by Samuel Owens. Owens had quickly been judged legally insane and sent to the mental hospital at Penetang. That Dancer had survived at all was remarkable, but he had never competed again. He was now retired at Hogscroft, the James' farm.

Abby sniffed the air; they were minutes away from a downpour. "Okay, ladies, gotta get back." The light was fading fast. Trying to radiate calmness for the horses' sakes, she gently pulled Moonie's head up from the grass and turned her around. Leggy followed on the lead line but hopped around nervously, afraid of the changing weather. Just then, something dark and furry darted out from the trees.

"Hey, Cody!" A small grey coyote looked up at Abby adoringly, eyes shining. This girl was his best friend.

Abby returned his gaze. She'd found him when he was only a few days old and dying of starvation. She'd fed him a special mother's milk substitution every few hours until he could eat on his own. Cody survived and grew into a small but healthy adult. Abby constantly marvelled at his intelligence and ingenuity. He was completely devoted to her; her shadow.

Abby, Moonie, Leggy, and Cody headed toward home. Old trees groaned and strained against the wind as the little group trotted down the path through the woods. Overhead, branches blocked what little remained of the light, leaving them to ride in near darkness. As they came out of the woods into a hay field, a strong gust of wind hit them. Angry-looking clouds were rapidly closing in, and the sky was turning black.

The rain started suddenly. Stinging, cold, driving rain. The wind howled, and Leggy lurched away in fear. "Leggy, honey, don't you worry, we'll be home soon."

A long serpent's tongue of lightning shot from the heavens in front of them, followed by a deafening, horrifying crack. Abby counted five seconds between lightning and thunder, which meant that the lightning had struck approximately one mile away, very close to home.

They were now galloping across the Wick property. It had been for sale for over two years, and the place was neglected and overgrown. The house had long been empty and there were "No Trespassing" signs posted on trees. The barn was said to be haunted, and a shiver went down Abby's spine at the sight of its dark looming shape.

Cody, nose down and tail flat, turned sharply and made a beeline toward the barn. Abby called after him, but the coyote didn't look back.

A streak of electricity lit up the sky and thunder crashed simultaneously. Moonie reared in fright, and Leggy squealed a high-pitched alarm. The rain was coming down hard, pelting them mercilessly. Abby made a quick decision. She turned Moonie and Leggy toward the barn, following Cody's lead.

The barn was a huge weather-beaten structure, about a hundred and fifty years old. The main floor was fieldstone, and faded grey barn boards housed the hayloft. Through the curtain of rain, Abby noticed a more solid shed, which stood on the other side of the farm lane. Dutch doors opened to a small paddock, and Abby thought that it must once have been shelter for horses. Since it was accessible and looked far safer than the barn, Abby headed for the shed.

Young trees were now bending with the force of the gale, and the rain came down in sheets. Abby's face stung, and her hands were red and cold. Carefully, the group made its way through soggy, rotten debris and tangled vines. At the paddock gate Abby dismounted and threw the reins over Moonie's neck. She led the two mares through the rusted gate and hurried to open the Dutch doors.

A hinge had come loose from one of the top doors, and it hung askew. Abby pulled it open and reached over the bottom door to feel for a latch. The horses were restless, eager for shelter. "Quiet, you two, I'm trying my hardest." Abby found a hook and released it. She pushed. The door was stuck.

Cody, who'd been patiently waiting at her side, leapt over the bottom door into the shed and began digging. Looking over, Abby saw that manure and old straw were blocking the door.

Abby went back and closed the paddock gate, then ran up Moonie's stirrups and tucked her reins under a stirrup leather so she wouldn't become tangled if she dropped her head to graze. She removed the dangling lead shank from Leggy's halter and, satisfied that her horses were temporarily accident-proof, climbed over the half-door. "Don't you move, ladies," she ordered the nervous mares.

In the gloom she spotted an old pitchfork leaning against the far wall. It was rusty, but the handle was firmly attached and it had all its tines. She quickly went to work, aware that another bolt of lightning would set off Leggy. If she jumped the fence and made a run for it . . . Abby didn't even want to speculate on the kinds of trouble the young mare could get herself into. She kept digging.

"Okay, girls, I think we're in business," Abby said to the mares, who had their heads over the door watching her work. She pulled at the door, scraping it open enough for a horse to enter. Moonie, followed closely by Leggy, burst into the dry shed and away from the storm. Leggy immediately shook herself off and lay down for a roll. She scratched her back happily on the bedding, then stood and shook again, sending old straw and dust everywhere. Abby chuckled, delighted to have everyone safely under cover.

She untacked Moonie, propping her saddle against a post and hanging the bridle over a nail on the wall. She draped the saddle pad over an old barrel to let it dry. The leather would be a mess to clean, she thought, and her riding hat was soaked. In fact, all her clothes were soaked, and she was feeling the chill. She took off her riding hat and hung it on another nail. She shook the rain off her windbreaker and hung it over the handle of the upright pitchfork. Hopping up and down and rubbing her arms didn't help much. "What I need is a blanket," Abby said to Cody, as if he'd understand. He stared at her earnestly, intent on deciphering her meaning.

Moonie lay down on her side and rubbed her coat in the dusty straw. She rolled back and forth until all the water had been absorbed. She stood and shook, just like her daughter. "You're so smart, using dirt as a towel," said Abby, shivering. "Do you think it would work for me?"

The horses were settled nicely, and the next great flash of

lightning didn't bother them at all. They felt protected and safe, and were drying off quickly, but they didn't have food or water. Abby hoped that they wouldn't have to wait long for the storm to pass.

"In case we're here for a while, it wouldn't hurt to see what I can find." There had to be a bucket in the barn, and if there wasn't running water, a moment under the eaves would fill it up. Also, she was cold. Maybe there were empty burlap grain sacks stored somewhere or, better yet, horse blankets. They'd be musty and filthy for sure, but they'd help retain her body heat. Abby patted Moonie and Leggy on their noses and set off to the barn with Cody.

The light was dim as they ran into the rain and dashed for the barn door. Wind whistled through an empty, broken window. The barn, standing starkly in front of them, seemed sinister. "This place is spooky," Abby said, feeling only slightly reassured by Cody's presence.

There were two huge doors that opened in the middle for tractors and haywagons. Cut into the one on the right was a smaller, human-size door with a latch. Abby took hold of the handle and pressed down firmly with her thumb. It opened.

Abby pushed the door wide and peered in. "Cody?" she called quietly. Immediately she felt him nuzzle her hand. "Stay with me, boy. I'm scared." Cody had no intention of leaving her side. He knew when Abby needed him.

Abby took one tentative step inside. The door swung shut behind her with a great slam.

"Cody!" she whispered, urgently. Cody nudged her with his nose. "Holy. I can't take this." Her heart pounded. She didn't dare move. She couldn't see a thing, and she didn't know where to step. Abby held Cody's coarse ruff tightly in her left hand. "Let's get back to the horses. I don't need a blanket."

Teeth chattering with cold and nerves, Abby backed up,

feeling for the door behind her. Her left shoulder bumped the wall. Suddenly, yellow radiance replaced the gloom. Momentarily blinded, she covered her eyes with her hands. Glancing at the wall she realized that she'd accidentally backed into the light switch. When she looked around, she gasped in wonder at what she saw. Abby could not believe her eyes.

In front of her was a theatre. A wooden stage with a small orchestra pit in front. Curving rows of seats covered with worn and faded burgundy velvet. A real theatre with a real proscenium arch over the stage and ragged burgundy velvet curtains hanging from it.

"Hold on," muttered Abby aloud. "This is a barn. In the country. On a wrecked-up old farm. What's a theatre doing here?"

Fiona Malone was worried about her daughter. Abby had been gone for hours, the storm was building, and the temperature was dropping. Spring storms were unpredictable, Fiona fussed as she nervously pushed back her grey-blond hair. She turned the radio to the weather station. "Exactly three years ago, a spring storm with less intensity than today's became a funnelling tornado, causing damage in the hundred thousands of dollars and claiming the lives of . . ." *Great*, she thought. *I really need to hear that. This could drive a person to drink.* It was one thing for Abby to be out on Moonie, a sensible mare, but to have to cope with Leggy, too . . .

The phone rang, startling Fiona out of her bleak thoughts.
"Hello?"
"Mrs. Malone?"
"Speaking."
"Hi! This is Hilary James. May I speak with Abby?"
"Mousie James! Are you home?"
"Yes, for the weekend. I got in last night."
"Your mother must be thrilled. How's Montreal?"

"Great, thanks. I'm working hard on my thesis, and exams are going well. How are things with you?"

"Fine, but I'm a little concerned just at the moment. Abby's out in the storm on Moonie, with Leggy on a lead."

"Wow." Hilary knew from first-hand experience how frightened a young horse might be in this weather, but she didn't want to add to Fiona's worries. "I'm sure they're fine, Mrs. Malone. Abby's smart. She's probably somewhere dry, waiting it out."

"I sure hope you're right, Hilary."

"How long has she been gone?"

"Over two hours."

There was a short pause. "Would you like me to look for them?"

"No! I don't want you out in this storm, too. Abby's father'll be home soon, and he'll go out if she's not back. Thanks anyway, though."

"Is Cody with her?"

"I assume so," Fiona answered. "He always is."

"If there was any reason to worry, he'd come find you."

"You're right. He would. Hilary, thank you. I feel better."

"Well, tell her I called. I want to talk something over with her. But I know my way through all the trails so please call me if you want help. I'm serious."

"I know you are. Thank you."

As Hilary returned the receiver to the kitchen wall Christine waited for an explanation.

"What's wrong, Mousie?" she asked.

"Abby's out in the storm."

"Are you worried?"

"Well, it's wild out there, and she's got the two-year-old with her." Hilary walked to the window and peered outside. Pepper, a little brown and white Jack Russell terrier, stood beside her with her paws on the windowsill. The sky was dark and it was only three thirty in the afternoon. The rain poured down heavily and the wind sounded like a giant in pain.

Hilary absently rubbed the small dog's head. "She's tough, Mom, but this is crazy weather."

"Don't even think of going out there, Mousie. You wouldn't know where to begin to look. You'll just have to trust that she's as smart as you were at her age."

As the storm raged outside, Abby slowly walked down the aisle of the little theatre toward the stage. The air was dusty and smelled moldy, but her nose picked up a hint of something else. She couldn't quite define it, but it was exciting, tantalizing. Was it the smell of greasepaint, she wondered, like in the song? Was it adrenalin, left over from a thousand first night panic attacks? Or maybe it was a combination of hairspray and makeup and sweat and old costumes and fear and delight. Whatever it was, Abby liked it. Her back straightened and her legs moved with more grace as she approached the stage. Then, head high, she stepped up the four risers to the left of the stage.

She strode to the centre and turned to face the seats. She imagined them full of people; smiling people, eagerly waiting for a performance that would touch them, move them, make them laugh. A performance that would allow them to forget about their troubles, their problems, their dreary jobs.

"Hello, out there," she said aloud. Her voice sounded feeble and thin to her ears. She took a deep breath. "Hello, out there!" That was better. The sound resonated from the back wall. "I welcome you all to a very special show. For the first time on any stage, anywhere in the entire world, A-a-bby Mal*one*!" She stepped briskly to the right and grandly swept up her right arm, placing her left foot behind her in her own version of a regal curtsy. Holding out a splendid, imaginary gown with her left hand, Abby bowed deeply to her adoring fans.

When Abby raised her head, the people were gone. The seats were dusty and drab, dirty cobwebs drooped from the lights, and the whole place was in bad repair. But the magic still hung in the air. Abby smiled, understanding that nothing, not even time, could remove it.

A movement in the back seats caught her eye. A blur of bluish light spread up the right aisle and settled in a seat two rows from the back and two chairs in from the aisle. Abby stared, mesmerized.

Cody howled softly, breaking Abby's trance. She looked at him, sitting obediently in the front row, paw raised and head tilted. He howled again, but not fearfully or with any sense of urgency. Abby looked at the back of the theatre again, but the blur was gone. *Hmm*, she thought. *Strange*. Maybe she'd imagined it.

Without warning, Cody dashed up onto the stage and stood protectively in front of Abby. He bared his teeth and growled fiercely.

"Cody, what's wrong?" Abby asked. Something was threatening them, and it was out there in the theatre. She backed up slowly until she could feel the thick curtains against her back, then quickly ducked under the heavy fabric. Cody scooted under, too, and Abby dropped the curtain to the floor.

Heart pounding, Abby crouched motionless, straining her ears for any telltale noise. A minute went by. Cody stiffened and growled again.

Attracted by a spot of light showing through the curtain, Abby crept over and found a small hole a few feet off the ground. Peering through, she saw nothing but empty seats and bare walls. She kept her eye to the hole, and arranged herself to settle in and watch.

Abby had a troubling thought. Were her horses safe? Was she hiding here, afraid for herself, while the horses were in danger? She fidgeted, uncertain of what to do, when the latch on the door lifted with a sharp click.

The door slowly opened. Holding her breath, Abby waited to see who or what would come in.

It was the old farmer, Robert Wick. Relief spread through Abby's body. She took a deep breath, realizing that she'd forgotten to breathe. Farmer Wick was a weathered man in his seventies, tall and lanky with a slightly spreading belly. His red and black checkered jacket was wet from the rain, and he wore green rubber boots and a soaked olive-green cap with ear flaps. He looked as frightened as Abby felt. Step by tentative step he sidled into the theatre, sliding his back along the wall, darting his eyes all over the large room. He carried a shotgun.

"Mr. Wick?" Abby called.

The old man jumped. "What?" he blurted. "Who's there?"

"It's me, Abby Malone. I'm behind the curtain, and I'm coming out. Cody is with me. Please don't shoot. Can you hear me, Mr. Wick?" Abby was nervous. She knew that a person with a gun could make a mistake when frightened, even Mr. Wick.

Robert Wick lowered the shotgun. "Abby Malone." He took a deep breath. "The gun's not loaded. Show yourself. Where are you?"

"I'm here, behind the curtain," she repeated. "Here." To show Mr. Wick where she was, she poked the fabric with her hand and shook it.

"Okay, Abby, I see you. Come on out."

Abby lifted the heavy velvet, then emerged cautiously with Cody, trusting that the gun was empty.

"Now, what the blazes are you doing in my barn, on my property, without permission, in the middle of a whopping big storm?"

"I'm sorry, Mr. Wick. I can explain everything . . ." Abby began.

"I can't hear you. You're mumbling. Speak up."

"I can explain everything," Abby projected loudly. "We, that is my two horses and Cody and me, got caught in the storm and we needed to get out of the wind and rain but especially the lightning, so we found shelter in your shed, but I was cold and I thought there might be an old horse blanket in the barn, but when I got here I realized it wasn't a barn but a theatre, so I couldn't help but look around, and I hope it's all right." Abby took a breath. She'd been speaking very quickly, and when she stopped the theatre resonated with the echoes of her voice. Wick took his time.

Finally he spoke. "I guess that's fine."

Abby was relieved. "Thank you so much. Well, I'll go now. I'm sorry. I really am. I'll never do it again."

"I must say you scared the living daylights out of me," Mr. Wick said, relaxing.

"And me, too. You scared the living daylights out of me." Abby and Cody had come down the stairs and were walking toward the door.

"I come to check on the farm every few days," said Mr. Wick, feeling more talkative. "It's been empty for a long time, since my wife died and I moved into the bungalow, but until today nobody's bothered with it, if you don't count the ghost. That's why, when I saw the lights on, I grabbed my shotgun. It's not loaded, but it's scary. I had no idea what I'd be facing. I apologize for that, Abby."

Abby stopped dead. "A ghost?"

2

THE RETURN
OF SAMUEL OWENS

HILARY JAMES CONTINUED TO STARE out the kitchen window at the rain. Her reflection stared back. Tall with shoulder-length, light brown hair streaked with blond, Mousie had grown into an attractive, intelligent woman of twenty-two. The show-jumping passion that had taken her and Dancer to the top of that world had been replaced by a love of ancient civilizations, a love that she shared with Sandy Casey, her fiancé. The two planned to join an archeological dig for a year in Belize, and they were practising their Spanish in anticipation.

She was thinking about Abby Malone, the girl she'd first met two years earlier. Abby had been riding bareback, chasing hunting dogs away from her beloved Cody. *Such spunk*, Hilary thought. She remembered the day of the steeplechase, when Abby competed against some tough riders on her little quarter-horse mare. Mousie admired the younger girl's uncanny ability with horses; but more than that, she liked her spirit.

Now, Abby was somewhere out there with two horses and her coyote. Mousie thought over the options. The first, and most sensible, would be to wait and hope that they got back okay. And likely they would. Plus, as her mother said, where would she begin to look? They could be anywhere. Should she risk herself and Dancer getting struck by lightning, or mired in mud?

The other option was to saddle up Dancer and go. Doing something, however rash, was easier than standing idle. At least if something awful happened, she could tell herself that she had tried.

Hilary pulled on her rubber riding boots and zipped up her waxed canvas slicker. Pepper hopped around in excitement, thrilled at the prospect of an adventure. "No, Pepper. You stay." Immediately, the little dog's ears dropped and she slunk away to her tiny basket in the corner of the kitchen. Hilary threw on her hard hat and hollered, "I'm going to look for Abby, Mom. See you later."

"Mousie? Did you say something?" Christine's voice floated up from the basement, where the laundry was in full gear.

Hilary walked to the top of the basement stairs. "I'll be back soon. I'm going to find Abby."

"You're crazy!" The pounding of feet sounded on the stairs. "Where are you going to look? It's dangerous to be out there on a horse with the lightning!" Christine anxiously wiped her soapy hands on her jeans.

"I can't just sit and wait. I'll be careful."

"How can you be careful of where lightning strikes?"

"Mom, what are the chances? Abby might have a broken leg or something."

Christine could see that her daughter would not be deterred. "Then don't take Dancer, he hasn't been ridden in ages. He'll be too fresh. Take Henry, he'll be much calmer in this storm."

"Mom, I've got the cell phone." Hilary patted her pocket. "I'm taking Dancer. He'll follow anyway if I take Henry, and then I'll have two horses to worry about, like Abby." She put on her riding gloves, turned to the door, and headed out to the barn.

The wind was powerful, and the rain felt like needles prickling her face. If her mother hadn't been standing at the window worrying, Hilary might have been tempted to turn back.

Dancer stood in the barn out of the rain. His coat was totally dry. Dancer's barnmate, Henry, was lying down in his stall. A solid bay gelding of Clydesdale and thoroughbred origins, Henry was dreaming happy horse dreams, ears twitching and lower lip flapping. He looked comical, like a talking horse.

Hilary carried her newly cleaned saddle and bridle from the tack room and placed them on the rack in the aisle. "Dancer, don't look at me like that. I know it's bad out there, but we're going to look for Abby and Moonie, your girlfriend, remember her? And your daughter, Moon Dancer." She laughed at herself, talking to Dancer like he was a person. She'd always done that. Somehow, he'd always seemed more like a person to her than a horse.

With Dancer tacked up and ready to go, Hilary walked into the pelting rain. Dancer tucked his tail between his legs and hunched his back when the strong wind surprised him, but he stood quietly at the mounting block as Hilary hopped on. She put her feet in the stirrups and tightened the girth.

It was good to be up on his back again. It seemed like she'd been there all along, like she'd never gone off to university. She felt his power and his strong personality through the saddle, just like the old days.

Lightning flashed diagonally across the sky and thunder boomed and crashed. Dancer spooked sideways and started to prance.

"Let's try the woods behind the Caseys' and travel along the ridge above Saddle Creek. Come on, Dancer, don't wimp out on me now."

Fiona Malone paced the kitchen, trying hard not to pour a drink. A small drink to calm her nerves, just a sip. Nobody would know. Couldn't she be excused, with the worry of Abby out in the storm? The radio was playing "Rubber Ducky" in an effort to make a joke out of the severity of the weather. Fiona took a glass out of the cupboard and threw in some ice cubes. Her husband, Liam, thought he had gotten rid of all the liquor in the house, but Fiona always had something hidden away, just in case. When she'd bought the bottle of gin, she convinced herself that it was only to test her willpower.

The song ended and the news came on. World news about suffering and war and hunger. Fiona knelt under the sink and felt for the bottle amid the cleaning supplies. Her fingers clutched it, and she pulled it out. Local news about the firemen's strike and the fundraiser for the animal shelter. She cut open the seal around the mouth of the bottle. An interruption for a news bulletin about wealthy businessman Samuel Owens being released from the mental hospital after being judged sane.

Fiona stared at the bottle. The glass was ready for the clear, numbing liquid. Samuel Owens? Released? The man who tried to kill Dancer? Fiona wondered if Hilary knew. She should be warned.

Quickly, Fiona found the number and dialed. It was answered on the first ring.

"Hello?"

"Christine? It's Fiona Malone."

"Fiona, how are you? I'm already collecting things for the big garage sale at Someday Farm."

"I'm not calling to harass you about that, Christine," said Fiona, smiling briefly. "Yet."

"Has Abby gotten home?"

"No, not yet. I'm hoping to see her any minute. I'm calling because there's something on the news. I don't know if you've heard. Samuel Owens has been released from the mental hospital."

Christine took a deep breath. "When?"

"I don't know. It was on the radio a minute ago, and I wasn't paying close attention until I heard his name."

"Thank you, Fiona. I'll turn on my radio and listen for more details."

"I'm sorry to call with such bad news. It'll be better next time. I promised Hilary that I'd let her know the minute Abby gets home."

"Well, she went out on Dancer, looking for her."

"She didn't!"

"Oh yes, she did. There wasn't anything I could say to stop her."

"My God! It's horrible out there."

"I know, Fiona, but she's got the cell phone. If she reports back, I'll let you know, and if she's gone too long, we can always call her."

"Thanks so much."

"Why don't you come over and wait here with me?"

Fiona looked at the gin. "Thanks, but I want to be here when Abby gets home."

"Of course."

"If she gets home before Hilary calls on her cell, I'll call you."

"Good plan."

Fiona hung up the phone and continued to stare at the gin. Finally she rose from her chair. She untwisted the cap and carried the bottle over to the counter, where the glass of ice stood ready. With a shaking hand she began to pour. As she lifted the glass to her lips, she was suddenly overpowered by self-loathing. What was she doing to herself? And to her family, who had been so supportive of her rehabilitation? Fiona threw the glass into the sink as if it was too hot to hold, smashing it into fragments. She dumped the entire bottle of gin after it, listening to the chugging sound with satisfaction as it emptied.

"Fiona, girl."

Fiona swung around, startled.

"Well done, my darling. I couldn't be prouder." Liam Malone stood at the kitchen door, dripping water onto the mat. His face was tender, and his eyes were moist with tears. Fiona flew across the room into his open arms, ignoring the soaking wet jacket as she clung tightly to him.

Samuel Owens sat at his large mahogany desk and looked out of the big picture window over his hundred acres of rolling land. It was good to be home.

Gazing through the rain-spattered glass, he admired the sweep of the land as it melted into the woods that abutted the Casey property, which gently rose to the horizon. Even in this ghastly weather, the view was majestic.

It was so good to be home. Owens' hands greedily rubbed the rich leather arms of his favourite chair. He tilted it back and stretched out his legs, resting his slipper-clad feet on the desk.

Just this morning, upon his release, the director of Penetang had subtly inferred that he was one hundred percent sane. As if he had ever been insane. Owens' large, handsome face creased into a foxy smile. The silly doctor had basically apologized for the inconvenience of his incarceration. He didn't exactly say it, but Owens could read between the lines. His antennae were always up, and he knew that the doctor's stern warning to take his pills faithfully was merely rote. He couldn't really expect a sane man to take mood-altering drugs. The lithium dulled his senses. It reduced his pleasure. Even his taste buds didn't function in the same way.

Owens had patiently served his time, but now it was over. Things could get back to normal.

Lightning lit up the sky, and for a brief second, the lane through the lower woods was visible. Owens gasped. In that blink of an eye, he imagined that he saw Dancer and Mousie James, riding down the lane through the woods, from the direction of the Caseys'. Just like they'd ridden many times before.

Owens blinked. His forehead beaded with sweat and his pulse raced. He could almost feel his blood pressure rise. He dropped his feet to the floor and peered out the window, squinting. He grabbed his binoculars off the hook and focused them on the lane. No sign of horse or rider. He breathed deeply, calming himself. It had been a long, tiring day.

He turned the binoculars to Wick Farm, and then toward the Casey property. This is what he'd thought about again and again at the hospital. He would own all the land he could see from any window in his house. He would purchase total privacy. It was essential to his happiness. This was his goal, and he was going to achieve it. He'd thought a lot on how to proceed.

He would give the beautiful divorcée, Helena Casey, a call. In the next few days, he'd drive over for a little visit.

He rang the silver bell for his manservant. It was time for a Chivas, his first in five long years. Owens dangled his arm over the wastebasket and deliberately dropped the full bottle of lithium. It landed in the empty brass container with a satisfying clunk.

Hilary and Dancer were thoroughly soaked, but not cold. They were moving quickly. They'd run along the road and cut cross-country toward the trail. When they got to the point where the paths crossed, they headed south. First they checked the fields north of the Caseys' where her stepfather, Rory, had pastured his prize Herefords. The fields were empty now. Rory had sold the beef cows after his divorce from Helena.

They had galloped past the Casey mansion, where Helena continued to live. The lights were on in the sitting room, but the rest of the house was dark. Hilary imagined Helena sitting elegantly in the pink Queen Anne chair, wearing a tastefully expensive couturier ensemble. She'd be sipping her drink and clinking her ice cubes as she harboured resentments toward

Hilary for being engaged to her son, and toward Christine James for marrying her ex-husband.

Hilary had never understood how such a cold mother could produce a son as warm and understanding as Sandy. And Rosalyn, Sandy's sister, was growing into an engaging young woman. She was fourteen now, and when Mousie had seen her last Christmas, she could hardly believe how the chubby, insecure little girl had changed into a confident, bubbly teenager.

On they ran, through the fields behind the mansion and into Samuel Owens' woods. Hilary noted the exact spot where Dancer had been stabbed. The memory was fresh, even five years later. Suddenly a surge of raw fear shot through her body. She felt that someone was watching her. Her eyes darted toward Owens' house at the top of the hill. The lights were on, and she detected a slight movement in the large window.

Was Owens home? *Not possible*, she thought. *He'd be locked up for years to come. It was likely a servant.* A flash of lightning lit up the woods, momentarily blinding her. The following thunder rattled the trees, scaring Dancer and sending him lunging forward. "Okay, Dancer. Let's get out of here. This place gives me the creeps."

They sped through the woods and over the fields, up the rise and past the craggy bluffs with the river below. Hilary slowed Dancer as they started into the woods, trotting him through the trees as trunks groaned and branches bent and swayed with the storm.

"A forest isn't always the safest place in a storm, but neither are the open fields," Hilary said aloud to Dancer. She was trying to keep them both calm by talking. "A branch can break off and kill you in the woods, and lightning can strike when you're the tallest thing around. Right-y-o. I think I'll shut up before I scare myself to death."

Once out of the woods and onto the Wick Farm fields, the ground became treacherous with mud. Hilary slowed Dancer to a trot, and looked around for signs of Abby. The rain continued to pour down, obscuring any possibility of tracks.

"I wonder what we thought we'd accomplish, Dancer," said Hilary to the steaming stallion. "We might as well go back and count ourselves lucky to get home safely."

Dancer stopped dead. His ears pricked up and his head raised sharply and swung to the right. Hilary felt tension travel throughout his body.

"Steady, boy." Dancer spun to the right and stopped again. Abruptly he whinnied loudly and deeply. He listened. A far-off echoing whinny caught Mousie by surprise.

It came from the old Wick barn. Hilary knew that no animals had been there for years. She heard another whinny, followed by a higher-pitched call. There was definitely more than one horse over there.

Excited, Hilary strained her eyes, trying to see what Dancer saw across the dark field. Ears alert, Dancer trotted hard through the thick muck toward the abandoned barn, heading directly to the nearby shed.

Hilary could now make out the heads of two horses looking over the Dutch door. The one on the left was definitely Moon Dancer, with her looks so strikingly like Dancer's. And that was Moonlight Sonata, for sure, with her fine, dark head and beautiful, dreamy eyes.

"Good work, Dancer!" She praised him as she slid to the slippery ground. "Bloodhounds have nothing on you." Hilary led Dancer through the gate up to the Dutch doors. The horses sniffed and blew their introductions.

"Abby?" called Hilary loudly. No answer. She could see that the horses were dry and untacked. A saddle and a bridle were neatly propped up and a saddle pad was hung to dry. A riding cap and windbreaker confirmed that Abby had arrived with the horses, but she was nowhere to be seen.

Hilary walked Dancer into the shed, out of the pelting rain and raging wind. At the rear were two narrow stalls where horses could stand. She backed Dancer into one and closed him in securely. He could watch the action but be separate from the mares. She didn't want any trouble while she searched for Abby.

Hilary looked outside through the rain, wondering where to begin. A light was on in the barn. She hadn't seen it when she arrived. As she looked more closely, she saw why. Black-out drapes covered all the windows except the one beside the door.

3
THE GHOST

"Don't worry, Abby," reassured Mr. Wick. "He's been here for years and has never harmed a soul. Which nobody knows, by the way. Don't let on he's a friendly ghost, Abby."

"Why is there a ghost? How long has he been here? Were there plays in here and all that? Why was the theatre ever closed down, and when? Actually, *who* is the ghost and how do you know there is one?"

Mr. Wick chuckled. "One question at a time!"

"Well, then," replied Abby seriously. "The first question is about the ghost. Who is it? Or who was it when it was alive? And why did it come here?" Abby was fascinated. She was talking to someone who actually knew a ghost. She wasn't going to let this opportunity pass her by.

"You're still asking more than one question at a time, but I'll answer anyway," said Mr. Wick with a smile. "His name is Ambrose Brown and he was a real person. He was an actor who for some reason preferred this theatre to any other. He was absolutely wonderful on stage. He had a commanding presence and played an amazing range of characters."

"Did you know Ambrose Brown?"

"Sure did. He worked here for twenty years, as often as there was a part for him. He loved this stage. Said he wanted to be buried here."

Abby's eyes grew large. "And is he?"

"No. His family has plots in Mount Pleasant Cemetery. They buried him there."

"Is that why he haunts this theatre? Because he wants to be buried here?"

"Could be. I've wondered that myself. But you can't just dig up a body and move it. There's a lot of paperwork involved and his next of kin won't even consider it."

"That's too bad, but it might not help, anyway."

"That's the thing. How are we to know why he's haunting us?" Mr. Wick's brow furrowed. "He was devastated when we had to close the theatre down. It may have been the saddest thing that ever happened to him."

"Why do you say that?"

"Because he died on closing night, after the final show."

"Really? Can people die of sadness?"

"I honestly don't know."

Mr. Wick looked so sad himself that Abby changed the subject. "Why did you have to close the theatre?"

"It wasn't making enough money to sustain itself. I'm not a rich man and I couldn't afford to subsidize it."

"When was it closed down?" Abby asked, absorbed by the story.

Mr. Wick scratched his head under his hat. "Must be fifteen years or more. Maybe close to twenty."

"And you said the theatre ran for twenty years?"

"Yup, about that. Those were the days, Abby. I wanted to go into show business myself, you know, when I was a boy."

"You?" Abby realized after she spoke how that must have sounded. "I mean, I always thought of you as Farmer Wick, not really showbiz, you know?"

Mr. Wick laughed, stopped, then laughed again. He laughed so hard, he started to scare Abby. Tears rolled down his face, which had grown quite red. Abby began to worry.

"Don't look so, so, so alarmed!" he managed to sputter. "I can't stop. Oh! Oh! I haven't had such a good laugh in years. In the theatre days, people who came here were so refreshing, so jolly. We laughed like this all the time. I love actors. They're mimics, they're monkeys, they never grow old and cynical. They're always hoping for the big break, and it's always coming tomorrow. It's always Christmas Eve, with big presents ready to open the next day. Oh, Abby, how I miss those days."

Abby now feared that the old man would start to cry. She wanted to avoid that altogether. "Tell me why you built this place, forty years ago," she said.

"That's a long story." Mr. Wick's eyes misted over and a lovely smile crossed his face. "Gladys always said it was nuts to do it. She was my wife. But since I was a child, I had dreamed of acting in theatre.

"My father thought I was weird because I was interested in the arts, and tried to beat it out of me. He was a tough old goat, my dad. I gave up to keep the peace in the family. Became a farmer just like Dad.

"He was suspicious of me all his life, just because I wanted to bring life to the written word. He never understood why I wanted to create magic for people. Lights and illusion. I read about famous actors in England, who were honoured and knighted. Why couldn't I get just a little respect at home?

"Anyway, with the money he left me when he died, I converted the barn into this theatre. Call it my own form of revenge, if you like."

Watching Mr. Wick as he spoke, Abby saw the young man under the old farmer's face. She felt his hurt, his turmoil over his father, and his great love for the theatre.

"Why did you laugh so hard just now?" Abby gently asked. She didn't want him to laugh again, or to cry, but she wanted to know.

He paused before he answered. "Because I have become my disguise. We all wear disguises, Abby, in one way or another. You made me see myself as you see me, and that's not what I am underneath."

"That wouldn't make me laugh, Mr. Wick. It sounds kind of sad." Abby examined her dirty, chipped fingernails. "And anyway, now that you've revealed your true self to me, I'll always see you differently."

"Will you? Good. You should always look for the person under the disguise, Abby."

Abby nodded, wondering how many people had disguises. "Can we get back to the ghost? Is he friendly?"

"Absolutely. He keeps me company when I'm here and I always know where to find him. If he wants to be found, that is."

"Don't tell me," said Abby, excitedly. "Second row from the back, second seat in, on the right side of the theatre when you stand on the stage looking into the seats."

Mr. Wick stared. "You've met him? He showed himself to you?"

"Yes! Well, I didn't see a person, really, only a sort of a light."

"Then you have a special quality, Abby. Ghosts know." His eyes reassessed her as he spoke. "And it's called stage right."

"What is?"

"The right side of the theatre. When you stand on the stage and look out into the *house*—that's what you call where the audience sits—what's on your right is called *stage right*, and what's on your left is called *stage left*. And when you're in the middle of the stage, you are standing at *centre stage*."

Mr. Wick walked up to the stage and climbed the stairs. He stood in the exact middle of the stage. "You see? I'm at centre stage. If I go back a step or two, I've gone upstage. If I step forward, like this, I've moved downstage." Mr. Wick stepped as he spoke, illustrating with his actions. He swung his right arm out.

"Stage right." He swung out his left arm. "Stage left. Upstage, downstage, centre stage."

Abby was transfixed. As she watched, Mr. Wick turned from a farmer into an actor. Not a sloppy actor, either. His motions were economical, his voice was clear and well-modulated, and his bearing made even this rudimentary lesson in stage direction fascinating. His farmer's clothes were the same. What was different was underneath.

"If you upstage someone, that means you've forced an actor to look back at you by standing upstage. If his face isn't visible to the audience, his importance in the scene is diminished. Ham actors are often guilty of this." Mr. Wick illustrated this by becoming the upstager, and then the upstaged actor, looking away from the audience.

Cody's head popped up from under a seat on the other side of the house, where he'd been hiding. He let out a low, rumbling growl of warning and bared his long, white canine teeth.

"Your coyote scares me, Abby," said Mr. Wick softly as he backed away toward the stairs.

"Don't worry. He's like your ghost. You have to get to know what he's all about. What he's saying now is that someone is coming. And whoever it is is cautious and creeping around, making Cody suspicious."

"So, Cody himself is no threat?" asked Mr. Wick as he cautiously moved off the stage and back to his seat beside Abby. "He's not angry?"

"No, he's being protective."

"Good. So now we must find out who's creeping around."

"Right," said Abby. "Why don't I turn off the lights, and we'll wait for him to come to us. We'll have the advantage of surprise."

"You are one brave girl, Abby Malone," said Mr. Wick admiringly. "With a great sense of the dramatic." He chuckled with pleasure. "I like your plan."

Abby crept quickly over to the wall with the light switches and turned them off. The theatre was immediately pitch black. Abby felt her way back to sit beside Mr. Wick. They waited.

Hilary saw the lights go off. She had been about to open the door, but now she waited, unsure of what to do. It was windy and she was starting to chill in her wet clothes. Taking a deep breath, she pressed the thumb latch. The door opened. Now what? It was very dark inside, with the windows covered in thick black fabric.

"Hello?" she called feebly. "Hello? Abby?" Hilary called out louder with each word she uttered. She was gaining confidence, since nothing had sprung out at her. Yet, she thought.

Abby called out. "Who's that?"

"Me. Hilary James."

"Hilary? Mousie?"

"Yes. Is that you, Abby?"

"Yes! Just a minute, I'll get the lights. Don't move or you might stumble." Abby was at the switch within seconds and the theatre was bathed in light. "That's better, isn't it?" she said, grinning.

"Much better. Thanks, Abby."

The two young women smiled at one another. In the two years since they'd last met, Abby had grown taller and filled out. They were the same height now, and of similar builds.

"It's good to see you," said Abby. "It's been a while."

The older girl nodded. "Since the steeplechase, I think. Just a minute, what is this?" Hilary took in her surroundings. She looked around, amazed. "Holy! The old theatre! I heard about this when I was a kid."

"Yes!" confirmed Abby. "Oh, and this is Mr. Wick, the man who owns it."

Mr. Wick had risen from his seat and was making his way up the aisle to the girls. He put out his hand for Hilary to shake.

"Robert Wick," he said.

"I'm Hilary James. Pleased to meet you," said Hilary as she took his hand.

"I've heard all about you, young lady. You and that sensational beast of yours. You made us all proud." His blue eyes glittered in his smiling face. Abby could see that it was sincere praise.

"Thank you," said Hilary. "I've heard about you, too. From my grandmother, Joy Featherstone."

Robert Wick blushed. "Well, I'll be. Joy Drake. She's talked about me?"

Hilary grinned. "She said you were the one that got away."

"She didn't! Well, that's nonsense. She turned my head from the moment I spied her. She was a little young for me, that's all. I was in my last year of high school when she started grade nine."

"Four years difference doesn't seem much now, though, does it?" commented Abby slyly.

"You stay out of this," said Mr. Wick. "You girls are ganging up on me. It's not fair."

They all laughed, happy to share a joke and ease the tension.

"Now that the threat of a monster is over, girls, I must be on my way. The rain seems to have stopped, so you can get home dry." He looked fondly at Abby. "It was nice to see you again, Abby."

"I feel like I've met you for the first time, Mr. Wick."

He smiled. "I guess you have, too." He turned to Hilary. "Take care of that horse of yours, young lady. And say hello to your dear grandma for me."

"I will," Hilary promised. "She'll be pleased."

Robert Wick doffed his cap and started to leave the theatre, feeling much younger than when he'd arrived. He remembered his shotgun just in time. "Oops. Can't leave this old thing lying around. Loaded or not." He smiled at the girls and waved good-bye.

"What do you make of that?" asked Abby once the door had closed. "I can't imagine Mr. Wick having romantic feelings, but did you see him blush when you mentioned your grandmother?"

Hilary nodded. "I know what you mean. Grandma told me that he was a heartthrob in high school."

"A heartthrob?" Abby laughed. "It's hard to imagine him making any hearts throb, but he's very nice. He wanted to be an actor, or at least be in show business. Can you imagine that?"

"Grandma said he was a good actor, too. But hang on." Hilary reached into her pocket. "I forgot to call my mother. Everyone's worried about you being out in the storm with the two mares."

"You came looking for me?" Abby asked.

"Yes."

Abby was struck by Hilary's kindness. "But you could've been hit by lightning!"

"No kidding! It was awful. And all along, your horses were warm and dry and you're in here chatting it up with Grandma's old heartthrob." She chuckled. "My mom'll call your mom, and they can all stop worrying."

Hilary turned on the phone and dialled. It was answered after one ring. "Hi, Mom . . . I'm fine . . . Abby's fine, the horses are fine, everyone's fine . . . At the old Wick farm . . . Yes, we're in the old theatre . . . No, never, but I remember you and Dad talking about it . . . We're on our way . . . Don't worry, the storm's over. We'll be okay . . . Yeah, my cell was off the whole time . . . Mom, I just forgot to turn it on. I'm sorry . . . Love you, too. Bye." Hilary pressed the off button, shaking her head. "Once a mother, always a mother. I've been away for four years, and as soon as I'm home, she worries."

"I think that's kind of nice." Abby opened the door and looked out. "It's sure cleared up."

The two girls walked through the mud and old straw toward the shed. The mares nickered to them as they approached.

"They're hoping we found food," chuckled Abby.

From the stall at the back of the shed came a deep, booming neigh and the crash of a hind hoof on the wall. "Dancer!" called Hilary. "Don't be so impatient."

Three horses, two riders, and one coyote set off toward home. Miraculously, the sun was starting to peek out of the drifting clouds, causing the whole wet world to twinkle and shine. There was a vivid rainbow, its colours enhanced by the angle of the sun as it dipped lower in the western sky. The girls rode quietly for a time, taking in the beauty around them.

"Are you riding much?" Hilary asked.

"Maybe three, four times a week. Moonie likes to go out hacking, and I've started training Leggy."

"She's two now?"

"Just."

"What are you doing with her?"

"I've taught her to lunge on the line both ways, and she's picking up voice commands. Walk, trot, canter, and whoa. She's smart."

"Are you driving her?"

"I'm just starting. Mr. Pierson helps me. He swears it's the best way to train them. He likes it better than lunging because there's no chance of damaging her joints."

"By the circling, you mean? Stressing her knees and hocks?"

"Uh huh," Abby nodded. "I attach a lunge line to each side of her halter and run them through her tied-up stirrups. Then I walk behind her, and Mr. Pierson walks at her head. I steer her with the lines, and he makes sure she doesn't get confused. Soon, I'll do it on my own."

"When are you going to get up on her?"

"I've already laid across the saddle with Mr. Pierson leading. Mr. Pierson wants to be sure that she's not going to buck before I sit up on her. And once she understands about being ridden, we'll leave her until she's three before working her every day. He keeps telling me there's no rush, but I get impatient."

Hilary laughed. "I know what you mean. You're lucky to have Mr. Pierson helping you."

Abby nodded vigorously. "He's the best. He helped me train Moonie." She patted the mare's neck.

"The Piersons must be getting old."

"Close to eighty, I think. But neither one is slowing down much." Abby considered this. "Well, Mr. Pierson's got arthritis, but he says that's life."

The little entourage moved companionably across the terrain. They followed the old deer path through the lower meadows and up the hill toward the high field. The Wicks had kept sheep there until the coyotes ran the foxes out of their dens and took over the area. Foxes rarely go after healthy lambs, but coyotes find them tempting when the rodent and rabbit populations get scarce. They finally became enough of a problem to force the sale of the remaining sheep.

Abby noticed Cody sniffing the air and looking around carefully. *He'd best stay close*, she thought. Cody was trespassing. He'd be an easy target for a family of wild coyotes intent on defending their territory. Especially now, when the pups were young. Also, Abby had heard that old leg-hold traps were sometimes still found up here.

"Hilary, can I ask you a question?" Abby asked.

"Sure. Fire away."

"How's Sandy? It's none of my business, so please . . ."

Hilary laughed. "He's fine. And we're still engaged. Is that what you meant?"

"Yes. I'm glad. You seem so perfect together."

They rode along in silence, each thinking her own thoughts. After a while, Hilary spoke.

"Have you ever thought of showing?" she asked.

"Show jumping?" Abby was surprised. "Not really."

"Why? You're a natural. It wouldn't take much to teach you how to get around the ring. It's timing and getting into the jumps right. It'd be fun for you. A challenge."

"Moonie's never done it. She's only done cross-country, but I know she could learn."

"How about Dancer?"

"Dancer?" Abby stared at Hilary. "You've got to be kidding!"

"No. I wouldn't joke about something like this, and I wouldn't ask just anybody." Hilary looked at Abby, hoping that the younger girl would be interested. "I've been thinking about this a lot. My mother called me last Thursday, scared out of her wits because Dancer jumped the big stone wall. That's why I came home this weekend, in the middle of exams and everything. I really think he's bored, and if you're willing and have the time, you could be the solution to the problem. Do you want to try?"

"For sure you're not joking?" Abby croaked.

"No, Abby, I'm not." Hilary smiled broadly. "First let's see if you get along, that's important, and then we'll talk about it. Can you come over tomorrow morning around ten?"

Abby couldn't speak. She could only nod.

Samuel Owens had his second crystal tumbler of Scotch at his side as he searched the landscape with his binoculars. As he looked, he made mental notes of the land he would purchase to complete his view. The Casey land, of course. *This will be fun*, he thought. Testing his charm on a lady, especially a beautiful and vulnerable lady, would be a thrill.

The small dump of a place next door was an embarrassment. He'd look after that tomorrow. It was only an acre, and the woman living in the shack with her cats would be easy pickings. Hardly worth his time.

And the Wick farm. He could clearly see the high field. Only a part of it, mind you, but his goal was clear. He would own every piece of land along Saddle Creek that he could see from any window in his house. It had become his mantra.

The Wick farm had been for sale, he knew. Owens wondered if it was still on the market. If it was, he'd snap it up cheap. That was another call for the morning.

He found himself looking for Dancer again.

Owens put his binoculars down with a jerk. He must forget about Dancer; that piece of no-good trash in a horse suit! He scowled. He couldn't waste time imagining the wretched animal all over the place, running through the woods, then up on the Wick's high field just moments ago with two other horses. He had better things to do!

He hadn't thought of Dancer in a long time. Perhaps coming home had restimulated that obsession. He decided to take action. He would concentrate on his new goals, not his old goals. He would not wait another minute. He would visit Helena Casey this evening, and put Dancer completely out of his head.

"Walter!" he hollered, ringing the bell. "Walter, get out my grey flannel pants, the yellow paisley ascot, and my navy cashmere blazer. I'm going out!"

"I'll leave you here, Abby," said Hilary, as Abby's farm came into view.

"Thanks for walking me home."

Hilary smiled. "It was fun."

"And thanks for coming out to find me. I might have needed help."

"It was a nasty storm, all right."

Abby and Hilary waved their goodbyes, and Abby continued along the road. "Don't forget, Abby," Hilary called back. "Tomorrow morning!"

Abby yelled, "I'll be there!" and grinned broadly. She looked around for Cody. He was nowhere in sight. Abby hadn't seen him since the Wick's sheep field.

She could not get the thought of riding Dancer out of her mind. She'd never even allowed herself to dream of it. Dancer! Mousie James herself had asked her to ride him. Amazing. She shook her head. Too amazing!

Since Abby was a small girl, the legend of Mousie and Dancer had grown bigger each year. The team was almost mythical to the legions of young riders in Caledon and the surrounding areas. The powerful, dangerous stallion with only one rider.

There were many stories circulating about Dancer, some fact, some fiction. Gossip about the money offered for him and turned down. Rumours about his tempestuous disposition. Stories about people who'd tried to ride him and got hurt. Abby hoped that she wouldn't be another of those. If the fall didn't crush her, the disappointment would.

After untacking and grooming Dancer, Hilary went into the house. Her mother was on the phone. She covered the mouthpiece with her hand and said, "Hi, honey! I'm on the phone with your grandmother."

"Tell her I want to talk to her," said Hilary, smiling.

Christine nodded. "Mom, come visit. We'll put our heads together. Mousie wants to talk to you. Bye." She passed the phone to her daughter.

"Grandma!" she said.

"Hi, beautiful. I hear you went out on a rescue mission. Well done! How's everything?"

"Fine, now that the sun's out and everyone's safe. It's hard to believe there was ever a storm! Grandma, I just met someone who remembers you, shall we say, fondly?"

"Fondly, Mousie? Am I to start guessing, or are you going to tell me?"

"You have to guess, but I'll give you clues. First clue, he loves theatre."

"Christopher Plummer?"

"You know Christopher Plummer?"

"No. Next clue."

"Very funny. Clue number two. He thought he was too old for you."

"Are we talking about my visits to the old age home?"

"We're talking high school days, and that counts as clue number three."

"Then I think I know. Theatre plus high school equals no one else but Robert Wick!"

"Bingo! Three clues. Not bad."

"Where'd you see Robert?"

"At his farm. There's a theatre in his barn. It's incredible."

"It is, isn't it? How's he look after all these years?"

"Probably all right once he's cleaned up."

"You could say the same for me. Isn't his farm for sale?"

"Yes. Apparently it's been on the market for ages."

"Hmm. You know, I might come take a look. I need a new project. I was talking to your mother about that just now. Things are far too boring around here, and I'm not ready for Florida."

"You'd buy a run-down old theatre, Gran?"

"Give me one good reason why not."

Abby was getting a little worried. She'd brushed down the horses and watered them, and Cody had still not appeared. The last time she'd seen him was in the upper Wick field. She turned from the shed toward the house. She'd ask her father to drive her back to Wick Farm to look for him.

Cody! The small grey coyote jumped the fence and barrelled over to her. Abby reached down to pat him, and Cody licked her hand. He wiggled all over with excitement. Abby kneeled and hugged him.

"Good boy," she cooed, rubbing his ears. "Clever boy. You came the long way, didn't you, and stayed away from the wild coyotes. I'm so happy to see you." Relief flooded over her, and the empty feeling in her stomach disappeared.

With Cody safely at her side, Abby stood and surveyed the field where her horses grazed. She sighed with contentment. The grass was soaking wet, and shone a vibrant emerald green in the fading light.

The horses stayed at Merry Fields, the Piersons' farm, for the winter because it had a barn. Her father had built a loafing shed and repaired all the fences so that Abby could bring them home for the summer. Some day the Malones would rebuild their barn, which had burned down two years earlier, and Abby would be able to have them with her all year. Mr. Pierson said he loved taking care of them, but Abby knew that mucking out and lugging water was becoming more and more difficult for him.

Abby thought about the Piersons and how they'd helped her through all the trouble she'd had two years ago. Her father had wrongfully been sent to jail, Abby was having problems at school, and her mother was drowning her sorrows in alcohol. Mr. and Mrs. Pierson had been her dear and loyal friends throughout, her support when she had nowhere else to turn. It all seemed so long ago, Abby mused.

Moonie and Leggy peacefully grazed in the front field. Abby leaned on the fence and admired them. Their coats, one mahogany and one copper, shone in the light of the setting sun. Abby took a deep breath, relishing the sight.

"Beautiful, aren't they?" asked a cheerful voice with an Irish lilt.

"Dad! You startled me!" Abby turned to look into the handsome, smiling face of her father. Slimly built and agile, Liam had passed his athletic genes on to his daughter.

"I'm glad you got home safely, Abby my dear." His green eyes twinkled as he spoke. "That was a storm and a half. Your mother was worried about you."

Abby smiled at him. "I was fine. We found shelter at Mr. Wick's." Her face lit up. "Dad, there's a theatre in his barn! It's terrific. Did you know there's a ghost in it? Mr. Wick told me about him. His name is Ambrose Brown and he was an actor who loved that theatre and wanted to be buried there."

"I remember Ambrose Brown. Your mother and I went to several plays there before you were born. He was great. Very funny, and very moving, too. They say he died unhappy."

"Why, Dad? Because the theatre was shutting down?"

"There was more to it than that, but I really don't recall. Something about unrequited love. Maybe your mother will remember. Oh, yes. That's why I came out. Your mother asked me to tell you that dinner's ready. You can ask her about Ambrose Brown right now."

"Oh, Dad! The best thing of all—Hilary James wants me to ride Dancer!"

Liam's eyes widened. "Goodness!" He was cautious. "Is it safe?"

"I'll find out. I'm going over in the morning."

Liam was stern. "You be careful, my girl. He's not a toy. He's a big, strong stallion, and he's dumped more people than any horse I know."

"Don't worry, Dad. I'll be careful. I'm a good rider. You told me yourself." She grinned at him, challenging him to contradict his own words.

"You are, indeed." His face softened. "A chip off the old block, if I say so myself."

Abby and Liam Malone linked arms and turned toward the red-brick century home. It seemed to welcome them, even beckon them, as they walked up the path to the kitchen door.

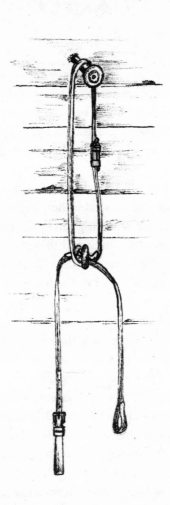

4

DANCER

SUNDAY DAWNED WITH a startling freshness. Saturday's rain had washed away the last traces of winter grime. Each leaf bud, blade of grass, and tree trunk had a clear definition that made the countryside appear to have undergone a massive spring cleaning. The sky was flawlessly blue and robins were singing their joyful song.

Abby woke much too early, filled with excitement about riding Dancer. She got dressed in her breeches and boots, and went outside swinging her riding cap by the strap. Cody crawled out of his lair under the porch and they stood together against the fence, watching Moonie and Leggy graze in the weak morning sun. Time ticked slowly by. Finally, Abby figured it wasn't too early to go.

As a last-minute precaution, she ran inside to get her Tipperary crash vest. Better safe than sorry, she thought. She'd heard too many stories about Dancer's uncertain temper.

Abby pedalled her bicycle along the road to Hogscroft, feeling the soft, cool spring air on her face. Her father had wanted to drive her over and watch, but Abby didn't want any distractions, even her father's supportive face. Riding Dancer would require all of her concentration. She guessed that Cody would be watching from a secret place, but that was all right.

She checked her watch as she neared the farm. Nine twenty. She'd still be early, but she wanted a chance to give Dancer the apple in her jacket pocket. Bribery never hurts when it comes to horses.

Turning up the lane at Hogscroft, Abby got a shock. Just sixty feet in front of her, the mighty Dancer flew over the four-foot split-rail fence, landing in a spray of gravel on the driveway. He stopped dead, then spooked at the sight of Abby on her bike.

"Whoa, Dancer," she said. His body was tensed, ready to take flight. Slowly she rested her bike on the ground and pulled the apple from her pocket. "Steady, boy."

The surprise in Dancer's eyes was replaced by wariness. Abby walked slowly toward him, apple offered, eyes down. Humans are predatory animals, and horses are prey, and Abby did not want to appear threatening. Knowing that horses see better peripherally than straight on, she came to his side, not his head.

Dancer sniffed the apple. He snorted. He pawed the gravel. He seemed to be torn with indecision. Abby tried to understand. Did he not want food from a stranger? Was she making him nervous by doing something wrong? Unsure, Abby continued to hold out the apple. Dancer refused, yet stayed beside her.

Abby decided to put it down at his feet. He looked at the apple, then at her, and snorted again. He seemed amused. Puzzled, Abby turned to retrieve her bike. *This is a very strange horse*, she thought. Most horses gobble treats, regardless of who offers them. Abby picked up her bike and looked back at Dancer.

He was gone. So was the apple. Abby looked around. She'd had her back turned for only a few seconds.

"This is going to be even more difficult than I thought," she said to Cody. "I have no idea what's going on in his head."

Abby pushed her bike up the lane and leaned it on the barn wall, keeping an eye on the house. She expected Hilary to come out any minute. Abby wondered what she'd got herself into.

While she stood there, a big bay head appeared over the fence around the corner of the barn. The large gelding eyed her appraisingly. This person smelled of apple. He sniffed her pocket.

"You must be Henry. I'm Abby. I'm glad to see you're a normal horse. I'm so sorry," she said as she rubbed the long white blaze running down his face. "I only brought one apple, and I gave it to His Highness, the Ungrateful. If I'd known better, I'd have given it to you. At least you'd appreciate it." Abby liked this horse. He had a kind eye and a calm intelligence. And she thought he looked handsome, too, in a friendly Clydesdale way.

"I'll look in the barn for a treat," she told Henry. "Wait here." Abby walked into the barn, looking for something she could give him. In the feed room was a huge sack of carrots. *Perfect*, she thought. Filling her pockets, she went outside. Henry stood, watching her.

Abby pulled out a carrot and offered it to him. Suddenly, Dancer appeared out of nowhere and bodychecked Henry, pushing him away rudely and snatching the carrot out of Abby's hand.

"You greedy pig!" Abby shouted, as soon as she'd recovered her composure. She climbed over the fence, walked to Henry, and gave him two carrots, patting and consoling him.

Dancer came charging, head down menacingly. Henry bolted away in a hurry, leaving Abby standing alone. She stood her ground, staring directly into Dancer's eyes. He didn't slow down. Abby waited until he was three strides away, then she punched her arms out quickly, and yelled, "Whoa!" in a deep, loud, gruff voice. Dancer swerved to the left, missing her by inches. Abby stood with legs shaking, then casually turned and walked to the fence as quickly as she could without appearing to be frightened. She kept Dancer in her sight as she climbed the fence, not trusting him one bit.

Abby pondered her next move. *I should get on my bike and go home*, she thought. *He's a stallion. He has a bad reputation. He's certainly unlike any horse I've ever known*. Abby was unsure of herself. She wished she'd let her father come. He'd give her good advice. Liam would tell her to leave it alone, to stick with Moonie and Leggy. They were enough of a challenge for anyone.

Abby nodded sharply. She'd made her decision. She would go to the house and tell Hilary that she'd changed her mind. Hilary would try to convince her otherwise, but Abby would remain firm in her resolve. There was absolutely nothing Hilary could say that could change Abby's mind, and that was that.

As she was gathering her courage and rehearsing what she'd say, Dancer sauntered up and touched her shoulder with his nose. "What do *you* want?" she asked, coldly. Dancer nudged her again. "What?" Abby stayed where she was, unresponsive.

Dancer tilted his head to the left, then to the right, studying her carefully. He put his nose to her nose and gently sniffed and blew.

"You say you want to be friends? How do I know you're not playing with me?" Dancer had just let her know that he was curious, but Abby was not about to forget the scare he'd given her.

They looked at each other for a couple of minutes, each sizing the other up. Abby searched for the scar on his neck where Samuel Owens had slashed him. It was hardly visible. There was a slight indentation about six inches long, but the hair had grown in and the wound had healed well.

Dancer made the first move. He quietly lifted his front feet off the ground, balancing on his mighty haunches. Softly he dropped down. He gracefully stretched out his neck and bent into a full curtsy, front knees crossed. He held this position for two or three seconds, then lifted his head and looked at Abby.

"Okay, I'm impressed. Let me return the compliment." Abby stepped back from the fence and performed a flourishing bow, mirroring Dancer.

Dancer repeated his act, ending once again with his nose on the ground.

"Okay, you've won me over, Dancer. Here's a carrot." Abby held out her hand, smiling in spite of herself. Dancer delicately took the carrot in his teeth. He accepted the two small ones that remained in Abby's pocket, then rubbed his head gently on her arm.

"I think you just made a friend."

Abby spun around and came face to face with Hilary James.

"I didn't know you were here!" she sputtered. "How long have you been watching?"

"I just came out. Why?"

"Nothing. Nothing, I just wondered." Abby decided to keep Dancer's behaviour between the two of them. He'd tested her, that much was certain, and she'd passed. Abby felt a healthy respect for this smart, powerful stallion. He was unusually clever and unpredictable. She vowed to stay alert.

"Well, Abby? Are you ready to try him out?"

Who's trying out who? she thought. *Or is it whom?*

"Yes," Abby said aloud. "I think I am."

"Good. Let's get him tacked up and we'll start in the jumping paddock." Hilary casually threw a rope around Dancer's neck and walked him into the barn. Abby followed, noting how docile he was with Hilary. He seemed quite ordinary and horse-like.

Hilary talked to Abby while she placed the saddle pad and saddle on Dancer's back and tightened the girth. "You're a sensitive rider, Abby. I know you'll get along. I wouldn't have asked you otherwise. Actually, you're the only person I can think of who could ride him."

"Why?" Abby gulped, her eyes intent on the older girl.

Hilary laughed. "I didn't mean to put it quite like that. Once you get to know him, he's really quite simple. He doesn't need much urging. He reads your mind, then does it. He seems to know what I want him to do before I know myself." Hilary smiled at Abby reassuringly.

Abby didn't doubt that Dancer would do anything Hilary wanted. The question was if he'd do anything at all that Abby wanted. Her stomach was in knots.

"All set," said Hilary, after she slipped on the bridle and fastened the buckles on the nose band and cheek strap. She led him out to the riding ring, through the gate, and over to the mounting block.

With shaking hands, Abby put on her hard hat and tightened the safety strap around her chin. She zipped up her Tipperary crash vest and prepared herself. *Breathe in, breathe out*, she told herself. *Calm down*.

Dancer stood placidly at the mounting block while Abby stepped up. He seemed bored, but Abby knew that sometimes a certain bored look comes before an explosion, and she had just witnessed him in action.

Hilary stood at his head, still talking. Abby tuned in. "Today, we'll just get you both acquainted. Just a walk and trot, and see how it goes. Okay?" Abby nodded.

As she grabbed the saddle and started to put her foot in the stirrup, Dancer swung his rump away from her, leaving his head in Hilary's hands. Abby stumbled off the mounting block, almost falling onto her face.

Before Hilary could say a word, Abby had scrambled up onto Dancer's back from the ground. She threw her leg over and settled into the saddle in a flash. Her face held a firm resolve.

"Stirrups okay?" Hilary asked as though nothing had happened.

Abby nodded.

"You okay?"

Abby thought about it. Then she smiled. "Yes, I am."

Abby *was* okay. After his second little test, Dancer felt fine. Now that she was on his back she could sense his sanity and willingness. There was no hint of the craziness and untrustworthiness that Abby had expected. Her father always told her that a good rider knows the second he gets on a horse if he should be there. If his instinct questions it, he should get off right away, before he wishes he had.

Abby tightened her legs slightly, asking Dancer to walk.

He responded immediately. His stride was long and steady. He walked out nicely, neck flexing of its own accord. Abby stopped him and turned to walk in the other direction. She thought about trotting, and before she'd decided if she was ready, Dancer picked up a trot.

It was like floating on air. His action was long and low and rhythmic. Abby could ride like this forever.

"You can stop smiling anytime," called Hilary, happy with what she saw. "Nice, isn't he?"

"Nice is an understatement," Abby answered. "He's incredible. I didn't have any idea how powerful he was."

"Try him in a canter, if you like," Hilary said.

Abby merely pressed Dancer lightly with her right lower leg, and he went into a canter on his left lead. He rocked gently as he cantered, smooth as a ship on the ocean. His well-muscled legs lifted and fell, lifted and fell. They circled the ring twice, then changed leads and went to the right.

After three times around, Abby slowed him to a trot, then a walk. "He's beyond anything I expected, Hilary. He's magical. He's . . . I don't know what to say." Abby looked at Hilary in alarm. "Why are you crying? What am I doing wrong?"

"Absolutely nothing, Abby," Hilary answered, wiping her nose with her sleeve and sniffing. "It's just that he's so beautiful. I've never seen anyone ride him before."

"Thank you so much for letting me." Abby took her feet out of the stirrups and prepared to dismount.

"You're not finished, are you?"

"You wanted me just to walk and trot today, didn't you? To see if we got along? We cantered, too, so I thought . . ."

"Dancer has been bored for years. He wants to do things. You know how smart he is. He'd love it if you'd ride a little longer."

"Sure! I'll ride him as long as you say."

"Great. Let me set up a couple of rails to make him happy. And ignore me if I start to cry again." Hilary grinned as she spoke.

Abby and Hilary worked with Dancer for close to an hour. Hilary asked Abby to jump one jump, then two, and by the end of the hour, she'd added four more. Dancer was happy to be working again. His eyes were bright and focused. Hilary watched him carefully for signs of fatigue, but there were none.

A small crowd had gathered. Christine and Rory came out of the house to watch. Christine had phoned Liam and Fiona to tell them how well Abby and Dancer were getting along. Too excited to keep it to themselves, the Malones had asked the Piersons to join the fun.

Hilary's grandmother, Joy, had arrived earlier that morning. She stood at the fence with the others, her fluffy dog Diva close at her heels. An attractive, intelligent woman with short grey hair and a flair for fashion, Joy was a loving, supportive mother and grandmother. She was thrilled by Abby's success with Dancer, knowing how much it meant to Hilary. If Abby could exercise the feisty stallion, it would take a big weight off her granddaughter's shoulders. Joy had come up to the country to see the Wick property; this was an added bonus.

"Do the whole course, Abby," requested Pete Pierson, resting both hands on his cane to support his back. He'd been having trouble with his right hip, but he held his tall frame proudly, and his look was one of determination.

Abby looked at Hilary. Hilary nodded. "Only once, though, he's had enough for today."

All the fences were the same height. They were under three feet; a good height to start with on the first day. Abby collected Dancer into a slow canter and headed him squarely into the first fence, which was an X. They landed, took one stride, two strides, three strides, and jumped the rails, as Abby looked for the third hurdle. Land, one, two, three, four, she counted, and they soared over the oxer—two, identical jumps set together to form a box. Land, one, two, Abby counted, and over. Now she turned to look at the jump set on an angle. It was higher than the rest, and Abby hadn't thought she'd jump it, but Dancer was so keen, and they were having such fun, that she went straight for it. One, two, three, over. Perfect.

Abby eased him into a trot and patted his neck. "Good boy, Dancer! Good boy." She smiled from ear to ear. Now she would walk him out until his breathing returned to normal.

"Abby, that was great," called Hilary. "He certainly works for you, doesn't he?"

Abby nodded. "He's a great horse."

Liam and Pete stood together. They'd been conferring quietly the whole time they'd been watching.

"Well ridden, Abby," said Liam. "I'm proud of you, my girl."

"Me, too," agreed Pete. "He's not an easy horse to ride. Not many people have stayed on."

Liam added, "Not many people would even try."

"He never put a foot wrong," replied Abby. "He actually made it really easy for me."

"I wouldn't have missed this for the world," said Laura Pierson, fussing with her bright pink head scarf. "You're a very brave girl." A petite woman with fine features, Laura kept her bouffant hair blond with weekly trips to her hairdresser. She still liked to look attractive for Pete, even after almost sixty years of marriage. Her actions were quick and alert, and her good-natured, devilish smile could light up a room.

"Come on in for coffee and croissants," said Rory, motioning toward the house. "Joy picked them up at Le Petit Gourmet in Toronto just this morning."

"One hour ago," said Joy, pleased. "They're not still hot, but they're fresh."

Rory took Joy's arm. "I like having a mother-in-law who spoils me." With his generous nature and dark good looks, Rory was a natural leader. "Come on, everybody. Please come in. The show's over. You girls join us when you're ready." He put his other arm around Christine's waist, and they started for the house followed by the Malones and the Piersons.

Diva and Pepper had been racing around, chasing each other and anything else that moved. These two dogs were great friends, co-conspirators in mischief. Now they fell in with the group of humans, hoping for treats.

"You think those young girls can handle that wild horse?" asked Pete, tongue in cheek.

"Better than you and me," Liam responded proudly.

Abby kept Dancer walking.

"You rode great, Abby," Hilary repeated.

"Thanks," replied Abby. "He's the one who's great. I just sat on him."

"I wonder if you understand, Abby. If he didn't want you to be on his back, you wouldn't be there. Many people can testify to that." She laughed. "And if he didn't want to jump, you couldn't have made him budge." Hilary tilted her head, trying to find the right way to explain. "He likes you. It's as simple and as rare as that."

"I think I do understand. Before you came out, Dancer and I had sort of a testing. He passed my test. I must have passed his."

Hilary nodded slowly. "Yes, you must have. I've never seen him so good with anybody but me, aside from that little mounting-block avoidance tactic."

Abby grinned broadly, basking in Hilary's praise.

"Can you come back tomorrow?" Hilary asked. "I have to go back to school early Tuesday morning, and I'd like to work with you one more time. How's after school?"

"I'll be here." Abby felt good all over. The sky was the limit.

Samuel Owens put down the phone. He smiled. Things were going his way. His goals were about to be fulfilled. It was all so easy when you had money. His real estate agent had agreed to keep Owens' interest in Wick Farm a secret. He'd been told that there had been no offers in all the years it'd been on the market. Some woman was looking at it later in the day, but the agent assured him that it would come to nothing, and that Owens would get it for an extremely reasonable price. He had only to wait until Robert Wick became desperate, which should be soon, and lowball an offer. On the off chance that someone else should put in an offer, the agent would give him a chance to put in a higher one. Owens considered the matter done.

The acre property next door was a trifle. It was hardly worth thinking about. That old woman would take anything he offered.

Last but not least, the Casey property. Samuel Owens leaned back in his leather chair and sighed contentedly, savouring the events of the night before. Helena Casey had been receptive to his charms. He'd called on her around five o'clock for a visit and a drink, and had returned home at approximately two in the morning.

She'd had a drink or two before he'd arrived, but then again, so had he. Her pale, beautiful face had looked surprised to see him, but she'd invited him in without hesitation. Owens knew the type. She was lonely and bored and tipsy. A little flattery, a little charm. It didn't take much.

Owens stretched out his arms and yawned like a satisfied lion after a full meal. The April sun streamed through his large windows and fell across his rich oriental carpet, warming the library with the colours of the Far East. Gone were the dismal greys of the previous day.

How could she have been married to a man like Rory Casey? he wondered. *She needs a man of the world like me. A man who knows the ropes.* Helena intrigued him. Beauty, grace, and elegance, wrapped up with a wonderfully catty sense of humour and a piece of property that Owens coveted. She despised all the people Owens despised. She found the same things abhorrent. They had so much in common. She might be someone he could spend time with. There were opportunities here, beyond the mere acquisition of land.

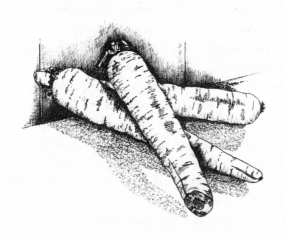

5
CALEDON HIGH

MONDAY WAS A GLORIOUS DAY, with the scents of crocuses and lilacs winning over the earthy smell of early spring. Birds called to each other noisily and insects buzzed and hummed. At seven forty-five in the morning, the sky was clear and the air was cool. Liam Malone pulled his car up to the school.

"Thanks for the ride, Dad," Abby called as she waved good-bye.

"See you later, lass. Have a good day."

Liam dropped off Abby on his way to work when their schedules matched. Otherwise, she rode her bike and took the school bus home when no one was going her way. Sometimes she got a lift home. Sam Morris had his family's old red Ford, but Abby never got a lift from him anymore.

With the excitement of the storm, the theatre, and Dancer, Abby hadn't thought about Sam all weekend. Now, walking up the wide stone steps of the school, Abby's heart plummeted in an all-too-familiar way. Sam had been her first boyfriend, and they'd dated for almost a year. Since their breakup the year before, Abby had dated several other boys and had had fun playing the field. It was great going to movies and dances with different people, and she'd really liked a few of them. But lately she'd started thinking about Sam again. With his beautiful brown eyes and his sweet smile, Sam had stolen her heart the first time she saw him.

His sister, Leslie Morris, was two years younger than Sam; Abby's age. Abby and Leslie had been best friends since the beginning of grade school. Leslie and another good friend, Lucy, were both very supportive when Abby confided in them. Lucy didn't want to see Abby hurt. The class comedian, she had likened the whole thing to ice cream. Abby had one favourite flavour. Why not sample all the others? In Lucy's opinion, it was very narrow-minded to insist that just because you like strawberry you shouldn't give butterscotch a chance. And chocolate fudge and rocky road.

Easy for her to say, thought Abby, making her way down the hall to her locker. Lucy was one of the most popular girls in grade ten. She was outgoing and funny, and she laughed riotously at all the boys' jokes. Abby figured that that was the way to a man's heart, forget the cooking.

And Abby *had* gone out with other boys. She *had* sampled other flavours. But Sam was, well, Sam. He was kind and thoughtful and insightful. He was smart and friendly and sensitive. He made her laugh. And he was so darned good-looking. But, quite obviously, Sam didn't feel the same about her. She sighed.

She got to her locker and dialled the combination of numbers. She pulled the lock open and started organizing her books for the morning classes.

"Abby?" asked a sugary sweet, little-girl voice. Abby clenched her teeth. She didn't have to look around to know who was standing behind her. The strong smell of cheap perfume almost made her gag.

"Hey, Pam. What's up?"

"Just wondering who you're going out with now. I mean everybody knows it's not Sam."

"What?" asked Abby angrily, turning to face her.

Pam Masters put her hand to her mouth in mock horror. "Oh, I'm so sorry. Did I upset you? I just wanted to know."

"Pam, I'll tell you what *I* know. I know that whenever you say anything to me, it's to make me feel bad. It's been like that since public school."

"So sorry." Pam made a good effort at looking sheepish, but Abby could see that her mission had been accomplished. She'd pressed a button. She'd gotten a reaction from Abby and confirmed her suspicions. Now she knew how Abby felt about Sam. *Is it so obvious? Is that the gossip?* Abby blushed, horrified that people were talking about her. *When will I ever learn to keep my temper?* she asked herself, turning back to the locker.

"What did she want?" asked another voice, this one friendly.

"Leslie!" said Abby with real warmth in her voice. She hugged her friend. "One day I'm going to murder Pam."

"What did she say to you? Your face fell to the floor."

"Oh, nothing. Just about Sam."

"Hmm. You know I'm not getting in the middle because he's my brother and everything, but I did some digging on the weekend. He isn't seeing anyone right now, I'm positive."

"Leslie, it's over. It's been over for ages. I shouldn't have said anything. And I wouldn't have if I'd known you were going to ask him."

"But you were so good together. And I didn't ask him! I just listened to his phone calls."

"His phone calls? You're crazy! You picked up the extension?"

"Easy peasy. I heard him tell Jon he wasn't dating anyone. With my own ears."

Against her better judgment Abby considered this piece of news. Then she looked intently at Leslie. "Leslie, listen to me. Sam and I are finished. Read my lips. I wouldn't go out with him if he begged me, not after the way he dumped me."

"He didn't dump you, Abby, and you know it."

"Okay, then, he didn't dump me. He just stopped asking me out and started avoiding me."

Books in order, Abby snapped the lock back into place, and the two girls walked down the hall to their first class. There was so much noise that their conversation had to be postponed. Cheerful banter, heels thumping on tiles, locker doors banging, books crashing to the floor, all mixed together to create a boisterous Monday morning cacophony.

"Hey, Abby! Hey, Leslie!" called out Lucy, going the other direction.

"Hey, Lucy!" returned Abby and Leslie, in unison.

"See you after second class?" Lucy bellowed. "We have to talk!"

"Who? Me?" yelled Abby.

"Yes!" Lucy was swept away with the flow of students, leaving Abby wondering what she wanted to tell her. Her brow furrowed. It was likely more gossip about Sam. She didn't want to hear it.

That morning, Christine James was on the phone in her home office.

"Is Mr. LeFarge there, please?"

"Speaking."

"Gus? It's Christine James calling."

"Hello, Christine. How can I help?"

"My client, Joy Featherstone, would like to put in an offer on the Wick property."

"Your mother? You must be kidding. She's seen it?"

"Yesterday afternoon. You left the key for me, remember?"

"Sure I do, I just didn't know it was for your mother. Excuse my surprise, Christine, but this is the first offer in three years."

"Then it must be good news. Shall I stop by in an hour?"

"Well, just to warn you, there's a first refusal on it."

Christine paused, startled. "Usually, out of courtesy, that would have been mentioned when I asked for a viewing."

"Quite right. Quite right. An oversight. I didn't think Mrs. Featherstone would be interested, nobody else has ever been. I'm very sorry."

"No problem. How would you like to proceed?"

"Well, why don't you drop by? I'll look at the offer, check back with the gentleman who has the first refusal, and call my client. We can go from there."

"You're not going to make this into an auction, are you, Gus?"

Gus LeFarge snorted. "Mr. Wick deserves the best price, and with a first refusal on the property, is there another way to do this?"

Christine hung up the phone. Who had the first refusal? She shrugged. There's always something. She returned to the stack of papers on her desk, sorting out which items of business required her immediate attention, and which could wait. The phone rang.

"Hello. Christine James speaking."

"Hello, Mrs. James. I want to know what my house is worth."

"Certainly. I'll come out and give you an evaluation. What is your name, please?"

"Gladys Forsyth."

"And where do you live?"

"Right beside Samuel Owens' place. I've got an acre. It's a small house. My name's not on the mailbox, but you can't miss it. It's the first lane past the Owens' big black gates."

"Is there any time that would be convenient for you?"

"I'll be here all day. You know why I'm calling?"

Christine took the bait. "To get your house evaluated?"

"Yes, but, strange thing. You know LeFarge Realty?"

"Yes, I do."

"Some young man called me from LeFarge Realty and offered me cash for my house. I would've taken it, but my son told me to check it out. You're the first real estate agent I saw in the Yellow Pages, so that's why I called."

"It's always a good idea to get a second opinion."

"That's just what my son says."

"Well, Gladys, I've got to make a trip close by anyway, so why don't we say eleven thirty or twelve?"

"Any time you get here is swell."

Christine hung up. She knew exactly where Gladys lived. The shack. Old car carcasses, rusted metal junk, and cats. Dozens of cats. Off the top of her head she couldn't think of who would be putting in an offer. She took the price of an acre of land in Caledon, then multiplied it by six because a severed acre with hydro and sewage was worth that much more. Since the house was worth nothing, she planned to give that base figure as her estimate.

She checked her watch. She'd have to leave soon. Hilary came into her study, followed by Pepper.

"Hi, Mom. Busy?"

"Never too busy to talk to you."

"I brought you a coffee."

"Wonderful. I've got just enough time for a coffee, then I've got to go."

"What are you doing?"

"Running around. Real estate stuff."

"Will you be back by three?"

"I'll be home well before that. Why?"

"Because Abby's coming to ride Dancer after school, and I could come with you if we'd be back by then. I'm leaving tomorrow and I have nothing to do but study and I know the stuff backward. Plus it's too nice a day to stay inside."

Christine smiled. "I couldn't think of nicer company."

Lucy caught up with Abby between classes. "Abby! Over here!"

"Lucy, if this is about Sam, forget it. I don't want to hear about it." Abby kept walking, face straight ahead. She spoke harshly. "I don't care a thing about him, and I wish I'd never said a word about liking him again. It's all over the school! It's embarrassing. I'm over him, totally!"

Lucy regarded her friend with skepticism as she kept up with her pace. "Liar. Anyway, it's not about Sam, so you don't have to be so touchy."

Abby stopped and looked at her. "What's it about, then?"

"Dancer. My grandfather told me that you rode him yesterday. Cool!"

"Yeah." Abby's face softened. "He's a fantastic horse. How did your grandfather hear?" Lucy's grandfather, George Farrow, had given Abby her first job riding Moonlight Sonata.

"No secrets around here, Abby. Everybody knows. It's news, whether you know it or not. Old Pete Pierson was all excited about it. He told my grandfather you could win any competition, hands down, and he's prepared to put money on it as long as Mrs. Pierson doesn't find out. Nobody but Hilary James could ever ride him without being thrown off."

"Lucy, I'm flattered that Mr. Pierson said all that, but Dancer basically allowed me to look good. It was his choice not to throw me. I'm not kidding. He did everything."

"That's what I mean." Lucy moved flat against the locker to avoid a running boy, presumably late for class. "The way I see it, all horses do that for you."

"Never mind, Lucy. It's hard to explain."

Leslie came around the corner, arms full of books. "Hey, guys!"

"Hey, Leslie," answered Abby. "When's your next class?"

"I have a spare. I'm going for tea in the cafeteria."

"Great!" said Abby. "My French teacher's got the flu. I'm taking a spare, too."

"And that's my French teacher, too. Hooray for the flu. Let's go."

The three friends hurried out of the hall, where the pushing and running and darting bodies were making it impossible for them to linger. They got their tea and sat down at a table.

"I know something I'm dying to tell someone," Abby said quietly.

"Tell! Tell!" shrieked Lucy.

"Quiet!" hissed Abby. "It's really private. You can't tell a living soul. Understand?"

Leslie nodded seriously. "Absolutely. On my honour."

Lucy swept up her hand, drawing a cross on her chest. "Cross my heart and hope to die."

Satisfied, Abby leaned across the table and asked, "Do either of you know the Wick farm?"

"Sure," said Lucy. "The haunted barn."

"Ooooh," said Leslie, wiggling her fingers. "Spooky."

"You make fun, Les," said Abby, "but it really is haunted. I saw the ghost, and Mr. Wick told me he's real, too. It's the ghost of an unhappy actor, Ambrose Brown, and I saw him."

"You are so weird," said Lucy. "I can't believe you're trying to make us believe you saw a ghost. We're not babies."

"Believe it." Abby took a sip of her tea, as Lucy gave Leslie a wink.

"I saw that, Lucy. You don't have to believe me. I saw what I saw."

"Hold on, Abby," said Leslie. "I didn't say I don't believe you."

Lucy snickered. "You believe in ghosts, Les?"

"Sort of. And if Abby saw it . . ."

"You're just being nice. There's no such thing as ghosts."

Abby sat quietly while Lucy and Leslie argued. Then she said, "Let's go. I'll prove it."

The other girls were stunned.

"Now?" asked Leslie. "I can't miss English."

"And Mr. Saunders will kill me if I skip math."

"Okay, then," responded Abby. "We'll go at lunch. Who can get a car?"

"I have my grandfather's truck today," answered Lucy. "I'll drive."

Abby nodded. "Good. We'll meet in the parking lot as soon as the lunch bell rings. We can eat on the way."

One minute after the bell, Lucy stood beside her grandfather's truck, waving to her friends. "Over here!"

Abby and Leslie came running.

"Let's hurry," said Abby. "We've only got forty-five minutes."

Lucy started the truck. "Destination, Wick Farm," she said as they pulled out of the parking lot.

Seven minutes later, they bounced up Robert Wick's pot-holed lane, splashing mud all the way up the sides of the truck and torturing the suspension. Lucy stopped beside the barn, where the lane ended.

"This better be worth it, Abby," Lucy said. "I'll have to wash the truck."

"Oh, it'll be worth it." Abby smiled knowingly.

Abby led the way. She unlatched the door and slowly pushed it open, finger to lips. "Shhh."

"What do we have to be quiet for?" said Lucy, loudly. "It's a barn. It's noon. There's nobody around."

Abby closed the door again. "This is a bad idea. You have no respect for ghosts, Lucy. He's not going to show himself if you come barging in, yakking away. Let's go back to school."

"I want to see him, Abby," pleaded Leslie. "I haven't said a word. Can't Lucy wait here while we go in?"

"No way! I drove. No way I'm waiting out here."

"Lucy, will you keep quiet if we go inside?" asked Abby, sternly.

"Okay." Lucy's posture indicated submission, but her eyes sparkled with mischief. "I promise."

Abby opened the door again. She entered silently, followed by Leslie and Lucy. They stood for a minute in the dark.

"What now?" whispered Lucy.

"We wait."

"For what?"

"The ghost, for goodness' sake. Lucy, you promised to keep quiet."

"I just wanted to know."

They waited. Two minutes passed. Three. Four.

"Okay," said Lucy loudly. "That's enough. There's nothing here."

Leslie was angry. She whispered hoarsely, "Lucy, that's so unfair! You keep breaking the silence! How do you ever expect to see a ghost?"

Abby switched on the lights. Lucy and Leslie covered their eyes in surprise.

"You're right, Les," said Abby. "We won't see the ghost as long as Lucy's around. But look at this."

Lucy and Leslie stared at the sight before their eyes.

"Wow," murmured Leslie.

"Double wow," said Lucy. "This is amazing. This is incredible." Lucy propelled herself up the stairs and onto the stage in a couple of bounds. She twirled around and danced and laughed. "Abby, this is great! What's the big deal about a ghost? This secret theatre is worth a hundred ghosts! To see this is worth having to wash the truck!"

Abby couldn't help but be pleased at Lucy's reaction. She laughed out loud, joined by Leslie, who threw her arms around Abby and twirled her. Dancing around the stage, Abby celebrated the fact that her friends found the theatre as enchanting as she did.

Cody was investigating the intriguing smells he'd ignored when he'd been in the upper Wick field two days before. These were dangerous smells, and very exciting. Cody's ruff was up, and he sniffed and circled and ran, getting nearer to the place where they gathered. They were wild. They were like him, but different. This confused Cody. It drew him, and repelled him.

Even in his excitement, he felt the eyes upon him. Suddenly, silently. He didn't look. Two, three, four. More. Many of his kind were here. They were drawing nearer. He must leave. Now. Not toward home. Leave no tracks that lead to home.

Cody headed north as fast as he could. He was gone before the wild coyotes devised their strategy, before they knew that he knew they were there. He ran out of their territory. Still running, Cody felt Abby's presence. Stronger and stronger as he neared the old barn where they'd waited in the storm. Nose in the air, concentrating on finding his Abby, Cody didn't watch where he was stepping.

By twelve thirty, Christine and Hilary James had delivered Joy's offer to Gus LeFarge, and then dropped in to assess Gladys Forsyth's place. They had a few more stops to make before driving back to Hogscroft.

"Do you think Gladys expected more for her house?" asked Hilary.

"Hard to say. I don't know what she was offered, or by whom, but she didn't look surprised at my assessment."

"She didn't look disappointed or pleased, either," replied Hilary. "She just stared at you. I couldn't tell what she was thinking, behind those taped-up, smudged glasses. It's a wonder she can see through them."

Christine smiled. "It takes all types, honey."

"It certainly does." Hilary was thinking. "Some types are better than others. I'd take Gladys over Samuel Owens any day."

"Amen," said Christine. "I haven't heard anything more about his release. Have you?"

"Other than seeing the lights on at his mansion last Saturday, nothing. I feel it in my bones, though. It's creepy. He's creepy."

"Mousie, you're feeling this way because we just drove past his house. He's been in treatment, don't forget. Hopefully, he's seen the error of his ways. They wouldn't have let him out unless he was better."

Hilary stared out the window and shivered. "I wouldn't put any money on that."

The thought of Owens back in the community upset Christine as much as it did Hilary. They sat in silence, each remembering the damage he had inflicted on their family.

They passed the Wick farm, just around the next bend. There was a muddy truck, empty, sitting in the lane beside the barn.

"Whose truck is that, Mom?"

"Looks like George Farrow's."

"What's he doing there?"

"I don't know. Maybe he's checking the place for Robert Wick. Or maybe he's our mystery competition."

"Maybe, but why? Actually, now that I think about it, why does Gran want it?"

Christine laughed. "Mousie, your Gran has always been full of surprises."

"It's great, the way she looks at things as challenges. Will she start the theatre up again?"

"Ask Gran."

"Does she have enough money? If she starts it up and it fails?"

"That depends on how much she can buy it for, and how much she puts into it. The land alone is an investment, no matter what happens to the theatre, so she wouldn't lose everything if the theatre doesn't succeed."

"I guess I'm really asking if it's wise for her to buy it."

"She's put in a reasonable offer. One she can afford. She's not a rich woman, Mousie, but she's been careful with her investments, and now she wants to play a little. Don't worry. She won't do anything that would jeopardize her finances. She's smart."

"I know." Hilary took a deep breath before she spoke. "Mom? I have something to tell you. Actually it's why I came along."

"Yes?" Christine continued to drive, waiting. She shot a glance at her daughter. "What is it, Mousie? Is anything wrong?"

"Not at all, Mom. In fact, it's great." A crooked smile tugged at her mouth.

"Then what is it? Don't keep me guessing."

"Sandy and I want to get married by the end of the summer."

Christine's eyes widened. She gripped the steering wheel tightly. "You're serious?"

Hilary nodded, now smiling widely. "Very. Sandy wanted me to tell you today, and tonight he'll call Rory and Helena from Montreal. Do you think you can keep it secret until tonight?"

Christine pulled the car over to the side of the road and put it in park.

"Is this what you want?"

"Yes, Mom. Sandy and I have been in love for five years."

"But you're very young, Mousie. You're only twenty-two. There's so much more to learn about life."

"But I want to learn it with Sandy."

"Mousie, you've never really dated other men. How can you be sure?"

"I never wanted to date anyone but Sandy." Hilary spoke with conviction. "He means everything to me. We want to get married, and we want to go to Belize as husband and wife. I hope you can understand, Mom."

Christine gave Hilary an enormous hug, which her daughter heartily returned. "Of course I understand, Mousie. I just want you to be happy."

6
CODY AND THE WILD COYOTES

LUCY DROPPED ABBY OFF at the end of her driveway after school. Abby's head was buzzing with the day's adventure and the prospect of riding Dancer again. She ran up the lane to her house, hurrying to get into her riding clothes before bicycling over to Hogscroft.

"Hi, Mom!" she hollered as she raced up the stairs two at a time.

"Hi, Abby! Did you have a good day?" Fiona asked.

"Great! Lucy drove Leslie and me over to the Wick farm at lunch. They couldn't believe how fabulous the theatre is! We want to put on a play and charge money and start a theatre company!"

"Does Mr. Wick know?"

"Know what?"

"That you were there."

"No."

"Hold on, Abby!" Fiona walked up the stairs to talk to her daughter. "You were trespassing. The place is empty and for sale, but it doesn't belong to you. It belongs to Mr. Wick. You need permission to be on someone else's property, and you should never go into other people's buildings. Would you like it if someone was snooping around here when you weren't home?"

Abby's face fell. "I didn't think of that." She zipped up her riding pants and grabbed her gloves. She faced her mother, realizing her mistake. "You're right. We won't go there again."

"I'm sure there's no harm done," said Fiona, reacting to Abby's deflation. "For today. Just make sure you ask Mr. Wick next time."

"I will, I promise." Abby was contrite, but anxious to go. "I'm off to ride Dancer. See you later." She kissed her mother on the cheek as she rushed past her and down the stairs.

Fiona followed her. "Do you want me to drive you over?"

"No thanks. I'll take my bike. I don't know how long I'll be."

"Be careful!" Fiona called to Abby's back as she jumped on her bicycle and started down the lane.

"I will!"

Abby thought of Dancer as she made her way along the road to Hogscroft. The gorgeous chestnut stallion had totally captured her imagination. The day before, he'd allowed Abby to make some progress. Today might be quite different. He was a smart horse. Too smart for his own good, the farmers around here said.

Abby had the sense that she'd forgotten something. Something was missing. She went through the list of things she had to remember. Breeches, boots, gloves, hat, Tipperary vest. She had everything. What was this feeling about?

Cody! Cody was missing. Abby slammed on her brakes. Cody always met her in the lane when she got home from school. Every day, without fail. No matter what time, however late or early, he always seemed to know when she was coming. Today, he had not been there to meet her.

Abby's stomach twisted with anxiety. Was he in trouble? How could she be so selfish, so preoccupied with her own dreams of stardom on Dancer that she could forget her most loyal friend?

She was almost at Hogscroft. Abby knew she couldn't ride until she found Cody. She sped the bike down the gravel road and tore up the lane to the barn.

Dancer was brushed and shiny, all tacked up in the aisle.

"Abby!" exclaimed Hilary. "What's the rush? You're early! I was about to take Dancer for a ride . . ."

"Hilary. Cody's missing. I have to find him. Can I ride later, if I find him before dark?"

Hilary was puzzled. "Doesn't he just turn up when he feels like it?"

"Yes, but he always greets me after school. He just seems to know. And he wasn't there." Abby was flustered, knowing how unconvincing she must sound.

Hilary realized that they wouldn't get any work done with Abby so unsettled. "Take Dancer. You start looking up that way and work down through the trails toward Saddle Creek." She gestured toward the woods to the northeast. "I'll start down at your place and work north. I'll tack up Henry, and we'll keep to the road." As she talked, she took Henry out of his stall and began to get him ready. "If you find Cody, come out to the road, but let's check back here in one hour. I'll bring Pepper. She'll warn me if he's around. She's been frightened to death of coyotes since the time she was almost eaten."

Abby nodded, satisfied with Hilary's plan. She buckled her chin strap and zipped up her vest. She led Dancer over to the mounting block and hopped lightly onto his back.

"Abby!" Hilary called. "If either of us finds him, we'll do a yip yip yippee at the top of our lungs and come back here. Okay?"

"Okay. Thanks, Hilary." Abby asked Dancer for a trot, and got a canter. He had sensed her impatience. He was like an enormous rocking horse with his powerful action, restrained but eager. He allowed Abby to keep him in check as they travelled north up the road.

Abby turned east onto the trail that wound behind the Caseys' farm. Cody might very well have gone on the paths that he and Abby and Moonie usually took. But if he was anywhere within miles of her, he'd have shown himself already. Abby's mind was spinning. Something was very wrong.

Cody lay still. *They* were getting closer. His shiny, terrified eyes darted around, as he desperately sought a solution, an escape. He mustn't breathe. He shouldn't move a muscle. He wanted the horrible thing off his leg. The thing that snapped its teeth and hurt badly. He'd dragged himself as far as he could until the horrible thing got caught on a rock. He could go no further. He worked his body into a small dip between two rocks and tried to disappear from sight. He needed to get away from this evil place. But he couldn't move, and he shouldn't move, or *they* would find him faster.

Hilary leisurely rode Henry south toward Abby's house. Cody might be sleeping under the porch in his little den, oblivious to all the fuss. It was worth a look. He simply might have come home after Abby had left to ride. Even Cody could misjudge arrivals and departures once in a while.

Pepper was delighted to be out on this beautiful spring day. She sniffed everything in sight, and hopped and scooted from here to there. Her comical antics made Hilary laugh. They'd find Cody at home, reassure Abby, and get on with the lesson. An hour's hack for Henry wasn't a bad idea, anyway.

Hilary thought of her new student with pride. Abby had good instincts on a horse. She'd turned out to be the perfect solution to Hilary's problem with Dancer. If Abby could commit to ride him three times a week, Dancer would feel useful again and settle down.

As they rode up the Malones' lane, Hilary called, "Cody!

Here boy!" Pepper was going berserk, sniffing and barking and circling around the porch.

Fiona came out of the house, drying her hands on a dishcloth. She had a puzzled look on her face. "Hilary! Abby's already gone over on her bike!"

"I know, Mrs. Malone, I saw her at the barn. But Cody's missing, so she's out looking for him on Dancer, and I'm looking for him on Henry. He's not here, is he?"

"I wouldn't know. He shows himself only when he wants to, so I can't be sure." As Fiona spoke, she walked over to the entrance to Cody's lair under the porch. "Cody?" she called. "Cody!"

There was no sign of the coyote.

"Hilary, you're very kind to help look for him, but in truth, he only comes to Abby. You might as well go back and wait. He certainly doesn't come to me when I call."

Hilary nodded. "Pepper! Come!" The Jack Russell lifted her head, cocked an ear, then continued what she was doing, which was digging frantically under the porch.

"Pepper doesn't come to anyone when she's called unless it suits her." The two women smiled at each other. "If Cody shows up, would you mind calling my house?"

"Not a bit. He could show up any minute." Fiona waved goodbye as Hilary turned Henry and trotted down the lane. Pepper realized that they weren't waiting, and furiously raced to catch up.

They knew where he was. *They* were playing a game with him. It was only a matter of time before the leader would give the signal and it would be over. Cody was ready. He was already dying. Blood soaked the coarse grass beneath him, and insects from the earth were smelling food. His only regret was for his Abby: He could protect her no longer. His heart broke. His body slumped. His will to live drained.

STAGESTRUCK

Dancer and Abby continued along the paths and trails. Abby called Cody's name. There was never a responding yip. No magical appearance of her coyote friend. Abby worried that he might be dead, hit by a car, mangled by a wild coyote. On they trotted, slowing only to listen for Cody's call.

As they travelled along, Abby and Dancer were getting used to each other. They began to respond without thought or tension to each other's signals. Before long, there was no misunderstanding between them; only an innate single will. Never did Abby bully or push him. Never did Dancer balk or resist. They were united in the mystical, timeless fashion of man and horse.

At the boundary of Samuel Owens' property, where it abutted Wick Farm, Dancer suddenly became uneasy. He pranced on the spot and shook his head. He refused to go further. "What's wrong, Dancer?" cooed Abby as she stroked his tensed neck. "What is it?"

Dancer only got more fretful. He backed up and scooted sideways, twisting his neck and trying to tell Abby that they must leave. The harmony between them was broken in a struggle of wills. After urging him every way she could think of, and pleading with him to go forward, Abby realized that Dancer was not going to change his mind. He was legitimately frightened. Abby must respect that, and search for Cody alone.

She dismounted, wondering if Dancer's fear might be a sign that Cody was near. "Is it the smell of coyote that frightens you?" Abby detached the reins from Dancer's bit and put them in her pocket. She ran the stirrups up, tucked the leathers through, and tied them tight to keep the stirrups from flapping on his sides.

"Home, Dancer! Home!" Abby waved her arms and clapped her hands, urging Dancer to follow his instincts and flee. A horse always knows where home is, and Abby knew that Dancer would run directly to his barn. Dancer hesitated, stunned by his new freedom. Then he turned and ran.

Now Abby was alone. The April afternoon was sunny and the air was fresh, but Abby felt dread in the pit of her stomach and fear caused sweat to trickle down her arms.

"Cody!" she called. "Cody!" She walked deeper into the neglected field, feeling the brambles catching on her breeches. The Wick land hadn't been tended in years, and stubbly bushes, stunted thorn trees, and a mess of weeds made walking difficult. "Cody!" Abby looked carefully for any signs of a tussle.

The hairs on her arms bristled. She looked around quickly. Nothing. She took a deep breath and continued walking. There was a sturdy stick lying on the ground. *This might be a useful thing to have.* She weighed the heft of it in her hand and felt better armed.

"Cody!" she called as she moved along into a small clump of straggly growth. The ground was rocky and uneven, suitable for grazing animals but not for growing a crop. Abby looked at her watch. It was four thirty; she had another two hours or more of light.

The tall grass rustled behind her. She spun around. Nothing. A rustle to her left. Nothing. Abby felt danger all around her, but couldn't see a thing. "Take a pill," she told herself aloud. "It's all in your imagination."

Just then, she saw the glinting eyes of a large, grey coyote. He strode out of his hiding place with the confidence of a prize fighter. Abby knew what that meant. She was surrounded. This handsome, shaggy animal with the manic eyes and the grinning snout would be the chief, the alpha male, coming out to challenge her. *Why would he do this?* she asked herself. Normally they watch but never show themselves to humans. Was she too close to the den and a litter of newborn pups? Or had the coyotes gathered for another purpose? One that she interrupted?

Abby swung the stick and surprised the coyote, yelling at the top of her lungs. "Get out of here! Get lost! Yahhh! Hahhh!"

As the chief jumped away, another coyote came up from behind, teeth bared. Abby swung at him with all her strength, still screaming in her fiercest voice. "Rahhh! Get away! Hahhh!"

A third and fourth coyote came at her from the tall grass. Abby continued to yell and holler and swing the stick. The coyotes were taking turns jumping at her, wearing her out, playing with her. One grabbed the stick in his strong jaws. Abby felt the pull and knew she was in trouble. She let it go and kept screaming and waving her arms. The coyotes smelled victory and began to close in.

Abby blinked. She couldn't believe her eyes. There, struggling toward her, just twenty feet away, was Cody. His back right leg was bleeding badly, and he was dragging a rusty, nasty-looking leg-hold trap. He pulled himself toward her, using every ounce of his strength. Half-dead from blood loss, and delirious with pain, he was coming to save her.

Abby's throat constricted. "No, Cody! No!" He reeled back, chastened by his mistress. "No!" Abby repeated. "Stay!" Cody would be killed in an instant if the coyotes turned their attention to him. She would be powerless to do anything about it.

Cody threw back his head. He howled and yipped a challenge to the pack. Abby was shocked. He was trying to distract them. Unsteadily, he rose to his feet, wobbling and swaying. Cody bayed again, trumpeting his superiority and howling his dominance. This was an insult to the pack, a direct affront.

Abby watched in horror as the alpha female turned to face Cody. Ignoring Abby's shouts, each coyote turned to Cody. Slowly, they surrounded him. Abby counted five. She bent to pick up her stick, abandoned for this newest amusement. She wasn't sure what she was going to do, but she couldn't leave Cody to die.

The coyotes stood poised, still as death, every eye on Cody. The moment was near.

At the exact same second as Abby chose to raise her stick and go for them, the sound of pounding hooves shook the ground and startled her.

Abby looked behind to see the magnificent charge of the stallion. Dancer came galloping, ears pinned back, teeth flashing, anger shooting out of his eyes like lightning bolts. The stirrups had come loose and they flapped at his sides, making the spectacle even more unearthly to the coyotes, who stared at him with terrified eyes.

On he came, over the rocks and bushes and brambles. No obstacle caused him to falter or vary his direct line. His knees reached up past his lowered nose as he covered ground, each huge stride bringing him closer to the astonished pack.

He didn't slow. He raced right through the pack, scattering them every which way, kicking and roaring and twisting until each one had turned tail and headed for safety.

Shaking with spent adrenalin, Abby collapsed on the ground beside her wounded coyote and hugged him gently. "We'll get you home, Cody. We'll fix you up." She rested with him, waiting for the shaking to subside.

Dancer thrust his nose down into Abby's face and sniffed and blew. His sides heaved. Abby held his head and stroked his sweaty face. Tears rolled down her face.

"You saved us, Dancer. You saved us. Thank you for coming back."

Abby knew she needed to get Cody help before it was too late. She checked his gums: They were white. He was in shock. Along with the blood loss, that added up to an emergency situation.

Abby examined the trap. The rusted steel jaws had ripped the flesh on Cody's leg and were digging into the bone. Abby didn't know if she should try to get him home with the trap attached to his leg or try somehow to release it. That question was answered when she lifted Cody. He yelped in pain. The old trap was very heavy, and its weight pulled on his injured leg. It had to come off.

The spring mechanism bowed in the centre. Abby guessed that when the trap was open, the spring would lie flat, like a mousetrap. If she stepped hard enough on the flexed steel, would it open? There was only one way to find out. Abby positioned the trap so that her weight would push down the spring. Cody whimpered.

Abby gritted her teeth. "Please, let this be the right thing to do," she prayed. She stepped down squarely, putting all her weight and strength onto the spring. If she was wrong, she feared that it would cut off Cody's leg.

The ancient trap snapped open.

Abby kept all her weight on the spring as she gingerly lifted Cody's leg out. The second she stepped off, the trap snapped shut with an awesome clang, sending particles of rust in every direction.

She gently scooped Cody up off the ground, careful to find the position that hurt him the least. Cody was stoic, but in a lot of pain.

The nearest house was Samuel Owens'. Abby didn't want to go anywhere near there, especially with Dancer. There was no one to help at the Wick farm. There was the little house on the acre lot beside Owens' driveway. Gladys Forsyth was usually home, and she loved animals, but Hilary would be riding on the road, or waiting for Abby at Hogscroft. Abby headed for the road.

Samuel Owens was on the phone.

"Dammit, Gus! You told me there hasn't been any interest in that piece of junk land in all the years it's been on the market!"

"There hasn't. This offer just came in, Mr. Owens. That's why I called."

"If I knew there'd be an offer, I would've bought the place yesterday. You should've seen it coming. I'm not happy, LeFarge. Now we'll have a bidding war."

"Not likely. The offer comes from Joy Featherstone. She's not a rich woman."

"Well, well. Joy Drake. I went to school with her a lifetime ago. What did she offer?"

"Close to asking."

"Gus, how much would it take for you not to mention Joy's offer to Wick? Pretend it's yesterday. I'll put in a good offer. When Wick accepts it, you get a handsome fee and we don't have to fool around with counteroffers."

"It's tempting, Sam. But you forget, I already had my licence suspended once for you. I won't be making that mistake again."

"You told me there'd be no problem. It's a problem if I don't get the property." Samuel Owens hung up, angry. Nobody wants to help a friend. He got up from his desk and took his favourite position by the picture window. Soon, all this would be his, but it was taking too long. There were more obstacles than he'd expected, and he was getting impatient.

Something was moving across his land. Way back, near the Wick boundary. Owens picked up his binoculars and adjusted them. A horse, no rider, but saddled up. A human, carrying something dark and heavy. The horse was Dancer. There was no mistake. Dancer, on his property. Mousie James wouldn't have the nerve to be on his land, would she? He strained his eyes to see. Didn't they learn their lesson last time? He was within his rights to shoot trespassers. There were signs posted. Couldn't she read?

The phone on his desk rang.

"Owens here."

"Mr. Owens? It's Gladys Forsyth."

STAGESTRUCK

Samuel Owens' eyes lit up. His voice took on a kindly, paternal tone. "Well, Gladys, how nice to hear back from you so quickly."

"I'll want more money for my house."

Owens' face darkened, but his voice purred. "That was a generous offer, Gladys. The price per acre is well-known. I offered twice the going rate."

"I had an estimate done. My son told me to do that. Mrs. James says it's worth six times the price per acre because it's a severed lot. That's three times what you offered, and that's what I want."

"You greedy—Christine James, eh? You called her in for an appraisal? She's been busy lately."

"Are you going to pay, or walk away? My son said to say that."

"Let me think on it, Gladys. Remember, this is a solid offer. A bird in the hand and all that, but I'll get back to you."

"Don't wait too long, or it'll be gone. Heh, heh."

"Your son is a funny man, Gladys. Goodbye."

Owens was furious. Dancer was walking across his property, and Mousie's mother and grandmother were messing up all his plans by putting in an offer on the Wick farm and telling Gladys Forsyth her acre was worth three times his offer.

That does it. Owens took his Remington hunting rifle off the shelf over his desk. Keeping his eyes fixed on Dancer, Owens slipped a cartridge into place. He closed the well-oiled chamber with a firm click. He threw open the casement window and aimed. That horse was not welcome on his property.

Boom! Boom boom! The sounds of a rifle discharging ripped through the air like claps of thunder. Abby dropped to the ground, her body covering Cody. Dancer jumped, startled. His muscles tensed, ready for flight.

Where were the shots coming from? Abby looked up at Dancer. The big horse's eyes were wild. She could duck low, but Dancer was a big target.

"Home, Dancer!" Abby commanded.

Dancer refused to go. He nudged her with his nose, urging her to get up. He nudged her again, this time pushing so hard that she was lifted to her feet. "Okay, Dancer. We'll run." Abby spied a wooded growth not far away.

As she gathered Cody into her arms, he whimpered with pain, then placed one paw over Abby's arm. "You can cry if you like, Cody," she told him. "I know it hurts." Abby headed toward the trees. She ran low to the ground with Cody tucked into her chest.

Boom boom boom!

They made it to cover. From the safety of the thick tree trunks, Abby scanned the horizon, trying to see where the gunfire had originated.

Boom!

Samuel Owens' mansion. Somebody was firing a rifle from his house. Abby's blood ran cold. He was back.

Missed again! Owens couldn't contain himself. He hurled his rifle out the window as far as he could, then ran out into the yard and jumped on it. How could he miss? He was a champion shot. Angrily he strode back into the house and slammed the door. He rang for his manservant.

Walter came running, his face pale. "Sir?"

Owens smiled at the man's fear. That made him feel a little better. "Can't take a little rifle noise, Walter? Never served your country? It shows, Walter. You're a snivelling coward, aren't you, Walter?"

"Yes, sir."

"Go out and buy a dozen red roses. Deliver them yourself to the beautiful Mrs. Casey. Write something clever on the card, from me." Owens threw a crisp fifty-dollar bill on the floor at Walter's feet. "And Walter? Act like a man."

"Yes, sir, Mr. Owens, sir." Walter's face was deep red as he stooped to retrieve the money, kneeling under the sneering face of his boss.

Hilary trotted Henry home along the gravel road, giving him a good workout. The amount of sweat that seeped through his shedding winter coat reminded Hilary that he was out of shape.

"You're a nice boy," she told him, "but you're fat. You need some work." Hilary wondered if she should hire Abby to exercise both horses. Henry would live longer if his heart and body were healthy. Abby might like the extra money, if she had time.

Hilary looked at her watch. The hour was almost up. Perhaps she'd meet Abby and Dancer coming back. Hilary fully expected Cody to be following them, and Abby would say she'd been worrying needlessly. Regardless, it had been a lovely ride. Henry needed the exercise, and Pepper was enjoying the run.

They walked up the hill toward Hogscroft. As the road straightened, Henry's ears shot forward. He whinnied loudly, a whinny of greeting. An echoing whinny answered his call. Hilary couldn't see anything yet, but she knew Dancer's call. She kept Henry walking, even though he badly wanted to trot.

Dancer whinnied urgently from down the road. Henry responded. Ignoring the reins, he grabbed the bit in his teeth. He trotted down the road, around the curve past Hogscroft.

That's when Hilary saw Abby, carrying a bleeding mess of grey fur, followed by the tall, elegant stallion.

"Oh, my God," Hilary muttered under her breath. She cantered Henry right up to the trio, stopped him, then slid from his back onto the road.

"Abby! What happened?"

"Cody was caught in a leg-hold trap and the coyotes were

coming to kill him. Dancer scared them off. Cody needs help. He's dying. Call Pete Pierson, Hilary. Now!"

"Can I help you carry him? He looks heavy." She reached out to help, but Cody growled and snapped. "No, I guess not," she said.

"He's in pain, Hilary, and he doesn't know you. Don't take offence."

"I won't, don't worry." Hilary remounted Henry. "I'll run home and phone Mr. Pierson. Give me Dancer's reins, and I'll pony him back."

"They're in my pocket."

"In your pocket? He's following you? I thought you were leading him. Dancer! Come!"

Dancer looked at Hilary, but stayed with Abby.

Squelching the enormous feeling of hurt that swelled up inside her, Hilary turned and cantered Henry back toward Hogscroft.

Tears ran down her face. She scolded herself. She'd wanted Dancer to like Abby. That had been her whole plan. She hadn't considered that he would choose Abby over her, though. It hurt. Dancer was more than a horse to Hilary. He had been her best friend when her father had died. His company had eased her loneliness when other girls had dates and were going to parties. They'd gone through danger together and had shared times of great excitement.

Now she had a different life. A life that excluded this great horse. She couldn't have it both ways, she told herself. If she wanted to be an archeologist and travel to exotic places, she could not have a horse like Dancer, who needed time and attention. She could not have everything. Choices must be made. The tears continued as she rode up to the house.

Christine and Joy were bundled up on the terrace enjoying the late sun with their afternoon coffee. Pepper and Diva perked up and ran to Hilary, tails wagging. When Christine saw that her daughter was upset, she stood up from the table.

"Mousie!" she called. "What's wrong?"

"Call Mr. Pierson, Mom. Tell him to drive his truck over right away."

"What happened, Mousie?"

"Cody was caught in a trap. Abby needs help."

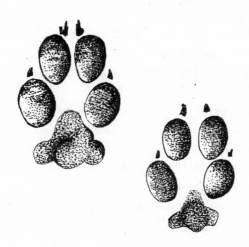

7
FIONA'S PROBLEM

PETE ARRIVED FASTER THAN Christine expected. Dancer and Abby, with Cody in her arms, were just turning up the lane when his old blue truck appeared. Pete came to a stop beside them. Christine opened the passenger door and Abby got Cody settled in the middle of the seat. Dancer stood still, attentive and protective. Before climbing in beside Cody, Abby patted the stallion and quietly thanked him. Dancer shook his mane and whinnied. He turned and trotted up to the barn.

Pete grimaced as he backed up and turned the truck around.

"Thanks for getting here so fast," Christine called as the truck pulled out. As it sped off, gravel flying, Pete waved his goodbyes. There was no time to lose.

Christine walked up the lane, thinking about her daughter. Hilary was very upset. Was it the shock of seeing the injured coyote? Or was there something else?

Christine noticed Joy entering the barn, where Hilary was untacking the horses. It was just like her mother to know when she was needed. Instead of going to the barn as she'd intended, she decided to head for the house to start dinner. She'd let the two of them have a chat.

"Gran, I need to be alone right now." Hilary continued brushing Dancer. The tack was still in the aisle, but Henry had been brushed down and was in his stall with a cooling blanket over him.

"I'm sorry, Mousie. I don't wish to intrude."

"You're not intruding, and I don't mean to sound rude. I just need some time to collect myself." She bent down and picked up Dancer's front left foot.

"Sure. I understand. We all have times like this."

"I know you understand. You always do." Hilary deftly cleaned the hoof with the pick.

"Not always, Mousie." Joy reached into her pocket. "Would you like my hanky? It's clean."

"Thanks." Hilary took the white linen handkerchief and wiped her eyes. "This is embarrassing. I'm twenty-two years old." She blew her nose.

"I'm seventy-two and I still cry."

Hilary laughed. "But not about stupid things."

"If it's making you cry, my dear, it's not stupid."

"But it *is* stupid. I'm crying because Dancer seems more attached to Abby than he is to me. And Abby just started riding him yesterday. I feel sad. I feel so . . ." She left the sentence dangling as she picked up his back left hoof and cleaned it. "I feel so *jilted*. And that's stupid."

Joy said nothing until Hilary finished picking out Dancer's feet. "It's totally understandable, my dear. There's nothing stupid about that emotion."

"Yes there is, Gran. I can't look after him anymore. I wanted Abby to ride him because she's the only person I can think of who could get into his head. And I was right. They get along great, so I'm sad? It doesn't make sense."

"Logically, no. But emotions aren't always logical. You feel that you've lost your best friend."

"But I haven't, really. And I know he'll only be happy if he's working, and I want him happy."

"You really love him, Mousie, if you're willing to let him go because it's better for him."

"Maybe, but I still feel jealous."

As Hilary led Dancer into his stall, Joy tried to explain. "It's like having a child. You love her, raise her, protect her, teach her how to look after herself. Then the time comes when he or she leaves you to discover the big, outside world. And you're left with a hole in your heart. But it's the best thing for her. You can't keep her with you for selfish reasons. So a mother who loves her child has to let her go."

"Maybe it's exactly like that, Gran." Hilary looked at her grandmother with questioning eyes. "Is this how you felt when Mom moved out?"

Joy nodded. "Exactly." She smiled. "I cried like a baby."

"And is this how Mom feels now? Now that I'm moving on?" Hilary's face suddenly crumpled. She ran out of the barn.

As she watched Hilary stumble into the house, Joy thought she'd made things worse. She picked up the bridles and hung them in the tack room. Wondering what to do about her granddaughter, she put Henry's saddle on the proper rack then returned to get Dancer's.

There was a bullet lodged in the back of Dancer's saddle. Joy breathed deeply, steadying herself. "Oh my," she muttered as she ran a finger over it. It was deeply embedded in the leather on the left side of the seat. "Oh my, my, my." Joy felt shocked as the realization of averted tragedy hit her. Her head was light. Trembling visibly, she rested the saddle on her hip and started for the house. Hilary would have to see it.

Joy wasn't looking forward to showing her granddaughter the saddle. She'd upset her enough already. When she opened the kitchen door, though, she saw Hilary and Christine locked in a hug, rocking and laughing and crying together. Joy smiled and wiped a tear from her own eye.

Colleen Millitch was the head veterinarian at Cheltenham Veterinary Hospital. Although she was only in her mid-thirties, she'd dealt with more than her share of animal crises. Tall and dark-haired with a ready smile, Colleen was attractive as well as capable.

As soon as she'd gotten the call from Pete Pierson, she prepared an operating table and disinfected herself. Colleen smiled. A vet's life was full of surprises. This had been just an average Monday afternoon until now. She remembered working on Cody before, the night Pete Pierson had brought him in, full of Colonel Kenneth Bradley's buckshot. Cody had been a good patient, but he was still a wild animal. Colleen would be very careful. She was pulling on her latex gloves when the receptionist buzzed.

"They're here, Colleen. What should I do? It's a real coyote!"

"Send them in." Colleen opened the door to the operating room and studied the animal as Abby carried him in, followed by Pete. Cody would need intravenous fluids immediately.

Abby held him close, hiding his face so he wouldn't see Colleen injecting him with a tranquilizer. Cody's head dropped. He was instantly asleep.

While Cody's rear leg was being operated on, Samuel Owens and Gus LeFarge were viewing the Wick property. They'd walked the land, gone through the house, and checked out the sheds. Now they were entering the huge old barn theatre.

"This would go up in flames with one match," said Owens as he examined the space with critical eyes. "Insurance would build another barn. A modern, functional barn." He swept his arm from wall to wall with a disgusted sneer. "It's a piece of garbage, the whole place. Wick was always crazy, but this takes the cake."

"Funny. Joy Featherstone wants the farm *because* of the theatre. Each to his own, I guess."

"Don't tell me she thinks she can make this theatre profitable! She's as crazy as Wick." Owens walked up to the stage and kicked the wood. "Solid. Some salvage here, but he'll be lucky to get it off his hands."

Gus stood quietly, watching his client. He was getting impatient with all of Owens' complaints, but he wanted the sale. "He'll be happy to sell it to you."

"Does Wick know I want it?" Owens asked, suddenly suspicious.

"No, but he'll know soon, if you decide to raise Joy's bid."

"Why? Wick will just jack up the price if he knows I want it. I told you, I demand anonymity. If you can't get this place for me on my terms, I'll find someone who can." Owens' face was dark with anger as he snapped out the threat.

Suddenly, the lights went out. The two men were plunged into complete darkness.

"What the—!" sputtered Owens. "The goddam electricity's out! Get me out of here."

A blur of dim blue light briefly appeared in the second seat in on the second row from the back, stage right. Then it was gone. It flickered in the fourth row from the front, stage left, then disappeared.

"Gus, are you playing games with me?" demanded Owens angrily.

"N-no, I-I promise." Gus LeFarge was terrified. He'd heard stories, like everyone else, of the ghost that haunted the theatre.

The blue light flared brightly right in front of LeFarge. He turned and ran, clumsily bumping into seats and bouncing off the walls in his haste to find the door. He pulled it open and fled.

"Coward!" Owens hollered as he walked to the door. "Chicken liver!" He was disgusted with Gus LeFarge. A grown man afraid of the dark. Owens grabbed the door latch. It was burning hot. "Yeowch!" he screamed, pulling back his hand and shaking it. He kicked at the door. "LeFarge! Open this door! I've had enough of this crap!"

Owens listened for Gus at the door, but heard nothing. He covered his hand with his jacket sleeve and reached again to open the hot latch. This time, an electrical surge shot through his hand along his arm, throwing him back into the seats. Owens was dumbfounded. He sat dazed.

The blue light flickered in the aisle beside him. "You'll never get out." The tone of this unexpected voice was flat and the pitch was deep. There was a slightly faraway sound to it, a husky echo. "You're like me, locked forever in a joyless void of your own choosing."

"LeFarge?" Owens called. "Is that you?"

"You'll never get out."

"Who said that?"

The dim blue flickering light moved closer. "Samuel Owens. You'll never get out of your own personal hell. Wherever you are, whatever you do, no matter how much land or how many horses you own."

"Get away from me!" Owens cried, frantically swatting the air. He jumped to his feet and ran to the door. Uncertain of what might happen when he grabbed the latch, Owens squeezed his eyes shut and lunged for it, ignoring the consequences.

The door swung open and Owens charged, right into Robert Wick, who was accompanied by Joy Featherstone and a quivering Gus LeFarge.

"Whatever Joy Featherstone offers, I'll offer more! Just for the pleasure of burning down that theatre!"

"It's a little late, Sam," said Robert Wick quietly, after he righted himself. "I'm not selling."

Owens was stunned. "You're not selling?"

"I'm not selling. I'm back in the theatre business."

"You're crazy! You're absolutely crazy. You think you can put your farm on the market and take it off when somebody wants it!"

"You never put in an offer, Sam."

"I was just about to."

"Like I said, it's a little late," answered Wick. "I've changed my mind."

"I'll sue. You'll live to regret this." Owens backed away, shaking with rage. "And what are you doing here, Joy Drake Featherstone? Have you two made a deal, or what? You and your daughter and your granddaughter are nothing but trouble. Let me warn you. I'm back, and you can't trifle with me." His face was crimson and rigid. His body was hunched and aggressive. "I expect a call within the next two hours accepting the offer that Gus was about to draw up, or you'll all regret it."

Samuel Owens walked stiffly to his car, rubbing his right arm. He got in and drove away, leaving Gus, Robert, and Joy puzzled and more than a little alarmed.

Colleen pulled off her surgical gloves and washed her hands thoroughly. It was getting late. She pulled off her cap, quickly brushed her hair, and changed into a fresh white uniform. Bloody clothes are not a comforting sight to nervous pet owners.

She smiled as she strode into the waiting room, now empty except for two worried people. "Mr. Pierson, Abby. Cody is going to be fine."

Pete and Abby both looked at her with the same expression of relief.

"His leg is badly broken and unstable at the moment," Colleen said. "I've set it and put a plaster on it, but I want to talk to you both about what we should do."

"What do you suggest?" asked Pete as Colleen sat in the armchair beside him.

"I believe that it's best to keep him here for a week, heavily sedated. That would give the bones a chance to begin to knit."

Abby looked at Pete. "Won't he be scared to be here alone?" she asked.

He looked back at Colleen. "What are our options?"

The vet pursed her lips and thought. "If the leg gets knocked, it'll need pins and a steel rod. I'd hate to have to re-operate on him."

"Can we keep Cody sedated at home?" asked Abby.

"I can give you pain pills for him, but they won't stop him from moving. He needs some days of immobility."

"So, you're saying that we don't have much choice. We need to leave him here."

"That is my strong advice. He needs to be sedated, and that means he should stay here."

Abby was worried. "If he starts to gain consciousness, he'll be terrified to find himself here."

"Don't worry. I'll look after him."

"We know you will, Colleen," said Pete. "Thank you so much. Do we pay the bill now?"

"No, the secretaries leave at six o'clock. It's seven thirty. Don't worry, we'll get you." She smiled.

"Can I come to visit him?" Abby wanted to know.

"Any time at all." Colleen Millitch rose wearily from her chair. "Now, you two better get something to eat. It's way past dinnertime."

Pete dropped Abby off at her front door and waved goodbye.

"Thanks, Mr. Pierson!" she called. She watched the headlights disappear down the lane with a heavy heart. She hated leaving Cody at the vet's. Abby took a deep breath and opened her door. The house was quiet. A few lights were on, but there were no cooking smells coming from the kitchen. Abby had a feeling that something was wrong.

"Mom? Dad?"

She heard footsteps coming out of her parents' room. Someone stopped and closed the door quietly behind them.

"Hello?" she called. "Who's there?" Abby stood at the open front door, ready to bolt.

"Abby, it's me," whispered Liam.

"What's wrong? Why are you whispering?"

Liam came slowly down the stairs. His face wore an expression that Abby instantly recognized.

"It's Mom, isn't it? She's drunk."

"It's not so bad, Abby. Come into the kitchen and let's talk."

Liam flicked on the lights as they walked into the kitchen. He opened the fridge door and looked inside. "Scrambled eggs on toast?" he asked.

"Sounds good. I'm starved." Abby cleared the table of the empty gin bottle and dirty glass with a disgusted groan.

"Tell me about Cody."

Abby had flung herself into a chair and was slumped over the pine table. Without lifting her head, she answered, "I can bring him home in a week, if the bones are knitting properly. He'll be so heavily sedated, he won't move around. Dr. Millitch says that's the best thing to do, but I feel sorry for him, locked in a small cage with only strangers around. He'll freak out. Even drugged, his instinct will be to panic."

"She's the best small animal vet around. She knows what's good for him."

"I hope so. I'll visit Cody every chance I get." Abby sat up and looked at her father. "Now Dad, tell me what happened here. With Mom. Not that I really want to hear."

"I got home about an hour ago. My meeting ran a little later than I thought. Your mother was sitting at the table with a glass in her hand. She raised a toast to me when I came in, then fell on her face."

"Great."

"Abby, we have to accept that this is an illness. A disease."

"Right, Dad. Like chicken pox? Or is it more like cancer? I've heard that before and I'm not buying it. She's weak, face it. You're late getting home so she pays you back by getting smashed."

"You can be as mad as you like. I don't blame you. I'm pretty mad myself."

"So, what are we going to do about it, Dad? Hold her hand and tell her we understand? It's just a disease?"

"In fairness, she's been pretty good lately, but she needs help."

"Help? That's an understatement, Dad. She needs brain surgery, a lobotomy. When you were in jail, she was drunk all the time. I'm sick of it! I don't have any compassion left. It's disgusting." She dropped her head onto her folded arms in defeat, exhausted after her long, emotional day.

"I'm taking her on a trip."

Abby's head popped up from the table. "What?"

"A trip. For at least a month. Maybe two. Only her and me. Sorry, but I think it should be just the two of us."

"Great! She gets pissed so she gets a big trip! What do I have to do to get some attention? Develop a drug habit?!" Abby was yelling, fists clenched and face red.

Liam closed his eyes and rubbed his forehead. "Abby, my girl. I wish it wasn't like this. I really do."

"What's taking her away on a trip going to accomplish anyway? She'll just come back again and everything will be the same."

SHELLEY PETERSON

"We're going to a clinic. A place where she'll learn new ways to cope with her urges. At least that's the hope." He spoke quietly, and Abby heard the despair and disappointment in his voice.

Abby stifled a sob. After a minute of thought she rose from her chair and walked over to her father where he stood tending the eggs. "I didn't mean everything I said, Dad. I love Mom, and I love you," she said as she hugged him. "I'm glad you're home to look after her."

"And I love you. Everything's going to be all right, Abby," Liam said as he returned the hug. "It'll turn out fine, you wait and see." Now he had to figure out how to look after Abby.

The phone rang, startling them both.

"I'll get it," said Liam, reaching for the wall phone. "Hello? . . . Yes, Hilary, just a minute." He covered the receiver and looked at Abby. "Do you want to take it?" he whispered. Abby nodded, wiping the tear from her cheek.

"She's right here." Liam passed the phone to Abby, kissed her on the forehead, and returned to his cooking.

"Hi, Hilary," said Abby.

"How's Cody?"

"Dr. Millitch says he'll be okay, but he has to stay there for a bit. He has a broken leg and he lost a lot of blood."

"You were right about something being wrong, Abby. I thought he was probably just out hunting."

"He could've been. But, anyway, thanks for helping. I'm sorry we didn't get a lesson today."

"No lesson would've given you what you got today."

"What's that?"

"Dancer's devotion."

Abby carefully considered this for a minute. "I'll never have the bond with him that you have. Not in a million years."

Hilary chortled. "I don't know about that, Abby." The older

girl wondered if her conflicted emotions had been transparent. "I have to go back to Montreal for my exams. Can you keep riding Dancer?"

"I'd be happy to. I mean, really happy. How often?"

"Maybe three or four times a week? When you have the time. And ride Henry, too, if you can. Or bring along a friend when you hack. Keep records so I can pay you."

"Pay me?"

"Of course. D'you think I'd ask you to exercise Dancer for free?"

"Yes! I don't want money, Hilary. I love riding him."

"Abby, I'm glad you do, but—"

"Let's figure it out later, okay? Right now I think I should be paying you for letting me ride him." Abby paused as she listened. "What's that noise, Hilary? Are you having a party?"

Hilary laughed. "No. My grandmother just came in with Mr. Wick. They're going to be partners in a new theatre operation, and they're telling Mom and Rory all about it."

"Really?"

"Really. And I just overheard that Samuel Owens is mad because he wanted to buy it."

"Samuel Owens?"

"Yes. He wanted to burn down the barn because the ghost scared him."

"Hilary, are you kidding?"

"No! I guess he shot out of the barn as white as a sheet!"

Liam's ears had pricked up at the mention of Samuel Owens. "What happened, Abby?"

"Hold on, Hilary, I have to fill Dad in. Actually, why doesn't he speak directly to your grandmother so we don't have to be in the middle?"

"Good idea. Good luck with Dancer, and I'll call soon. Any problems, get my number in Montreal from Mom. Now, here's

Gran to talk to your dad. And thanks, Abby. You riding him is the best thing that could've happened to Dancer, and I really appreciate it."

Liam took the phone from Abby. "Joy? It's Liam."

Abby popped the bread in the toaster and stirred the eggs while Liam and Joy laughed and chatted. Why did her mother drink? She didn't want to think about it.

She worried about Cody waking from the drugs and becoming frantic. She hoped nobody would be foolhardy enough to try to befriend him. Cody was wild. He would bite. That could be a problem. At least he'd gotten all his shots and had his teeth cleaned. Colleen had taken the opportunity while he was under sedation.

Her mother worried her, but Abby didn't want to think about it.

She started planning her riding schedule. Moonie would be kept fit at three rides a week: Monday, Wednesday, and Friday after school. Working Leggy twenty minutes each day before school would keep her training on target. And she would bike to Hogscroft directly from school Tuesdays and Thursdays to ride Dancer, and ride him again Saturday, Sunday, or both. Lucy could ride Henry sometimes; they'd have fun riding the trails together.

Her parents were leaving. She didn't want to think about it. The toast was buttered, the eggs were scrambled, and Abby arranged the plates with sliced tomatoes and parsley. She set them on the kitchen table with knives and forks and napkins, and two glasses, one with milk and one with water.

"That looks delicious, Abby!" praised Liam as he returned the receiver to its cradle. "I guess you heard everything?"

"No. I was thinking about other things. Why? What should I have heard?"

Liam sat down at the table and shook out his napkin, placing it on his lap. "First, a little gossip for you. Samuel Owens and Helena Casey are an item."

Abby snorted. "They deserve each other."

Liam nodded, smiling. "Aside from the age difference, I can't think of a better match." He dug into the steaming plate of food. "Maybe that's too harsh. I remember Helena Sandford when she younger. She was a great girl. A wonderful dancer, and an eyeful, too. But she changed."

He nodded his approval of Abby's cooking, then his face darkened. "Joy found a bullet in the back of Dancer's saddle."

Abby's face paled. "Oh my gosh, I forgot to tell Hilary about that. Someone shot at us when we came through Owens' place."

Liam stopped chewing. "You *forgot?*"

"Well, so much has happened today, and all I could think about when I got back with Cody was getting him to the vet's." She stopped. "Dancer. A bullet in his saddle? That was close."

Liam nodded. "Real close. Rory called the police and they're having the bullet examined. They'll want to talk to you. We were lucky this time, Abby my girl, but you stay off Owens' property from now on, you hear?"

Abby could only murmur, "I hear."

They ate in silence, deep in their own thoughts. Liam wiped his mouth with his napkin after a few minutes and tried to lighten the tone.

"Joy and Robert Wick have gone into partnership. In a theatre venture."

"Hilary told me." Abby was relieved that the topic had been changed.

"So Joy is going to be around a whole lot more."

"That's good. I really like her, although I don't know her very well."

Liam raised an eyebrow. "Would you like to get to know her better?"

"Sure." Abby looked up from her eggs. "Why? And why are you looking at me like that?"

"Because Joy could move in here while your mother and I are at the clinic. How would that be?"

"Dad, I can look after myself. I'm a very responsible person. I'll be fine by myself." Abby stopped herself from adding that she'd been virtually alone all the time that her father had been in jail.

"Honey, I'm not going to leave a sixteen-year-old girl alone on a farm. It's too isolated. You're too young."

"I could move in with Leslie."

"What about Cody? And how would you look after the horses if you weren't here?"

Abby looked at her father. She swallowed the last mouthful of toast. "If it would put your mind at rest, then do it. But understand, it's for your sake, not mine."

Liam laughed aloud. "That's my girl."

8

News

ON A WEDNESDAY MORNING one month later, Abby was riding her bike to school. Although there had been a spell of hot weather, this day in mid-May was fresh, and she was wishing she'd worn a sweater. But the sun was shining and soon the temperature would rise. All around her were signs of full-blown spring. The riotous flowers, the noisy nesting birds, the bright green leaves on the trees. Abby breathed in a lungful of fragrant air and smiled. It was a beautiful day and her spirits were high.

Before she'd left for school that morning, her parents had called from the clinic. Her mother was working hard in her treatment, and her father was using the time to finish a mountain of paperwork he'd brought from his office. Five weeks remained before her parents were due to return.

Joy Featherstone and Diva had moved in the day they'd left. Diva was a curious, friendly dog, given to mischievous jokes, like hiding one shoe or moving her food to a location of her own choosing. Abby had wondered if Diva would get along with Cody, but so far it wasn't an issue: Diva followed Joy everywhere, and Cody kept his distance.

Abby was growing quite fond of Joy, and admitted to herself that having her around was actually a great idea. Joy was always cheerful and had a quick, cozy sense of humour. The theatre project was keeping her totally absorbed, and Abby loved hearing about its progress at dinner, which was usually their only extended time together. No matter how busy Joy got, she always made time to prepare a delicious evening meal for Abby. Lunch became more interesting, too, with the tasty little treats that Joy would sneak into Abby's lunch bag.

Mr. Wick dropped in quite often, entertaining Abby and Joy with funny theatre anecdotes and stories. The story of Ambrose Brown intrigued them both, and there was much discussion about whether or not he approved of the refurbishings. Abby grinned to herself, thinking how much happier and better-dressed Robert Wick was lately. She suspected a little chemistry between the two older people, which amused her.

Cody had survived his stay at the vet's. He'd been extremely happy to see Abby every time she visited, but became very upset when she left without him. Finally, the day came for Abby to take him home. He could hardly contain himself, wiggling and whining and bumping into Abby's legs. Colleen Millitch was every bit as relieved as Cody when he left. Having a wild animal in a cage who glowered and growled and sulked and skulked did not make for an enjoyable work environment. But she pronounced that he had been as good a patient as nature would allow, and that the leg would heal perfectly. Now, Cody was once again following Abby to school and hiding behind trees to avoid detection.

Abby had rigorously kept to her horse schedule. She rode Moonie and Dancer at least three times a week, and trained Leggy daily. She could already see results in each one. Moonie was growing more responsive to leg aids, and jumping a three-foot course effortlessly. Dancer was getting much more fit. He enjoyed working, and met Abby at the gate to walk up to the barn with her. Abby got a big kick out of that. Pete Pierson helped with Leggy when he could, and expertly guided Abby in Leggy's training. Leggy was driving happily now, responding immediately to voice commands and steering with confidence.

Her attitude, haughty and proud and full of life, gave Abby great pleasure.

She arrived at the big red-brick school with time to spare. Abby swung her leg over the bicycle seat and dismounted. She waved to a couple of kids as she walked over to the bicycle rack. Everyone was in a good mood on this sunny, brisk day, she thought, noting the smiles on people's faces.

Abby was kneeling at her bike, snapping the lock through the spokes when she realized that someone was standing over her.

"Hey, Abby."

She rose slowly, combing her hair through her fingers. "Hey." She looked up into the handsome face of Sam Morris, hardly daring to breathe. His curly dark hair and deep brown eyes made her heart beat rapidly in her ears. She was sure Sam could hear it, too.

"Can I walk you in?"

"Sure. Are you going that way?"

"No. But you are, and I wanted to just, well, talk to you."

Abby willed her face not to blush. Too late. Fire-engine red, she knew. Her defences rose like thorns on a rosebush.

"Whatever."

"I don't want to bother you."

"You're not."

"Good. I want to tell you something. And I want us to stay friends."

Stay friends? Is that all it was to you? she thought. Glibly she said, "We're still friends."

"I'm glad."

They walked in silence to the front of the school. They started up the steps, heads down, arms clutching books.

Sam stopped.

"Can I give you a lift home? After school?" Sam looked at

her earnestly. "I've got the truck, I'll throw your bike on the back. We can talk then?"

"Sure," responded Abby. "Fine."

Sam smiled sadly.

Abby's insides melted. *He has such a beautiful smile. But I can't let myself fall for him again*, she thought. *What does he want to talk about?* She turned and walked straight to her locker, never daring to look back at the young man who stood watching her go.

"Abby! Good news!" Lucy yelled, wheeling around the corner. "Auditions! Tonight! Look! For the new theatre at Wick's farm! They're calling it 'The Stonewick Playhouse'!"

Clutched in her hand was a large green flyer. She thrust it at Abby.

Abby uncrumpled it and read aloud, "Open auditions for the first production of The Stonewick Playhouse. Come one, come all."

"Didn't I tell you? Isn't this the best thing you've ever heard in your whole entire life? I'll be a star! Can't you see me as Maria in *West Side Story*? Annie in *Annie Get Your Gun*? Mary in *Mary Poppins*?"

"I can see you as all of the above, Lucy, and you can throw in Juliet, too, in *Romeo and Juliet*. But what play are they doing? The flyer doesn't say."

"Who cares? Let's just go and audition!"

"How?" asked Abby. "What does a person do at an audition?"

"It says to sing a song that you know, and to recite something that you already know by heart, but I've never done an audition before, either. That's where you come in, Abby."

Abby looked at Lucy. She knew with a growing certainty what Lucy was going to say. "You want me to put in a good word with Mrs. Featherstone, don't you?"

"The 'Stone' in 'Stonewick'? And why not? You know I'd be fantastic in any part." Lucy smiled devilishly, and winked.

Abby laughed. "Actually I don't, but you get top marks for trying. What I *do* know is you'd put everything you had into it."

"So you'll do it?" Lucy put her hands together as if in prayer.

"If I see her after school, which I might not, I'll tell her you're interested and ask her for suggestions, but it's not like I have any strings to pull, and I don't imagine she's open to bribery."

"But you'll talk to her about me?"

"If she's there."

"As soon as you get home?"

"If she's there."

"And call me the minute you do it? I need at least a few minutes to get my act together. I mean this is *real* short notice."

"Yes, Lucy, the minute I talk to her, *if* I talk to her, I'll call you."

At this, Lucy started hopping around in a strange sort of victory dance, punching the air and racing her feet. "Hooray! I'll be a star! I'll be bigger than Julia Roberts!"

"You look more like Snoopy!" Abby called as she raced to her first class.

The three-thirty bell rang after a full day of classes. Abby packed up her books and strolled toward her locker. *Will Sam remember he offered me a lift home?* she wondered. She'd seen him a couple of times in the hall, and he'd hardly glanced at her. *He did want to talk to me*, she thought, *but maybe he was only trying to see if I still liked him.* She decided she'd slowly get her things ready to go, then amble out to the bike rack. She'd take a peek at the parking lot, and if Sam was around, and made the offer again, she'd consider it. She told herself to keep cool. Pam Masters was trying desperately to capture Sam's attention, and Abby didn't want to appear to be doing the same.

Sam saved her the trouble. His tall, lanky frame was leaning on her locker as she came around the corner.

"Ready to go?"

"In one second, if you wouldn't mind moving a little to either side so I can get my things?"

"Oops! Not at all."

Again Abby wished that she didn't blush so easily. She stuck her head right into her locker to hide until the red subsided, and noisily banged books around.

"Hi, Sam," said a smooth, seductive voice. Abby knew without looking that it was Pam. "What are you doing here?"

This will be interesting, thought Abby.

"I'm driving Abby home," said Sam.

"Can you drive me, too? I'm almost on the way." Abby heard the girlish pout that Pam was affecting. She thumped her books a little more.

"Maybe another time, Pam. I want to talk to Abby."

"Don't hurt my feelings, Sam." Pam sounded threatening to Abby, but she guessed that Pam knew how to handle men.

"I don't want to do that, Pam. Can I drop you off first, then drive Abby home?" *Aha*, thought Abby. *I knew it. She's getting her way. She pushed some button I didn't even know about.*

"It makes more sense to drop *her* off first, but whatever you think. See you at the truck, Sammy." Abby pulled her head out of the locker in time to see Pam saunter down the hall in tall strappy sandals, short red skirt swaying with an exaggerated motion. Every other pair of eyes in the hall was doing the same thing, including Sam's.

Abby couldn't help laughing.

It was Sam's turn to blush. "Why are you laughing?"

"I was thinking that I could use some lessons from Pam on how to handle men."

Sam shook his head. "She did it again. She's making me

drive her home, something I had no intention of doing."

"Your choice, Sam."

Sam stared at her. "You're right. It's my choice. I'll have to remember that and not let her push me around."

Abby snorted. "Do you really mind so much? She made it look easy."

"You don't need any lessons from Pam, Abby. You're devious enough," he retorted.

The ice was broken, and together they walked to Sam's truck. Pam was draped across the hood, shoulders hunched to show cleavage under her low-cut black camisole. One strap had dropped over her arm.

"Pam!" shouted Abby. "I'll buy one!"

"Buy what?" asked Pam with a scowl.

"Whatever you're trying to sell."

Pam huffily slid down from the hood of the truck.

Sam whispered in Abby's ear, "I don't think it was *you* she was trying to sell it to." Abby laughed with Sam, making Pam even madder.

"I want to sit beside Sam," said Pam breathlessly, not ready to give up.

"No," answered Sam. "You're first out, so you sit by the window."

"Maybe I'll get a ride from Jonathon, then." Pam winked tauntingly at Sam and ran her tongue over her lips as she turned to walk away, ignoring Abby completely.

"Oh, Abby," she called back. "Are you competing in the Grand Invitational?"

"What? I haven't heard about it," Abby answered.

"It was in all the newspapers. It's on June 26 and all the best riders have already been contacted. My mother's doing the invitations."

"So why ask? You knew I wasn't on the list, Pam."

Pam smiled. "Maybe. Fifty thousand dollars in prize money, Abby. Open jumpers. But that's not your thing, is it? You just do the wild eventing stuff."

"Pam, what are you getting at? Only the top horses compete in this event. Why would you think I'd be insulted by not being invited?"

"Maybe because Dancer is still qualified. And I've heard that you're riding him now."

"How can Dancer be qualified?" Abby was puzzled. "He's been out of action for years."

"Exactly five years, Abby. If he doesn't compete this year, he's off the list."

"How do you know all this, Pam?"

"I told you. My mother. An invitation was sent ages ago to Hogscroft. They haven't responded, and replies are due this week. The Jameses must feel that you're not capable of showing him." Her hand flew to her mouth in mock horror. "Oh, my. I didn't mean to upset you, Abby. That's the last thing I'd want to do."

Abby could only stare at Pam's retreating back.

The drive home was congenial but one-sided. Abby's mind kept returning to the horse show. It would take place a month and a half from now, just after her mom and dad got back from the clinic. Should she ask Mrs. James about it? Would that be too brash? Could she get Dancer ready by then? And herself, too? *Fifty thousand dollars! Wow.* That kind of money would get her nicely through university and leave some start-up money in the bank. It would take all the pressure off her father. *As if I'd really win*, she thought.

"What did you say? Sorry, Sam, I wasn't concentrating."

"Never mind."

"No, really, what did you say? I was thinking about the horse show."

"Abby, it's okay. There's something that I want to talk to you about, but there never seems to be enough time to get into it."

"We could talk now," Abby suggested.

"We're at your house. Do you have time to talk now?"

Abby thought about skipping her ride on Dancer, but with the news of the Invitational, she really wanted to ask Mrs. James what was going on. "Sam, I don't have time now, but can you come by later? After I ride?"

"No, sorry. I'm going to the auditions tonight."

"Oh, yeah," remembered Abby. "Me too."

"We can't talk there. What are you doing this weekend?"

Is he asking me out? She tried to sound cool. "I'm just riding and stuff. No plans."

"What about Friday night?"

Abby tried not to smile. "Sure."

Cody met her as she skipped gaily toward her house. She noticed how much healthier he was looking.

"Good boy. I'm glad you're all better," she said, stooping to stroke the coarse fur on his back and rub the much softer fur under his chin and around his ears. "Cody, I have great news. Sam just sort of asked me out for Friday night!" Cody seemed genuinely excited for her, hopping and scooting and dodging as Abby played tag with him up the lane and back. Abby was on top of the world.

When Abby walked into the kitchen, there was a note on the table from Joy.

Abby

Dinner's in the fridge, just heat it up. I've gone to the theatre to set up. If you haven't heard, we're doing impromptu auditions to-night, starting at seven. Why don't you come?!

Love, J.

I'd better call Lucy, thought Abby. She picked up the phone and dialled.

No answer. The answering machine clicked on.

"Lucy, it's Abby. Mrs. Featherstone has already left, so I couldn't ask her what you should do. I'm sure whatever you do will be perfect. I'll meet you there after I ride Dancer. See you before seven. Save me a seat. Bye."

After hanging up, Abby ran upstairs and changed into her riding clothes as fast as she could. Racing down the stairs she caught a glimpse of something out the window in the front field. A chestnut blur had leapt over the fence.

Abby halted, wondering what it was. It might be a deer. She opened the front door and looked down the lane in the direction the blur had been heading. Nothing. Did Leggy jump out? No. There she was, standing beside her mother as they both looked in the same direction, toward the road.

Abby shrugged her shoulders. It was probably a deer. There were plenty around.

Wheeling her bicycle out of the shed, Abby hummed a happy tune as she thought about riding Dancer. She hopped up onto the seat and happily started off toward Hogscroft, followed discreetly by her devoted coyote.

Samuel Owens was thinking of Dancer, too. He stood at the picture window in his study, binoculars scanning the path that wound over the top of the Casey property to the east, beside the woods in front of him, and into the woods to the northwest. He was watching for Dancer.

Dancer had been coming this way lately. Alone. Owens had spotted him twice in the last two days. He checked his watch. Eight minutes after four. It was four o'clock two days ago when he'd sighted Dancer, and four fourteen yesterday when Dancer had galloped west, through the Wick farm toward Hogscroft. He should be here any time now.

What the stallion was doing was of no concern to Owens. What concerned him greatly was that Dancer was there at all, reminding Owens of his past obsession, enraging him that he dared to trespass on land owned by a man that the stallion should fear. *Dancer should be terrified of me*, thought Owens. *He should be quaking in his iron shoes.*

He'd kept an eye out for Dancer all afternoon, but so far, no luck. Everything was ready. His plans were laid. He'd worked very hard all day, and was convinced that the bear pit was foolproof. All he needed was Dancer.

He scanned the path earnestly, slowly moving the lenses from left to right, then from right to left. His anger mounted, as always, when he cast his eyes on the Wick property.

"That land should be mine," he growled aloud. "Those bastards cut me out. They'll pay one day, and they won't even know what hit them."

"Hi, Mousie."

"Mom! I was just thinking about you! How are you?"

"Great. How was the exam?"

"I think I aced it."

"Congratulations!"

"Well, it hasn't been marked yet. I'm just heading out, Mom. Can I call you back?"

"No, no. Just let me ask you one question. You got an invitation in the mail regarding the Grand Invitational. It's been sitting here for a couple of weeks and I keep forgetting about it. What do you want me to do with it?"

"Mom, I won't be around. It's in June, isn't it?"

"Yes. Sunday, June 26."

"I start my job at the Royal Ontario Museum. I won't have time. Do you mind declining for me?"

"Not at all, honey, I thought you might be too busy. What about Abby?"

"Abby?"

"Well, Mousie, she's been coming here to ride him four times a week. They're getting along famously, doing all the courses you set out, and doing them well."

Hilary didn't reply.

"Mousie?"

"I can't believe you'd think that."

"Think what?"

"That Abby could ride him as well as me."

"I didn't say that!"

"But you think she should be entered in the Invitational. Wasn't the letter addressed to me?"

"Yes, it was, but it's the horse that qualifies in this show. Mousie? What's wrong? You sound . . . jealous."

There was a long pause on the line. Hilary sighed and said, "You're right. I'm jealous. Isn't it silly? I can't believe this. I'm not just a little jealous, I'm a lot jealous. I thought I'd gotten over this, but I obviously haven't. I guess I secretly liked being the only one who could ride Dancer."

"Look, I'll decline. Let's forget I ever mentioned it, and honey, I'm sorry. I didn't mean to be insensitive, and obviously I—"

"Wait, Mom. I have to get over this. Do you think Abby could do it?"

"Why don't you judge for yourself? Come home this week-end."

"When's the deadline for registration?"

"Let me check the invitation. It doesn't say anything about a deadline. It says that replies would be appreciated by May 23. That's the end of this week."

"Mom, why don't we let Abby decide. Does she come to ride today?"

"Yes. She should be here any minute."

"Ask her what she wants to do, and we'll go with it."

"Are you sure?"

"I'm sure."

"Mousie?"

"Yes, Mom?"

"I'm proud of you."

Hilary hung up the phone, glad that her mother couldn't see the tears falling down her cheeks. She wouldn't be so proud if she knew how much it hurt. She shook her head, unable to put her emotions into words. Rubbing her forehead with her fingers, she started to laugh.

"What an idiot I am!" she exclaimed to her empty room. "What a silly, ridiculous, jealous idiot! I have to let go, like Gran said, because it's good for Dancer. Of course Abby can do it."

Dancer didn't come to greet Abby when she rode her bike up the lane. This was interesting. Maybe he was grazing in the back field, Abby speculated. Maybe he didn't feel like working today.

She rested her bike at the side of the barn and called for him. "Dancer! Come on! Dancer!" No Dancer. Abby went into the barn and put some grain in a feed bucket. She came out and shook it so he could hear the food rattling.

"Dancer! Dancer!"

Hooves thundered toward the barn. Abby smiled to herself. When in doubt, offer food. Horses can never resist food, her father always said.

Henry, with ears pricked expectantly, wheeled around the fenceline as fast as his overweight body could run, sliding to a halt at her side. Without even bothering to acknowledge her presence, he stuck his nose into the pail and began to eat.

"Nice to see you, too, Henry, but you're not going out today. Saturday and Sunday are your days with Lucy. Where's Dancer?"

His noisy crunching was the only response Abby got. "You know, Henry, I'm getting a little worried."

Abby fondly patted his forehead and rubbed his ears. She put the bucket on the ground so Henry could finish his snack then ran to the James' house and knocked on the door.

"Abby! I was just on the phone with Mousie. We were talking about you."

"Really?"

"Yes. Mousie wants me to ask you if you'd like to enter Dancer in the Grand Invitational. It's entirely up to you."

"Really? That's super! I mean, really, really great! I'd love to take him! But Mrs. James, do you know where Dancer is?"

"Is he not in the field?"

"No. I called him and he didn't come. Henry did, but there's no sign of Dancer."

"I wouldn't worry too much, Abby. Dancer sometimes disappears for an hour or so. He always has. Why don't you get Henry's tack soaped and oiled. He'll be back before you know it."

"But since I started riding him, he's always come to meet me."

Christine smiled at the concerned young woman. "He's an unusual fellow, Abby. If he's not back by the time the tack is done, come and get me and we'll go looking. Okay?"

Abby could see that Christine wasn't worried. "Okay, Mrs. James. Thanks." She slowly walked to the tack room, the joy of being asked to enter Dancer in the Invitational totally eclipsed by worry. She felt trouble in her bones. And where did Cody go? If there was trouble, Cody would know. Maybe Mrs. James was right. Maybe Dancer would show up and everything would be fine.

Cody loped along the ridge of Robert Wick's high field above Saddle Creek. Nose high, he smelled the fear in the air. It was unmistakable. He would find the source. The wind changed direction slightly and Cody veered with it. He was distracted by another scent. Human. Male. From up the hill, and not close. He stopped, and put his nose to the ground. Horse scent. It was the trail of the Good Horse, the horse who'd saved him from the wild coyotes. The horse that his Abby rode at the other place.

Cody followed the trail, head down, running fast as the path led down into the meadow along the woods. The fear smell was getting stronger, but his ears could pick up no sounds of distress. He ran faster, following the trail and the fear.

The man scent again. In the air, not close, but not far. The man-den up on the hill. Cody cast a sideways glance and there he was. The man. Outside the man-den covering both his eyes with a black thing, holding it up with his hands. Cody's ruff went up. A deep growl tickled his throat. Bad Man.

The man suddenly moved fast. Cody crouched in the long grass and watched. The man dropped the black thing and picked up the long shiny stick that shot fire.

Cody waited until the man was looking the other way, then ducked into the woods. The man was coming down the hill. Cody tried to understand what was happening. He smelled fear, he smelled the Good Horse, and the Bad Man was coming.

Cody shot off through the woods, running for safety. He would be out of the trees and onto the road in no time, and off to rejoin Abby at the other place.

But the scent of fear. There it was again. Very, very strong. Cody stopped running and started to shake. He must help. He spun around and followed the scent. Suddenly, just beyond, he heard a scrambling noise, followed by a series of frantic thrashes.

His nose and ears brought him to the edge of a deep pit, dug right in the middle of the path through the woods. He looked down.

The Good Horse!

9
THE BEAR PIT

ABBY DECIDED TO CLEAN all the tack. She hung the dirty leather bridles, girths, and martingales on the hook that hung from the ceiling in the tack room. She put some warm water in a bucket, opened the large container of saddle soap, and took a clean sponge off the shelf.

Abby took a deep breath and closed her eyes. Please, please, please, let Dancer be all right. And please, please, please, let Cody's little coyote face peek around the tack room door, proving that everything is as it should be. Cody's clash with the leg-hold trap and the pack of wild coyotes was too recent. A sense of foreboding grew in Abby's chest.

She wet the sponge and rubbed it into the saddle soap, creating a thick lather at the top of the container. With speed that came from long practice, she scrubbed the leather with the soapy sponge, then wiped it thoroughly. After soaping and wiping the bridles and saddles, she threw out the water, rinsed out the sponge, packed up the soap, and opened the big jug of saddle oil.

Abby could barely contain herself. Her hands were shaking as she soaked the oil rag with neat's-foot oil and rubbed it into the leather saddles. As she completed each one, she felt more anxious. Cody was not to be seen, and Dancer had not returned.

Owens threw down his binoculars and, double-barrelled shotgun in hand, began striding down his lawn. A grim smile transformed his rugged face into a sinister mask. The horrendous crash of underbrush had been music to his ears. He'd fooled him. The mighty Dancer had been outwitted by a few branches cleverly placed over a gaping hole in the earth, littered at the bottom with jagged boulders.

Hopefully the wretched animal was now writhing in agony with a broken leg, or better yet, a broken neck. Owens would tell people that he had to put Dancer out of his misery, out of compassion for an injured beast in deathly pain. A mercy killing. Owens' smile got broader. Now he would finish the stallion off, once and for all. Once Dancer was dead, he could get on with his life. He could put his mind to other things. Like procuring his privacy.

Owens' valet came panting out of the mansion's side entrance and called, "Mr. Owens! There you are! I've been looking for you!"

Owens abruptly turned to glare at his quivering manservant.

"My apologies, Mr. Owens, but—"

"Walter," said Owens quietly. He spoke softly but in such a menacing manner that Walter was struck dumb in mid-sentence. "Walter, I'm busy. Can you see that, Walter?"

"Y-yes s-sir," he stammered. "But you were expecting Mrs. Casey, and you told me to inform you immedi—"

"Yes, I did, Walter. Good boy. Could you show her to the study and pour her a drink? I'll be along shortly. I have a little business to take care of."

"Yes, sir, Mr. Owens, sir."

"Samuel, darling!"

Owens turned his head and watched as Helena Casey floated across the lawn toward him. She was wearing a cream linen pant suit with a magenta scoop-necked blouse and matching pumps. Her blond hair was swept up in a glamorous French roll, and her teeth gleamed in her perfectly made-up face. Diamonds glittered at her throat and ears. She took his breath away.

Owens found himself hiding the shotgun behind his back. "Walter, take this," he ordered under his breath, shoving the weapon at the obedient man.

Dancer can stew in his own juice for a little while, Owens thought savagely, striding up to greet the vision in cream. *I have bigger and more delectable fish to fry. Let the creature die slowly, he's not going anywhere.*

Cody began to dig. His right hind leg was still not strong so he put all his weight on the left, and furiously dug with his two front paws. He worked steadily, creating an ever-growing pile of earth behind him.

Dancer was on his back, surrounded by sharp rocks. The hole was deep and it narrowed at the bottom. Dancer's legs were hidden by thick, leaf-covered broken branches with sharp points, and tangled in long, unyielding vines.

The mighty stallion lay there, stunned. The world was spinning in crazy circles. He couldn't get his eyes focused. Where was he? His legs scrambled, but to no avail. His head was bleeding and his legs were badly scraped.

Cody dug. Left, right, left, right, left, right. The man was coming to hurt them. He must get the Good Horse out.

Dancer rested. He closed his eyes to stop the spinning.

He slept.

Twenty minutes passed. The pile of earth behind Cody had grown into a small hill. Cody stopped to rest, panting hard. His front paws were bleeding, his muscles spent. He listened intently. No man-noise. He sniffed the air keenly. No man-scent. He looked down at Dancer. The Good Horse wasn't moving.

Cody slid down a little further. He grabbed a thick branch with his mouth and yanked on it, trying to lug it out of the hole to clear the way. The movement startled the horse, and he started thrashing.

Cody didn't let go. He tugged and pulled and hauled the branch up. He went back for another. And another. And yet another.

Dancer's head was beginning to clear. He realized that Abby's coyote was helping him. He began to understand the animal's plan. Dancer moved his front right leg. There was no pain. With his teeth he pulled on the vine that twisted around it, and removed it from his leg. He carefully tested his front left. It was sore, but it moved. His hips hurt when he moved his hind legs, but at least Dancer knew that once he could get himself righted, all four legs would support him.

Cody slid down the path he'd dug, into the pit. The steep wall was now a slope, and Cody thought that Dancer should be able to walk out. He sniffed at Dancer's head. There was a lot of blood. Cody couldn't understand why Dancer still lay there. He yipped.

Dancer flinched at the noise so close to his ears. He nickered, twisting his neck first to the left, then to the right.

Cody showed him how to get out. He bounded easily up the side of the hole, spun around, then stood looking down at him. He yipped again, and wagged his tail.

Dancer threw his head forward and paddled his legs. No good. He couldn't find a way to get his feet under him. He was like a turtle on its back. He was helpless.

Cody froze. Footsteps coming. Man steps.

He slid down beside Dancer and whined softly, pushing him urgently with his nose.

Dancer tried again.

The tack was cleaned and oiled. The time was up. Abby jumped on her bike and raced across to the farmhouse. She pounded on Christine's kitchen door, opened it, and hollered, "Mrs. James!

I'm going to look for Dancer! Bye!" and she sped down the lane.

Abby thought fast. *If Cody isn't here, he must be with Dancer, who must be in trouble. When Cody goes travelling, he takes the path past Wick Farm, Owens' and the Caseys'.* Abby headed north.

Christine rushed out of her office. "Abby, wait! I'm coming!" She threw open the kitchen door and looked outside. No sign of Abby. Christine grabbed her car keys and ran for the car, uncertain of where to go.

Cody whined with fear. The Bad Man was coming. He was already down the hill and entering the woods. Very soon he would be at the hole. Cody looked down into the hole. Dancer was still on his back, resting again. Maybe there was no hope.

Cody slid down the side and nudged Dancer. Get up get up get up! The exhausted, injured beast didn't move.

Cody's ears picked up another sound. His Abby's spinning machine! He could hear it coming toward them. No! She must not come! The man would hurt her, too. Cody leapt up to the top and looked for her.

Suddenly, with a huge effort, the valiant stallion arched his back, leaning all his weight on his bloodied head. He tucked his hocks under him as best as he could. With one mighty thrust he propelled his body forward, shoulders finally breaking free from the boulders. He sat on his haunches like a dog. With his front feet on the ground, he wiggled his back end until he had it positioned properly over his hind legs. With another great effort, Dancer threw his weight up and forward. He stood.

Cody vibrated with impatience. Let's go let's go let's go! His Abby was coming, and she shouldn't be here when the man arrived. He listened. The man was getting very close, too close. Cody's sharp ears knew he was only thirty seconds away if he continued to walk at the same pace. If he walked any faster, there was no time left at all.

Dancer stood still, gathering his strength. His head was spinning and his eyes were out of focus. The cut on his head had been reopened by his efforts, and blood was running down his face.

Cody hopped from leg to leg. His senses told him to run from danger; his loyalty kept him with Dancer. Dancer, rightside up but deep in the hole, shook his head and snorted.

Now now now! urged Cody.

Abby came racing from the direction of the road and appeared around the trees, panting hard as she pedalled her bike along the bumpy path.

"Cody!" she called, comforted and elated to see him.

In the same instant, Samuel Owens came crashing through the woods from the other side, double-barrelled shotgun at his side.

Cody stood in the middle, high on the mound of dug-out earth. He threw back his head and howled.

Owens raised the shotgun defensively.

Abby screeched her brakes to a halt.

Christine had driven back and forth along the road twice now. She had little idea of what might be happening, but she wanted to be at hand, just in case.

Suddenly, off the road directly beside her, the unmistakable sound of a gun shattered the peace. The hair all over her body stood on end. She stopped breathing. Slowing the car, Christine pulled over to the side of the road. She put it in park and waited, trying to reason out a course of action and fearing the worst.

When the shotgun came up, Cody dove for Owens' leg, throwing him off balance. The resounding roar momentarily deafened them all, but the buckshot flew harmlessly into the treetops.

Furiously, Owens began to hit Cody with the barrel of the gun. The coyote's teeth were imbedded in Owens' calf and he was not about to release his jaws. Owens aimed the gun, prepared to empty the remaining shot into the small grey animal. There were more cartridges in his pocket for Dancer.

Dancer was galvanized by the tremendous noise. He shook his head, clearing away the last remnants of dizziness. He gathered himself onto his powerful haunches and sprang up the side of the pit in one stride. He sized up the situation and took immediate action. His left hind leg shot out and thumped Owens sharply in the chest.

Owens' mouth formed an "O." Cody let go of Owens' leg and dashed to Abby, where he positioned himself squarely between his idol and danger.

Dancer gauged his target perfectly, striking again with his left hind, this time at Owens' abdomen. Doubling over in pain, Owens tumbled into the very pit that he had dug for Dancer. As he fell, the second shell exploded, the sound muffled by the walls of earth.

Abby stood immobilized. She looked at Dancer. Magnificent, incredible Dancer. He stood tall and bloodied, head up, ears forward, nostrils flaring. His gaze met Abby's. "Good boy, Dancer. Good boy," she whispered. Dancer appeared to nod, then, in the blink of an eye, disappeared along the path toward home.

Cody grabbed her hand with his mouth and began to pull. "You're a good boy, too, Cody. I'm coming, I'm coming."

Christine sat rigid in her car, hands gripping the steering wheel in a death vice. Two shots. She didn't have her cell phone with her to call the police. She'd have to go home to call, but she didn't want to leave. Should she go into the woods? Was Abby in there? She didn't want to rush in to face a person with a gun, but she couldn't just sit here and do nothing.

Her dilemma was solved as Dancer, bloody but sound, shot out onto the road in front of her car. With hardly a glance at her, he abruptly turned and galloped down the gravel road toward home.

Abby was next, frantically pedalling her bicycle, followed by Cody, blood dripping from his mouth.

Christine threw the car into drive and sped after them. Pulling up beside Abby, she hollered, "Abby! What happened?" Abby's frightened face looked back at her. She was breathing hard, and spoke in gasps while continuing to pedal down the road. "Oh my gosh, Mrs. James. It's Mr. Owens! I don't know if he's hurt or dead, or what. He has a shotgun and Dancer kicked him into the pit and the gun went off and we ran. I couldn't bear to look."

"Abby, stop your bike. I have to know what happened."

Abby did what she was told and unfolded the story as coherently as she could manage.

When she was finished, Christine thought for a moment. "Go up to Hogscroft and stay there. Call the vet. I'll be there shortly." She turned her car around. "Oh, Abby! Before you do anything else, call the police and send them here! I'll wait by the road to show them the location of the pit."

She parked beside the path. As the minutes passed, Christine grew more and more restless. She couldn't just sit here while a human being, even a despicable man like Owens, lay injured and needing medical help. He may have accidentally shot himself. Since Dancer had kicked him in the chest and stomach, Christine imagined internal bleeding, cardiac arrest, hemorrhage, punctured lungs. Finally, unable to wait any longer, Christine got out of the car and walked briskly down the path.

Christine reached the huge hole in the ground. The woods were silent. Not even a bird peeped.

Is Owens already dead? She could hardly dare to look, but she knew she must. Now that she saw the depth of the hole, she wondered about broken bones or a fractured skull. She listened intently. Not a sound.

Christine picked up a leafy branch and waved it over the mouth of the pit. Nothing. No gunfire, no yelling, no cry for help. Nothing.

Gathering her courage, Christine knelt at the edge and looked over. It was dark inside. She peered intently, trying to make out the shape of a body. She saw nothing.

"Samuel?" she called. "Mr. Owens?" No answer.

Duty done, she rose to her feet and began to hurry back to her car. But it bothered her that she couldn't see the bottom of the hole clearly. She turned, thinking that she should do a complete search. She didn't want to hear later that she'd left a badly injured man to die.

Christine slid down into the hole and carefully looked around. As her eyes grew accustomed to the dimness, she marvelled that Dancer could ever have gotten himself out. The boulders were large and rugged, and she could see where his steel shoes had scraped and scuffed as he'd tried to free himself. Owens was definitely gone.

Just as she began to climb out, a large shovelful of stony earth hit her on the head.

"Hey!" Christine yelled. "Stop that!"

Another load of earth came down, followed quickly by another, and another. More than one person was up there, filling the hole.

"Hey! Stop it! Who's there?"

A rock hit her on the head and she lost consciousness.

Police officers Milo Murski and John Bains pulled their cruiser up to the barn and parked it beside the veterinarian's truck. They got out. A very agitated Abby emerged from the barn.

"Abby Malone!" Milo greeted her warmly. Milo and Abby had become friends two years earlier when she'd solved the Bosco mystery, releasing her father from jail and putting Colonel Kenneth Bradley behind bars, where he still remained.

"Mr. Murski, Mr. Bains! I'm so glad to see you! We've got to go!"

"We got the call just a few minutes ago. We came as fast as we could."

"As fast as we could, considering we were making a drug arrest." John Bains interjected dourly.

Alan Masters, the vet, strode out of the barn to his truck. "I'll finish up soon and be off, Abby. You go ahead. Dancer should be fine." He opened the hatch and found the items he needed.

"Thanks, Dr. Masters." The experienced equine doctor would clean Dancer's wounds, give him penicillin and painkillers, and stitch the gash on his head.

"I'll change the bandages tomorrow morning at eight, Abby, and take a look at how his wounds are healing."

Abby answered, nodding, "Okay, I'll meet you here."

"Good day, Milo, John." Alan greeted the policemen gravely as he returned to his work in the barn.

"Good day to you, Alan," responded Milo as John nodded.

"Where's that sidekick of yours, Wile E. Coyote?" inquired Milo with a friendly smile.

"You mean Cody? He's around, but we have to hurry. Samuel Owens dug a pit—I need to show you; it's a long story. Can I tell it on the way?"

Milo ground his teeth. "Any story concerning that man is a long story, and it rarely has a happy ending." He opened the back door of the cruiser. "Hop in, Abby. Take us to the scene."

Abby filled them in as they drove. She tried to contain her impatience as the cruiser approached the path. They saw Christine's car parked at the side of the road.

"How long has she been here?" asked Milo.

"A long time. I'm not wearing my watch, but I'd guess half an hour."

"She should have waited for us," muttered Bains darkly.

"Abby," requested Milo firmly, "you stay in the car. Don't leave under any circumstances. And keep the doors locked. You hear?"

Abby nodded. She felt a chill go through her body. "You think something's happened to Mrs. James, don't you?"

The officers looked at each other. Milo spoke. "We'll look after this, Abby. Just stay put so we don't have to worry about you."

Abby could hardly sit still, but she stayed in the car, watching the path. Her eye caught Cody's tail as it rose above the roadside weeds. His inquiring face popped up to look at her.

Abby tried to open the window to reassure her coyote, but the car was off and the electric windows wouldn't budge. She opened the door just a crack.

Scraping sounds filled her ears. And sounds of rocks hitting metal. Shovelling noises, Abby deduced. What was happening?

One little peek couldn't hurt, Abby reasoned, as she got out of the cruiser. Followed by Cody, Abby tiptoed into the woods along the path.

It was almost seven o'clock. Auditions were about to start at the Wick barn, now officially called The Stonewick Playhouse.

Joy Featherstone and Robert Wick had completely transformed the theatre. The old, decrepit barn looked remarkable. The auditorium had been scrubbed clean. The walls were painted three shades of mossy green; the walls darkest, the wainscotting highlighted, and the trim the lightest. The chairs had been fixed and re-covered in a durable velvet of deep plum. A grand new purple curtain hung across the proscenium arch, sweeping the newly sanded and polished stage floor. The original sconces and overhead lights had been touched up and rewired, retaining the romantic atmosphere of old, and the rusted stage lights had been replaced by modern ones, all hooked into a state-of-the-art computerized lighting board. The smells of cut lumber, fresh paint, and new fabric intermingled with the exciting aromas of adrenalin and greasepaint.

Joy and Robert had set up a station for themselves four rows from the front of the stage in the centre of the auditorium. A little table with a light sat over the two seats in front to facilitate their note-taking, and their seats had been raised to a level where they could comfortably use the table. On the stage, the organist of the Inglewood Church sat ready at a grand piano to accompany anyone who wished his services. Sitting along the outside seats were dozens of nervous-looking people, all waiting for their turn to audition.

Among those people sat Lucy, saving the seat beside her. Every few minutes she looked around, studying the entrances. She hoped that Abby would show up soon, but she already felt a little better. Her spirits had lifted as she studied the crowd, for over there, near the back, were Sam and Leslie Morris. And there was Annie Payne sitting with Pam Masters. Even Leo Rodrigues and his mother had shown up. Everyone was coming to audition for the new playhouse.

All these people, and how many parts? Suddenly, Lucy felt deflated. She didn't have a chance. She thought over what she'd decided to do. She was going to sing her favourite nursery song "The Three Bears" because she remembered all the words, and recite "The Tyger" by William Blake, a poem she'd learned for school. But even though she'd been quite confident of her choices before coming, they seemed more and more inappropriate. Lucy wanted to get up and leave before she embarrassed herself beyond salvage. *"Tyger! Tyger! burning bright, In the forests of the night . . ."* The more she thought about the movements she'd rehearsed to go with it, the more demoralized she became. She'd never acted before. She'd never even auditioned before. For sure she'd be terrible. Lucy stood up to go.

A bluish-grey glow three seats away caught her eye. *Could it be Abby's ghost?* she wondered. Goosebumps prickled her arms. *It must be. He's really real. She wasn't making it up!*

Lucy looked at the people around her. Nobody seemed to notice the odd light but her. *He showed himself to me.* She thought for a moment. *He wanted me to see him. He must want me to stay!* She looked back at the ghost. He was gone. She shivered, but resolved to do her audition. She would forget about the live people watching. She'd play to Abby's ghost.

The auditions began at seven o'clock sharp. Everyone hushed when Robert Wick stood up, and their eyes followed him anxiously as he strode onto the stage. The great hall was silent. Mr. Wick began to speak, tones mellow and full, words carrying easily to the back of the house.

"Welcome to the first auditions of The Stonewick Playhouse. Let me introduce you first to my friend and theatre partner, Mrs. Joy Featherstone." Joy stood and smiled graciously. Her presence was somehow reassuring, calming the fears of a good many people.

"My name is Robert Wick, and tonight we'll have some fun. Intentionally, we called the auditions with little warning. We didn't want to give you time to get yourselves into a stew." Everybody laughed. "Relax, and remember, you're all in the same boat. Tonight we want to see you and figure out how to use your particular talent, which, we have no doubt, will astonish us." Again, the entire auditorium laughed, perhaps a little over-enthusiastically. "Let us begin. We want everyone here to get a part." He looked down at his notes. "Please take the stage, Mr. Ed Scaff."

As a short, roly-poly man with very little hair and a smile from ear to ear sprinted up the steps to the stage, Lucy assumed that Abby had chickened out. It wasn't like her, though, to promise to come and not turn up. Lucy was disappointed. She took a deep breath to curb her nerves, remembered the ghost for good luck, and waited for her turn.

Resting his bruised body in his favourite chair, Samuel Owens barked his orders. "Run! Don't dawdle, you ungrateful wretch! When I say I want more ice in my scotch, I want it now!" Walter was back in the den with ice in a small crystal bucket before Owens had finished his tirade. Using silver tongs, he dropped three cubes into the cut-glass tumbler and watched anxiously to see if Owens wanted more.

"Take it out! Two cubes only! You are such an idiot, Walter. Get me another scotch. I can't drink this."

The telephone beside Owens' chair rang. Walter rushed to answer it.

"Get out, Walter! Don't touch my phone!" Reaching to answer it, Owens groaned. His ribs hurt every time he moved. *That cursed horse*, he thought, remembering the impact of Dancer's hooves.

"Owens here," he growled into the mouthpiece.

"Payment's due. Look outside your window."

Owens turned his head sharply to see the figure of a stocky man, facing him with a cell phone at his ear.

"Payment in cash, or I don't leave."

"I need proof that the hole is filled. I want no trace left."

"Go look, then."

"Okay, okay," Owens grumbled, flinching at the prospect of moving his aching body from his chair. "I'll trust you this time. I'll want you for another job soon. Wait one minute." Owens put down the receiver. "Walter! Get in here!"

At the hole, Abby hid behind a thick maple tree and watched breathlessly. Secured to a big sugar maple tree were two men with resentful eyes. Milo Murski and John Bains had removed their police uniform shirts and were digging furiously. Their heads were visible above the ground, and Abby watched as shovelsful of earth flew over the lip.

"We didn't know anyone was down there!" yelled one of the handcuffed men.

"Tell it to the judge," snapped John Bains.

"We're here, Christine. Don't try to move yet. Take small breaths. You'll be all right." Milo spoke steadily in a calm voice.

Mrs. James? Is she down there? Abby was alarmed.

"Okay, John. I think we're ready. Easy now."

Christine James moaned. Then she started to cough. Abby couldn't see what was happening.

Suddenly the top of Christine's head emerged. Her body followed, completely supported by John Bains and Milo Murski. They carried her out, one at each side. She was covered in dirt, with her eyes, mouth, and nose black with mud. Her hair held clumps of earth where the blood from the blow to her head had hardened.

Abby's hands flew to her mouth. She stumbled backward, then turned and ran to the cruiser. She got in and sat quietly. An ambulance pulled up and stopped at the roadside. Its engine idled while two men took a stretcher out of the back and hurried into the woods.

The moment Hilary James got the message from her stepfather, Rory, she called Sandy. He'd also talked to his father, and within an hour they were on the last flight of the day from Montreal to Toronto.

"She was buried *alive*, Sandy. It must have been horrible."

"My dad's been with her the whole time, Hilary," Sandy said reassuringly. "He says there are no broken bones, no internal injuries, only bruising and a slight concussion. She's going to be fine."

"I know, Sandy. You keep telling me that, but until I see her myself, I'm going to worry. That's just the way I am."

"And that's just the way I like you. I only wish I could make you feel better."

"I feel better having you with me. Thanks for coming."

Sandy smiled. "Dad's meeting us at the airport, and we'll go straight up to the Orangeville hospital."

"Can't he stay with Mom? We could take a taxi."

"You know my dad. He insisted. He said your mom needed a break from him anyway."

"Well someone should stay with her tonight. She'll have nightmares, I'm sure of it. I'll ask the doctor to have a cot brought in for me. I can't leave her alone."

"So the worm has turned."

"What do you mean by that?"

"That the child is now mothering the mother."

"I guess that's true." Hilary thought about it for a minute then asked, "Did you talk to your dad about Dancer's condition?"

"Not much. I know nothing you don't know."

"Well, I'll feel better after I see him, too. Dr. Masters told me he'll be okay, but a crack on the head like that could be serious if it gets infected."

"If Dr. Masters says he'll be okay, he'll be okay. He's known Dancer a long time. Now, try to get a little rest. It's going to be a long night."

Hilary rested her head on Sandy's strong shoulder. Not for the first time, she felt lucky to have him in her life.

10
YOUNG LOVE

FRIDAY MORNING, ABBY AWOKE long before the alarm rang.
It was five o'clock. She had barely slept. There was too much on
her mind. She leaned across her bed and opened the drapes a
little to check on the weather. Just as she thought. It was still
raining. Ugh. Maybe Joy could drive her to school today.

Christine had come home from the hospital the day before.
They'd kept her in only one night, with Hilary sleeping on a cot
beside her. Christine was tired and bruised, and her ribs were
sore, but she was in great shape for a woman who'd been knocked
out and buried in dirt. Joy had gone to visit her Wednesday
night and arrived back at her bedside early Thursday morning.
Joy told Abby that Christine had survived because of the way she
fell. When she was knocked out, she'd slumped forward into a
ball and had somehow managed to create a pocket of air. Abby
didn't want to imagine if Christine had died. Indirectly, it
would've been her fault. Christine had gone to see if Samuel
Owens needed medical assistance because Abby was too frightened to look down the hole after Dancer had kicked him in.
Abby pulled the covers over her head. Too horrible.

She sighed, resigned to dragging herself out of her warm bed
in one hour to work with Leggy. She tried to fall asleep again.

It was difficult to get excited about training Leggy when the
ground was muddy. Abby could make the case that it was even
dangerous, but she knew better. There was always something to

do, and keeping to the daily schedule was almost as important as the training itself. She could groom Leggy and tack her up and walk her up and down the road, practise loading in the horse-trailer, or teach her to back up or to yield to each side.

Sam had virtually ignored her yesterday. Abby was more confused than ever. They had a date tonight, didn't they? Or was it a date? Sam had said he wanted to talk to her. He didn't call it a date. Why should Abby call it a date? Maybe she should just phone Sam and cancel. Abby rolled over. *Count sheep, you idiot,* she told herself. *It's way too early.*

Dancer looked better Thursday than Wednesday, and Abby felt hopeful that he'd look better again today. With Hilary home for the weekend, Abby wasn't sure how much she'd be needed, but she planned to go to Hogscroft directly after school to offer help in any way. She might as well forget about the Invitational, even though Christine had registered her. There was no way Dancer would be sound and fit in just five weeks. Abby calculated three weeks minimum for recovery, then at least a month to regain his muscle tone. She was sorely disappointed.

She turned onto her belly in an effort to shut down her thoughts.

Moonie wasn't her normal, perky, willing self. Abby had meant to ask Alan Masters about her, but so much else had been going on. She made a mental note to call him. Moonie and Leggy needed their rabies shots and worming medicine, anyway. Until Moonie got a checkup, Abby didn't want to ride her.

Everyone at school was talking about the auditions. Was Abby the only one who hadn't been there? The roles would be posted on the library bulletin board on Monday, but already people were sure they'd snagged the lead, or positive they'd embarrassed themselves terribly. Lucy went on and on about Ambrose Brown. He was now her personal ghost. He had appeared as a sign that stardom was beckoning, and vaporized as soon as he knew she'd got the message. Lucy was even talking about holding a seance. Abby smiled under the covers.

Mr. Owens was another matter. Abby shuddered, thinking that he made her old nemesis, Colonel Kenneth Bradley, look almost angelic. Well, not quite, but this man was looney-tunes. What could he possibly get out of trapping a horse or trying to shoot it? Was it all about trespassing? Abby didn't know how to read it, she only knew that he gave her the creeps. More than the creeps. He made her mad. Furious. The man was making people afraid. You never knew what he'd do next, and you couldn't prove his involvement anyway.

She'd never get back to sleep now. With a huge effort, she threw the covers off and leapt out of bed. She pulled on her old sweatsuit and hurried downstairs. Not even pausing for orange juice, Abby shrugged into her rain slicker and stepped into her boots. She might as well wake Leggy and get her morning training out of the way. Then she would reward herself with oatmeal porridge with raisins and brown sugar, and a soak in the tub before school.

Dawn was trying to break in spite of the thick cloud cover as Abby opened the gate and walked through the paddock. She entered the shed with the lead rope in hand. "Leggy, wake up. Time for work."

Three horses lifted their heads. One with a large white bandage.

"Dancer! What are you doing here?" Abby was amazed.

Moonie, Leggy, and Dancer stood companionably in the shed, for all the world like they were stable mates.

"What am I going to do with you?"

Dancer saved her the trouble of having to do anything. He nodded his head, snorted, and trotted away. Abby watched as he sailed over the four-rail fence and casually disappeared up the road to Hogscroft.

"Yeesus Murphy," she muttered. "I guess he's feeling better." Moonie and Leggy stood with her as the sky lightened, all mesmerized by this unusual horse.

The school day passed without incident. Along with her lack of sleep and the constant drizzle outside, other factors added to Abby's bad mood. Leslie was at home, sick with the flu. Lucy was on a science class retreat. Sam was still avoiding her.

Sam came to her locker after school, and asked if he could pick her up around seven. Abby answered yes, that would be fine, but wondered if his long face meant he might possibly be taking her to a funeral.

Abby caught the school bus to go home. She found a seat at the very back and hoped that nobody would join her. Nobody did. Perhaps low spirits act as a repellent, she contemplated. She didn't care.

The rain on the windows was soft but consistent. *It might be good for the flowers,* Abby mused, *but it's certainly hard on the gravel roads.* The sky was dull. The farms they drove past looked deserted and dirty. Every car on the road was covered in mud. The world through the school bus window was a study in sepia; brown was the colour of the day.

Abby got off the bus at the end of her lane and slouched toward her house. She pulled up the collar of her coat and stuffed her hands into her pockets.

Cody came running, tail wagging, delighted as always that his mistress was safely home. "Cody, you're the best," Abby declared. "But don't try to cheer me up. I'm too far gone."

Abby considered taking a nap. Curling up under the covers, making the world disappear. Bliss. Maybe she'd sleep for a week. Nobody would miss her. She sighed.

Lights were on at her house, giving it a welcoming and cozy appearance that cut through the dullness. Maybe things weren't so bad. *Mrs. Featherstone is home,* Abby thought. *Hmm. She always makes cookies when it rains.*

Abby noticed that the Hogscroft truck was parked in the turnaround. She opened the kitchen door to find Hilary and

Mrs. Featherstone at the kitchen table and Mrs. James cuddled up in a blanket in the overstuffed chair beside the cheerful fire.

"Abby!" exclaimed Joy. "Just the person we were talking about."

Tea, fresh-baked chocolate-chip cookies, apple slices, and cheeses were laid out on the blue-checked tablecloth with china and napkins.

"Get out of that wet coat and sit down," said Joy. "Would you like some hot cocoa? It's all ready on the stove."

Looking at Joy Featherstone as she bustled around the kitchen doing things to make people happy gave Abby a lump in her throat. Seeing Hilary's kind face as she pulled out a chair brought a tear to her eye. But it was Christine's bruised and lopsided grin that was the straw that broke the camel's back. Abby stood dripping rain as her eyes brimmed over.

"Abby, what is it?" asked Hilary, standing.

"My darling girl!" Joy rushed to her.

"Are you all right?" Christine called from her chair.

"I'm fine, really," Abby spluttered through her tears. "I don't know what's wrong with me."

"Here's your cocoa. Be careful, it's very hot." Joy set the steaming cup on the table, and helped her out of her coat and into the chair. Hilary grabbed the box of tissue from the counter and set it beside her.

Abby took a tissue and smiled as she mopped her cheeks. "Ignore me, please. I've had a bad day, and the sight of all you nice people made me cry. I'm just so happy you're all here." She blew her nose. "Mrs. James, how are you feeling?"

"Better than you, sweetheart," Christine responded, chuckling good-naturedly.

Abby laughed, joined by Hilary and Joy. She was amazed at how quickly her day-long misery had ended. The warmth and fellowship of her little farm kitchen was an island of contentment on this cold and rainy day. She drank her cocoa, gobbled up cookies, and joked with these women; three generations of the same family. Abby felt like one of them.

"More tea, Mom?" Hilary asked Christine.

"Thanks, dear, but I've had plenty. Don't want to float away."

"Gran?"

"No thanks, Mousie. Abby? More cocoa, or would you like some tea?"

"Thank you, but no. Oh, I'm going out tonight, Mrs. Featherstone, remember?"

"How could I forget? With that dear young man, Sam Morris."

Hilary smiled broadly at Abby. "Cool," she said.

"He's picking me up at seven. I didn't get much sleep last night, so I'm going to try to have a nap."

"I thought I heard you wandering around in the night. Is anything bothering you, dear?" Joy was concerned.

"No, nothing to worry about. But I'm glad to see that you're okay, Mrs. James. I feel really awful about the whole thing. You wouldn't have gone back there if I'd had the nerve to look down the hole to see if Mr. Owens was injured."

"Abby!" exclaimed Christine. "Get that out of your head! You aren't the culprit, Samuel Owens is. Don't forget that. He had a gun, and he tried to use it. You were right to get out of there as fast as you could. I was the stupid one. I shouldn't have gone there at all. I've gotten heck from my old friend Mack Jones, the police chief, about this several times already."

Hilary's face darkened. "I hope nothing disastrous happens before Owens is behind bars. I won't be happy until then."

"He's always been trouble," Joy opined. "From way back in school. He's a bad apple."

"He's sure got a thing against Dancer," added Hilary. "He's not over it, even after his time in the mental hospital. Can you imagine planning a trap?"

"How did he know that Dancer would fall into it?" asked Christine. "If that is what he had in mind, and it seems it was."

Abby thought for a moment, then spoke. "I might have the answer to that. This morning, Dancer was in my shed with Moonie and Leggy."

The women registered their surprise.

"I know, I was shocked, too. But then I remembered seeing something jump out of the field a while ago. It was chestnut, so I assumed it was a deer. Now I'm not so sure."

"And the path from your farm to Hogscroft is right through the woods behind Owens' house." Hilary was figuring it out.

"Right along the path and into the bear pit," Joy surmised.

Christine went the next step. "If Dancer has been visiting at regular times and Owens has seen him coming and going, there's our answer."

The kitchen was silent as the enormity of the situation sank in.

"Then Dancer's not safe," said Hilary. "Here we go again."

"How can we keep him from wandering into Owens' hands?" asked Christine. "Build a higher fence? Drug him? Move him away? Hire an armed guard?"

"We'd better come up with something," said Hilary. "And fast."

"He sure looked good jumping over the fence this morning," said Abby. "You wouldn't guess he was injured except for the bandages."

"He's healing remarkably well," agreed Hilary. "No swelling in his legs, no infection on his head. Dr. Masters was amazed when he checked him this afternoon. He said if Dancer continues to heal this fast, he might be fit enough for the Grand Invitational."

"Really?" Abby's eyes popped wide open.

"Only if he's sound and fit, so don't count your chickens." Hilary looked at her watch. "We'll put up electric wire this afternoon, and see if that keeps Dancer in. It's after four, so I'd better get going. Go have your nap, Abby, and tomorrow we'll talk strategy. I'll give you a program to follow once he's ready to work."

"Okay! Call me when it's a good time to come over," enthused Abby, completely back to her old self.

Seven o'clock arrived. Abby'd taken a short nap and was bathed and dressed and waiting. She'd worried about what to wear. She didn't want to look like she cared, but she wanted to look good. She'd decided on a new baby blue cotton sweater and her best jeans.

Joy Featherstone had promised Robert Wick that she'd go to dinner with him, but she wasn't leaving until Abby had been picked up.

"You don't look like a girl about to go on a date," noted Joy.

"And what does that look like?"

"Well, pink-cheeked and radiant, for starters."

"I'll let you in on a secret, Mrs. Featherstone. It's not a real date. He just wants to talk. I think he's going to tell me why he dumped me last year."

"Ahh," said Joy with a great deal of sympathy. "Why would he do that?"

Abby shrugged. "Who knows? But he sure hasn't been happy to see me in the halls. I don't know what to expect."

"You still like him, don't you, Abby?" Joy noted warmly.

"I'll let you know later. I won't be late."

Joy took Abby by the shoulders and looked her in the eye. "Whatever comes, remember, it won't be the best thing that will ever happen to you, and it won't be the worst. Take it in stride. Being dumped has happened to us all, and more than once to most."

"Even you?"

"Even me. In fact, one man who dumped me is picking me up tonight for dinner." She smiled slyly at the young woman. "It ain't over 'til it's over."

Abby laughed. "You always know exactly what to say to make a person feel better."

The doorbell rang. Abby and Joy exchanged a look.

"Do you want me to get it?" asked Joy.

"I'll get it," replied Abby with assurance. "I'm ready."

Sam Morris stood at the door, a tall young man with a handsome smile. Abby asked him in and introduced him to Mrs. Featherstone.

"You take care of her, now," Joy said pointedly as Abby put on her raincoat.

"I will, Mrs. Featherstone. It was nice to meet you."

"And nice to meet you, too, Sam. Have a pleasant evening." Joy watched from the window as Sam opened his umbrella and walked Abby to his father's car.

Joy sighed. "Young love."

They drove for some time in silence. Sam's face remained serious and he concentrated on the road. Abby watched the windshield wipers as they cleaned the raindrops rhythmically away. They reminded her of the metronome her old piano teacher had used.

"Where are we going, Sam?" Abby asked.

"To the Roadside Cafe. We can talk there. And their burgers are great."

"Sam, you're driving me nuts, you know that?"

"Abby, you'll understand better when I explain."

"Well, can I turn on the radio? I can't bear the silence."

"Sure."

Abby found a radio station that she liked, and they pretended to listen. Sam seemed more and more distracted.

"Sam, stop the car and let's talk. Let's get it over with. I know what you're going to say, and I can't sit here on pins and needles waiting for you to find the appropriate place to say it."

Sam pulled off the road.

"It's not like anything you say is going to be a surprise. I'll take it in stride. It won't be the best thing that ever happens to me, but it sure won't be the worst, so just blurt it out."

Sam looked puzzled. "What are you talking about?"

"I'm not an idiot, no matter what you think. And I'm not insensitive. I figured this out weeks ago."

"Figured what out?"

Abby looked down at her hands in her lap, letting her long hair cover her face. "You heard, didn't you?"

"Heard what?"

"This is so embarrassing." She took a deep breath. She figured she had nothing to lose. "Heard that I liked you again. I told my two best friends, and I can't believe one of them told, but then Pam knew, and then you heard and now you want to talk to me about all the reasons why it wouldn't work out and why it didn't before, but you don't have to tell me, I've already figured it out, and anyway I'm past all that and don't even care anyway and—"

"Abby, stop!"

"—I know that I'll never be your type. But that's okay because you're not my type either and we're way past it anyway. I only wish you'd never heard the rumour."

"Abby," said Sam slowly. "I never heard the rumour."

Abby stared at him. "You never heard the . . . . Then what's this all about? This 'date?' You didn't ask me out because you like me."

"Is that what you think?" He shook his head in disbelief.

"What else can I think? You look sheepish when you see me, and you disappear if I enter a room."

Sam crossed his arms and cleared his throat. "Okay, here it goes, and it's not going to be easy." He breathed again. "I've been thinking about you again, Abby. I can't get you out of my mind." He held up a hand. "Let me talk. When I see you at school I wish that we were together again. When I'm at work or at home, I wish I could see you. We had a lot of fun, right?"

"Right." Abby didn't move a muscle. She had no idea where this was going.

"There's something I have to tell you. Something crazy. Before I can even hope to ask you out again, you should know this about me. Something I didn't even know myself until recently."

"What, Sam?"

"Did you ever notice my name?"

"Your name? What about your name?"

"Sam. My name is Samuel. It's a family name."

"So?"

"Do you know any other Samuels?"

"No."

"Think."

"Only Samuel Owens, but that's ridiculous."

"How is it ridiculous?"

"You couldn't possibly be related."

"Why's that?"

"It's a small community. I'd know if you were part of the Owens family."

"What if we're related, but nobody is supposed to know?"

"You mean . . . illegitimately?"

"Yes."

"Wow." Abby sat thinking.

After giving it a moment to sink in, Sam continued. "The Owenses don't exactly recognize us as family."

"I can hardly digest this, Sam. How are you related?"

"Samuel Owens is my grandfather."

"No kidding." Abby paused to consider. "Your father's father?"

"My mother's father."

"But, Sam," Abby said. "Your mother's black."

STAGESTRUCK

"Half black. Her mother, my grandma, is black. Owens is white. Gran worked for the Owenses. She was very young. When she told him she was pregnant, he denied any responsibility and had her fired. Things were very tough for her. Then, when my mother was three, Gran met and married my grandpa and they had two sons, my uncles."

"Wow," she repeated.

"Yeah." Sam leaned back and stared at the ceiling of the truck. "I was at our family reunion last March. I overheard two of my aunts talking about mixed marriages. The Owens thing just sort of came out in conversation. Like it was a given. Then they stopped talking and looked at me. Leslie didn't hear." Sam was deeply troubled. "I can't believe they kept it from me all this time. Why didn't they tell me? I don't know which was more of a shock, Abby; to find out Grandpa isn't related or to find out that Owens is."

Abby was quiet for a long time. Sam watched her, wondering about her reaction.

"Have you talked to your parents about it?" she quietly asked.

"Yeah. My mother."

"I can see it's really eating you up." Abby said carefully.

"Wouldn't it eat you up? To find out you're related to someone like Owens? I wouldn't blame you if you never want to see me again." Sam's voice was harsh.

Abby was stunned. "Why? What's it got to do with you?"

"It's the heredity thing. Samuel Owens is my grandfather. What if I've got his evil genes? What if I turn into a psycho?"

"You won't." Abby spoke softly. "You are one of the nicest guys I've ever known. And you won't go bad."

Sam stared at her. His eyes shone. "You mean that?"

"Yes." Abby reached across the seat and touched Sam's hand. It was a beautiful hand, long-fingered and strong.

Sam placed his other hand over hers and held it tightly. "Abby, my grandfather threatened you with a shotgun last Wednesday. Can you honestly say it doesn't affect how you think of me?"

"Samuel Owens is a horrible, scary, mixed-up man. What he does affects how I think of *him*, not how I think of you."

"I was afraid you'd turn against me."

"I wouldn't turn against you because of something someone else did," Abby said. "Never."

"Thank you, Abby."

"Does Samuel Owens know that you're his grandson?"

Sam looked blank. "I don't know. I guess so. I mean, he'd know that my mother was his daughter."

"I'm going to guess he doesn't want to know," said Abby thoughtfully. "That he completely refuses to acknowledge his part in this. It'd be in his interest not to be accountable."

"You're probably right," agreed Sam. "Anyway, I'm certainly not going to tell him."

"This doesn't affect how you think of Samuel Owens, does it? Now that he's family?"

"Don't worry about that," Sam said. "I'll never think of him as family. He turned my grandmother out, and Grandpa is the only grandfather I know."

Abby nodded. Another question occurred to her. "Why would your mother name you after someone who'd treated her own mother so badly? Who'd used her, then threw her out into the streets to fend for herself in a world that would've been hostile, to say the least?"

"I asked her that." Sam paused. "She said our family had been living in shame over something that Owens did and got away with. It was always a dirty secret, and why should we help him hide it? 'Facilitate' was her word. She said that naming me Samuel kind of released her, was cathartic. 'Opened the windows' was how she put it."

Abby thought about how unfair it was. The more she knew about Samuel Owens, the more she disliked him. She sat looking through the windshield. It was nice sitting in the old red Ford, next to Sam again.

She turned to face him. "So. Is there anything else you want to tell me? Any more hidden secrets?"

"No. That's it."

"That's all? That Owens is related to you?"

"Yes."

Abby paused and smiled at Sam. "So?"

"So what?" asked Sam.

"Now that you've told me, aren't you going to ask me out again?"

Sam began to laugh.

"That's what you said, you know, before you told me."

"I did, didn't I?" Sam slowly stopped laughing. "Abby Malone, will you go out with me?"

"You're sure you want to?"

"Yes, Abby, I'm sure. I've missed you." He gently encircled her with his arms and pulled her to him. He slowly smiled as his lips met hers. They kissed, pleasant sensations tingling down to their toes.

"Forget the burger," Abby said dreamily.

11

PLANS AND SCHEMES

ABBY JUMPED OUT OF BED the next morning, humming. Life was good. It was Saturday, the sun was shining, and Sam was her boyfriend again. He said he would call when he awoke to make plans. He worked Saturdays and Wednesday nights at a video store.

"Sam, Sam, Sam, Sam!" she sang as she jumped into a sweat-suit. She made his name sound like bells ringing. "Sam, Sam, Sam, Sam."

"Someone sounds happy this morning," Joy called up the stairs. "Come on down! Breakfast is ready."

"Sam, Sam, Sam, Sam," she sang as she half-hopped, half-slid down the banister.

"Mousie called earlier. She and Sandy have some errands to run in town, but she wants to know if you can go over to Hogscroft after lunch."

"Perfect. Nothing could be better." Abby plunked into her chair and drank the glass of freshly squeezed orange juice. "Ahh! This is so good, Mrs. Featherstone. You're spoiling me with all your yummy food."

"That's the idea. You're worth spoiling, Abby. Besides, it gives me pleasure. I love to cook, and it's no fun cooking just for myself." She placed a plateful of steaming waffles covered in butter and maple syrup alongside aromatic sausages in front of the hungry girl.

"Thank you!" Abby bit into a sausage. "What are Sandy and Hilary doing in town?"

"Choosing an engagement ring, among other things." The older woman's eye sparkled mischievously.

"An engagement ring! They're getting married?"

"I don't know of any other reason to get an engagement ring, do you?"

"When are they getting married?" Abby dug into the waffles with her fork.

"They haven't set a date, but I think they'd like to be married before they go off to Belize this fall. Orange juice?"

"No, thanks. Well, okay, sure. Please. That means this summer. Holy." Abby cut a piece of sausage and dipped it in mustard. "Holy," she said again, then popped it into her mouth.

"What are you doing today, Mrs. Featherstone?"

"Theatre work, mainly. Robert and I are making our final casting selections. The list goes up this afternoon, tomorrow the cast meets for a get-together, and Monday evening rehearsals start."

"What play are you doing? Can you tell me? I know it's been a secret."

"Actually, it wasn't a secret at all. We wanted to see what kind of talent we had before we decided on a play."

"Smart move," nodded Abby. "You don't want to pick a musical if you don't have singers."

"Exactly. Turns out we have plenty of talent, and plenty of people interested in acting. It's wonderful, really."

"You and Mr. Wick are spending a lot of time together." Abby watched to see Joy's reaction. Her back was turned as she poured Abby's juice, but Abby saw her cheeks tighten into a smile. "What's the scoop?"

"We're friends. We have a good time," said Joy cryptically.

"That's it? A good time?"

"That's all I'm prepared to say at the moment."

"Are you going into politics, or what?" Abby asked, laughing.

Diva scrambled from under the table and started her high-pitched barking.

"Diva! It's all right!" commanded Joy. The little dog continued, "Yarf! Yarf! Yarf! Yarf!"

"Diva!" Joy hurried to the door.

Abby slid her chair back to see Robert Wick at the door, his freshly shaved face split by a smile. He held out a bouquet of colourful spring flowers with one hand, and placed the other behind Joy's back. They kissed. Abby quickly put her chair back into position and resumed eating.

Joy bustled to the sink and gaily arranged the flowers into a vase while Robert Wick whistled as he hung up his coat in the hall.

"Friends, eh?" whispered Abby. She gave Joy a stage wink.

"None of your business," Joy whispered back, smiling as she swatted Abby's head with a dishcloth.

Robert Wick entered the kitchen.

"Coffee, Robert?" asked Joy sweetly.

"Love some, Joy," he answered.

"You're looking more dapper every time I see you, Mr. Wick," said Abby. "I'd almost guess that you're in love or something."

"Abby!" Joy turned to Abby, shocked.

Robert smiled at Abby fondly. "I am. I'm in love with Joy Drake Featherstone. There." He looked at Joy. "I've said it. What do you think of that?" For a moment his eyes were vulnerable. Abby's heart went out to him.

"I think that's wonderful," said Joy softly. "Because I've been in love with Robert Wick for years."

"Okay," blurted Abby as she jumped up from the table, "I'm out of here! Time to go. Thanks for breakfast, Mrs. Featherstone."

Abby didn't look back. Humming her Sam song she ran out the door to say good morning to the world.

Samuel Owens drove up his lane cursing under his breath. It galled him that he'd had to pay full market value for the ratty one-acre property next door. He couldn't see it from his house, but since he had to pass it each time he drove up or down his lane, it had become an irritant. Now he owned it, but he wasn't happy.

"I hope Gladys Forsyth chokes on the caviar she's going to buy now that she thinks she's rich. That little cat-loving hermit! Thinks she outsmarted me! *Me!* All because she called that goody-goody broad for a second opinion. Christine James should keep her nose out of other people's business. That whole family better stay away from me. If they know what's good for them."

He held a burning anger within his chest against all of them. Against Mousie because of Dancer, and Joy Featherstone and Christine James because of the Wick farm. How he longed to get his hands on that property! His jaw tightened and his molars ground against each other as he tried to come up with a way to get that farm. It was central to his plan.

Helena Casey was making him miserable, too. She hated Christine James with a passion for marrying Rory, which was good. She couldn't care less what happened to Dancer, also good. She thought that Owens should buy all the surrounding property, again good. *But,* and this is where the good stopped and the bad began, she didn't like him lumping her precious son Sandy with the James family in his diatribes. He was engaged to one of them, wasn't he? That put him firmly in the enemy camp, no doubt about it.

And, if that wasn't enough, Helena was having qualms about selling her property. Now she was telling him that it had been in the Casey family for three generations, that maybe Sandy or Rosalyn might want it someday. It was her blanking house, wasn't it? Rory left her in it when he moved into his little love nest with Christine, didn't he? Well, get with it, Helena, he'd told her, or get off the bus.

Owens stopped his new steel-grey Mercedes coupe in front of his house. He'd have a Bloody Caesar with a cigar on the terrace before lunch. The thought cheered him up so much that he actually smiled. The smile disappeared as he began to get out of the car. His ribs hurt badly. All his muscles were stiff. *Damned animal!* he cursed.

"Walter! Walter! Get out here!"

The front door opened to reveal an extremely agitated manservant.

"A tall Bloody Caesar, on the double!"

"Mr. Owens, sir," he began.

"Did you hear? A Bloody Caesar! Now! On the terrace."

Walter went pale. "Yes sir! But Mr. Owens, sir . . ."

"Mr. Owens, sir," he mimicked. "Just do as you're told." With that, Owens hobbled past him into the house.

He bumped right into Mack Jones, the Caledon chief of police. "What the?" he bellowed. "Walter!" He struggled to get himself under control. He smiled, showing all his teeth. "Why didn't you tell me Mack Jones was here, Walter?"

Walter bowed his head. He tried to disappear into the woodwork.

"Good morning, Mr. Owens," said Mack courteously.

"What can Walter get you, Mack? I was about to have a drink before lunch. Join me?"

"No, thank you. I have a few questions. Where can we talk in private?"

"Anywhere we like. Don't worry about Walter. He's bought and sold! Ha ha ha." Owens laughed heartily at his joke, but Mack noticed Walter flinch as he scurried away.

Since his promotion to chief, Mack had rarely gotten involved in specific cases, but he'd known Christine James for years, and her husband, Rory Casey, was an old friend. Mack had been the officer in charge at Samuel Owens' trial five years before. There was no love lost between these two men.

"In that case, let's begin." Standing on the polished marble in the spacious front hall, Police Chief Jones started his line of questioning. "Inspector Murski and Detective Bains arrested two men on your property this week. Tell me what these men were doing on your property."

Owens smiled, eyes half-shut. "Can a person not hire labourers anymore?"

"A woman was almost killed. A girl was threatened with a shotgun. A horse was badly injured. Let me remind you, it might interest the court that the injured horse was Dancer. The horse you stabbed."

"I never threatened anyone. And let me get this straight. It worries you more that a horse was injured than that a woman was allegedly almost killed?" He spoke through a chilly smile.

"I repeat, it might interest the court. Need I spell it out?" Owens glared at Mack and shook his head.

"I thought not. What was your intention in digging the pit?"

"It's my property. I have a gun licence and a hunting licence. I can do what I like. But perhaps I was looking for gravel. My land would be worth a fortune as a quarry. Should I call my lawyers?"

"It would be a good idea."

"I don't owe you an explanation, Mack, but just to set the story straight, I was out with my shotgun, hunting for the rabid coyote that killed my cat." Owens spoke slowly, thinking out his story. "I heard strange noises. When I investigated, I was savagely attacked by Dancer, bitten in the leg by the Malone girl's coyote, and injured badly." He pulled his shirttails out of his pants and unbuttoned his shirt. "Bruises. Note the horseshoe shape." He lifted up the right leg of his pants. "Teeth marks. Deep. Potential for infection or worse, a horrible disease. I've been to the hospital."

He looked triumphant as he dropped the pant leg and buttoned up and tucked his shirt back into his pants. "I have pictures, of course. Since this happened on my property, and the girl was trespassing, *and* the offending animals were under her supervision, my lawyers and I are considering pressing charges."

"And you and your lawyers don't have a problem with a gaping hole with sharp rocks in the bottom, dug on a path where it might become a grave hazard?"

"A *grave* hazard. You're ironic, but you don't have a case. It's private property and well-marked with 'No Trespassing' signs."

"And the bullet in Dancer's saddle?"

Owens' eyebrows lifted. *So I did hit him,* he thought. "A bullet? In a saddle, you say?" *I haven't quite lost my touch.*

"You don't know anything about it?"

He pursed his lips, to keep from showing his pleasure. "No. Should I?"

"I'd like to take your rifle to the police lab. If you know nothing about that bullet, it shouldn't be a problem."

"The problem is that I might need it if that rabid coyote comes around looking for my other cat." His eyes glinted. "But if you had a warrant, I'd happily oblige."

Walter appeared, anxiously offering Owens a Bloody Caesar with lime on a silver tray.

"Ah, just what I was dreaming of." Owens lifted the frosted glass off the tray and took a big drink. "Excuse me, Chief, I must go rest. Walter, don't go away. I might just want another. More pepper next time."

Mack stalked from Owens' mansion to his unmarked car. He was upset. Where had this interview gotten him? Nowhere. Except now Owens knew that he was being watched. Maybe it would curb him. More likely it would make him more careful.

At the trial five years before, Mack had argued strongly that

Owens be locked up in jail. It didn't happen. *Fat lot of good the mental hospital did him,* Mack mused. Mack had been worried when Owens was released, but could not have guessed how quickly he'd make trouble. Starting with the bullet in Dancer's saddle, and leading to who knows where.

It'll only get worse, you can bet on that, he thought. *Owens is a slippery one. There's going to be trouble.* Mack vowed to watch him like a hawk. He'd take no shortcuts, make no assumptions. He knew how dangerous Owens could be. He wanted him in jail.

There was an excited crowd at the library bulletin board that afternoon. People of all ages were craning their necks to see what part they'd got in The Stonewick Playhouse's first show. It was going to be *Pinocchio.* The village and circus scenes could have countless participants, allowing everyone to have a part.

Volunteers for lighting crew, set building, props, wardrobe, and sound effects were asked to sign up on a large white piece of paper beside the cast list. Already there were dozens of entries. Petr Baloun had offered his considerable talents as an inventor and iron sculptor to create a movable giant dogfish for the ocean scene.

The joyful noises escaped the hall, causing Miss Smithers, now the librarian after resigning from her job as a supply teacher, to rush out shushing everyone.

"Remember where you are, please," Miss Smithers haughtily whispered. "This is a library, *not* a theatre." There was no mistaking her disdain for the latter, but even Miss Smithers at her most sour could not diminish the holiday mood in the hall.

Everyone was talking at once. "George Farrow! You got Geppetto!"; "I get to play the ticket-taker on Runaway Island!"; "How could they cast Leslie Morris as Trooper? It's written for a boy!"; "Do I have to sing?"; "My mother won't believe what I'm doing!"; "Do we have to do our own makeup?"

Joy Featherstone and Robert Wick watched in amazement. "What have we done?" wondered Joy aloud. She had not expected such a huge reaction.

"We've filled a need, it would seem," answered Robert proudly. "We've unleashed the child in each adult, and allowed the children to play."

Joy laughed. "Isn't it great? The whole township is here."

"Except Abby," noted Robert. "Wasn't she interested?"

"I didn't want to push, so we never talked about it. Maybe I should have encouraged her."

"Perhaps she didn't want to be seen as using your influence, so she stepped back."

Joy nodded. "Maybe so."

"We'll find a way to get her involved," Robert stated. "She has real stage presence. I saw it immediately, the day of the storm."

"The day you told her about Ambrose Brown?" Joy smiled.

"That very day. What are you doing for dinner tonight, Joy of my life?"

Joy Featherstone blushed with pleasure.

Abby and Hilary had a very productive afternoon. They sat at the round table in the Hogscroft kitchen charting Dancer's training schedule.

Abby was to start hand-walking Dancer daily, starting at thirty minutes and adding five minutes a day. After the walk, she would cold-hose his scraped legs and wrap them for the night. Christine would remove the bandages each morning. That was week one.

Week two, providing Alan Masters approved after an examination of his head wound, Abby was to start riding. She would walk only, with a loose rein, very relaxed. She would walk him longer each day until he was up to one hour.

Week three, she would hack him on a loose rein the first two days. Walk, trot, no cantering. Thirty minutes on day one, forty minutes on day two. Day three, she would hack out but start collecting his gaits slightly and ask him for a little canter. She would also do that days four and five. By day six of the third week, Abby would be in the ring, moving him along and asking for leads.

Week four was a gradually increasing course of jumps. On day six, Abby would hack him down the road. Week five was heavy jump work on days one and three. Days two, four, and five, Abby and Dancer would hack across country. The plan was that he would be rested and eager to jump on day six.

Day six of week five was June 26, the day of the Grand Invitational.

The plan was completely dependent on Dancer's health. If he wasn't happy working, Abby was to immediately call Alan Masters. Alan Masters would also check Dancer once a week. If at any time he thought Dancer wasn't handling the work well, Abby would call Hilary and they'd discuss whether or not to proceed.

Hilary and Abby walked out to the jumping ring. Hilary showed Abby how to place the jumps. She'd drawn charts of jumping courses with heights, widths, and distances clearly marked. They set up the first course that Dancer would do in week four. Hilary walked her through it, explaining how to pace to get the distances right. To make Abby's work easier, she gave her instructions on how to ride each jump, and tips peculiar to Dancer.

Abby's head was full of details as she cycled home. Her knapsack contained multiple instructions and intricate course maps. It was much more demanding than she'd realized. This exacting, technical, and extremely difficult sport looked so easy when it was done well.

Abby remembered when she'd first seen Hilary on Dancer at

a horse show seven years earlier. Everyone called her Mousie then. Abby was nine years old, and she'd never forgotten the impression they'd made on her. Dancer, effortlessly sailing over a course that others found treacherous. Mousie, guiding her mount with such light hands and quiet body that it looked like she was doing nothing at all.

After today's intense lesson, Abby knew it was artistry in its highest form. No rhythm was taken for granted, no corner unplanned. Every possible combination and permutation was considered and practised so that when faced with the course, horse and rider were prepared.

In competition, riders walk the course before they ride it. The horses see it for the first time when they come into the ring to be judged. It's part of the difficulty of the course, because by nature, horses don't like surprises. They like to be familiar with their environment, and each strange obstacle represents possible danger to them. There might be a mountain lion or a snake lurking on the other side, or the jump itself might wake up and turn into a monster. Therefore, the more confident and well-schooled the horse, the less stressed it will be when faced with a new course.

It was a lot to absorb, Abby thought as she pedalled along. She wondered if she was crazy thinking that she could even get around. Especially in a show as prestigious as the Grand Invitational.

She thought it out. Tomorrow, she'd start Hilary's program. After a week or so, she'd decide if she felt comfortable competing or not. She'd try her hardest, but it was a lot to ask of herself, and of Dancer.

Abby nodded to herself as she steered her bike up her lane. That was what she'd do. There was always the possibility that Dancer wouldn't heal quickly enough, and the decision would be out of her hands.

Cody greeted her enthusiastically, wiggling all over. Together they checked on Moonie and Leggy, who were lazing in the shed. Abby freshened their water trough and gave them a quick brushing and foot picking.

Satisfied with the sheen of their coats, Abby rubbed both horses' ears and patted them, then headed into the house. She found a message on the kitchen table.

Abby,

Your mom and dad called. Please call when you get in. Their number is 714-555-9137, extension 12. No emergency, just phoned to say hello.

Love, Joy

Abby immediately picked up the phone and dialled. Fiona answered on the second ring.

"Hello?"

"Mom! It's Abby!"

"You're the only one who calls me 'Mom,' Abby! Of course it's you."

"How's the spa, Mom? Are you doing okay? Is Dad there? Is he all right? What do you do all day?"

"Abby! One question at a time! The spa is really beneficial. The courses are terrific. They're trying to help me understand the root of my problem, then teach me how to overcome it. I'm getting lots of fresh air and exercise, and facials and massages, too. It's lovely. We're up at six every morning for yoga in the garden."

"Sounds good, Mom."

"It is good, Abby. Dad is here and he's doing fine. He wants to talk to you. It's so good to hear your voice. Are you okay? I miss you so much. Tell me what's happening at home."

"I miss you, too, Mom, and lots is happening! I'll fill you in.

I'm going out with Sam Morris again, I'm training Dancer to compete at a horse show, and Mrs. Featherstone is the absolute best. She's dating Mr. Wick! Hilary is going to marry Sandy this summer, and they're doing *Pinocchio* at The Stonewick Playhouse."

"Lots of news! It sounds like things are exciting in Caledon. Your father'll want to hear all about everything, especially the horse show. How's Cody? Is he all healed up?"

"He's perfect. One hundred percent."

"I'm so glad to hear it. Is he getting along with Joy and Diva?"

"They all ignore each other, so it works out great." Abby's tone became serious. "Mom, do you think you can beat this?"

"I'm trying, Abby. The spa has been successful with a lot of people. I want to be one of them."

"I'm rooting for you, Mom."

"I know, honey. I know."

The next voice was Liam's. "Abby, my love! I miss you!"

"I miss you too, Dad!"

"Your mother got choked up, so I took the phone. What's this about a horse show?"

"It's the Grand Invitational, Dad. On June 26. Dancer was invited to compete, and Hilary will be busy, so I'm riding him. Will you be home by then?"

"June 26? It's on my calendar. That's a Sunday, isn't it? Wouldn't miss it."

"I don't want you to come home early if Mom's not ready."

Liam spoke earnestly. "If Mom isn't ready, honey, she'll have to stay here until she is. But I'll be there to watch you compete. Count on it. Nothing can stop me!"

"Dad, you're great. I'm so happy you're coming."

"I've got to be back by then anyway. I can't be away from work any longer. If all goes well, we should both be back home."

"I hope so, Dad, I miss you both."

"Is everything fine, Abby?"

"Oh, it's great!" Abby grew serious. "Dad, do you see a change in Mom? Is the spa making a difference?"

"It's hard to say, Abby, my girl. But your mother's working hard at it."

"Are you working, too? At your law firm, I mean?"

"It amazes me how productive I am with fax, email, and telephone. I almost think it's better that people don't meet me face to face, but my partners want me back regardless."

Abby laughed. "Bye, Dad, see you soon."

12

THE DRESSING ROOM

IT WAS THE MORNING of the first dress rehearsal. Abby felt like a non-person. All her friends were involved in the play. Some were crew, some were wardrobe, some were actors. Everyone was involved but her. Caledon High reverberated with chatter about *Pinocchio*.

Abby's English teacher was away visiting her ill father. A perky, toothy young woman named Zelda Iman was taking her place for the next-to-last week of school. Abby had nothing against her, but there was something about Miss Iman's exuberance that was forced. It was almost scary. She talked loudly, as if the class had trouble hearing. She *emphasized* words *oddly*, hoping to *engage* their *interest*. She gestured broadly, trying to help them understand. Abby had wondered all week if Miss Iman might burst into tears from overexertion.

Miss Iman had always wanted to be an actress, she'd told them. Abby could believe that. The Stonewick Playhouse's production of *Pinocchio* enthralled her, and occupied a great deal of discussion time in class. Today, everyone in the class was to write a one-page essay describing what he or she was doing in or for the play.

"Don't be *shy*, class," Miss Iman enunciated, broadly sweeping her hand down her face to illustrate shyness. "*Reach* into your *heart* and *dig* into your *personal reasons* for being *part* of a *theatrical experience*. I'm *there* with you, I really *am*. Let it flow."

Abby stifled a laugh as the teacher reached and dug and flowed with each word. Miss Iman's gestures were hilarious, she thought.

Her empty page, though, was another matter.

Abby wrote, "I am not doing anything in or for the play."

Abby was tempted to hand it in like that. She picked up her pen again.

"I do other things, however, like ride horses."

That should do it, she thought. Abby crossed her legs and swung a foot while drumming her fingers on her cheek. She began to daydream.

Good thing the school year was almost over. Exams were finished, but the school had made classes mandatory until the very last day. Teachers were busy marking, so the students were given make-work projects, which were greatly resented. They attended, however, because marks would be taken off if they skipped. Next Monday the marked exams would be given back. Wednesday, school was out.

Abby's parents were coming home soon, and Joy Featherstone would move out when they were back. Abby and her parents wanted her to stay, but she insisted on moving in with Christine and Rory. It seemed a shame, though, because all her things were arranged in the guest room, and she was up to her ears in rehearsals and production. Abby had come to treasure Joy's warmth and perspective. She would miss her a lot.

Moonie had continued to be moody and lethargic. If Leggy bothered her, she risked a sharp kick from her mother, which surprised the young mare, because until now Moonie had always had an extremely sweet disposition. Abby knew the reason why. Two weeks ago, Alan Masters had confirmed that Moonie was in foal. She would be delivering a foal next May and Abby was thrilled. Another Dancer baby. She smiled.

Dancer was phenomenal. Riding him could not be compared

to anything on earth. Their training was proceeding exactly to the schedule that Hilary had drawn out. The horse show was just over a week away, on Sunday, four days after school let out, and Dancer was right on track. Abby shivered with anticipation and nerves every time she thought of the Invitational.

Hilary was lending Abby her riding clothes for the show. It was a nice surprise that they fit. Her simple, elegant black riding jacket was perfect. Her tight-fitting, stretchy, beige breeches were just right. Her tall, slim, black boots only needed an extra pair of socks and some insoles to fit properly. The white blouse, the rat-catcher tie and stock pin, the black gloves, everything looked wonderful. With pleasure, Abby pictured the dashing figure she'd cut.

She and Sam were seeing as much of each other as they could. On top of school and work, rehearsals were taking a lot of his time. Because of his tall, slim stature, Sam was playing the part of Sly Fox, who encourages Pinocchio to be truant. Abby enjoyed Sam's company tremendously. Imagining his delicious chocolatey eyes and slow smile had Abby slouching in her chair with a silly grin on her face.

"*Perhaps* we could get a *sense* of how we're *doing* on our essays. This person *here* looks like she's *finished*." Miss Iman stopped at Abby's chair and put a hand on her shoulder.

Abby froze.

"Stand *up* and read your *work*. You look very *pleased* with yourself. We're all *anxious* to hear it."

Just like grade seven, Abby thought. Her face was growing crimson. She stood up with her head bowed, hoping to hide the blush with her hair. To make things worse, she was a head taller than the teacher. She felt like an oversized goof.

"Actually," Abby croaked, "I was thinking about what to write. I was reaching into my heart and digging into my personal reasons. You said to let it flow, but I was completely stopped up."

Miss Iman was dumbfounded. The small, surprised chuckles from Abby's classmates became noisy laughter. It was Miss Iman's turn to blush.

"Read your essay," she commanded. Gone was any sign of perkiness.

Abby felt badly. "No, really," she said, looking down into the angry teacher's face. "I'm sorry, but I don't have anything to do with the play and I don't know what to write. But I'll try again." She sat down, dreading the punishment that surely was to follow.

Concentrating hard, and not looking up for fear of enraging the teacher further, Abby wrote two rough copies before finalizing her essay on a clean sheet. She proofread it once again, satisfied that it wouldn't embarrass her if Miss Iman made her read it aloud. In fact, thought Abby, it was pretty darned good.

Nothing happened until the end of the class. Just before the bell, Miss Iman asked Abby to come to her desk before she left. Several people in the class snickered knowingly. Others gave her sympathetic smiles.

Abby gathered her books and made her way up the aisle. She stopped at Miss Iman's desk. "I'm very sorry, Miss Iman. I didn't mean to be rude. It just came out that way. Here's my work." Abby placed the paper on the desk.

Miss Iman read the essay as the other kids streamed out the door. Abby tried not to notice their giggles and funny looks as each one passed by to drop their essays on the teacher's desk.

"Well *written*, Abby," said Miss Iman. "Very *good*. And very *imaginative*, too, creating a *ghost* for the theatre. It *almost* seems like you *believe* you saw him, which is *very* good writing, allowing us to *suspend* our *disbelief*. I *steal* that term, of course, from the *theatre*."

Abby waited. "What's my punishment?" she finally blurted.

"*Punishment?* Why, there's no *punishment*. You did your *work*, and did it *well*. You were just a little slow *starting*."

Abby smiled gratefully. "Thank you, Miss Iman. Thank you very much."

As she walked to her history class, Abby reflected on the whole incident. It turned out to be not at all like grade seven. For one thing, back in those days she would've been sent to the principal's office, then banished home with detentions, suspensions, the whole shebang.

Secondly, her opinion of Miss Iman had changed. Yes, she had her idiosyncrasies. Yes, she tried too hard. But all in all, she was a really nice woman who wanted to be a good teacher.

Thirdly, Abby hadn't realized how sorry she was about not being in *Pinocchio*.

"Oh well," she muttered aloud. "It was my choice."

"What was your choice?" asked a very familiar voice behind her.

"Mrs. Featherstone! What are you doing here?"

Joy walked along with Abby. "I just delivered one hundred posters for *Pinocchio*. Your drama club promised to plaster the area. Each member is taking five. I wonder if they could handle more?"

"Probably. I could bring more posters to school tomorrow if you'd like."

"Thanks. Maybe I will. Advertising is key."

"Absolutely," agreed Abby. "If you don't know about it, you're not going to buy tickets."

"So true," nodded Joy. Suddenly, she stopped walking. "Abby, you may be the answer to my problem. Can I ask a large favour?"

"Shoot," said Abby. "Your wish is my command."

"Just now, at the office, I heard that Margaret Small has come down with some sort of bug."

"Miss Small, the principal's assistant?"

"Yes. She's the actress playing Pinocchio's good fairy. We'll have costumes for the first time tonight, which makes it an extremely important rehearsal, but I called her at home and told her to stay in bed and drink lots of clear fluids. I'd love you to fill in until she feels better. For the other actors. Can you do it, Abby?"

Abby's eyes widened. "Are you a mind reader?"

"Why?"

"Remember you asked me 'What was your choice'?"

"Because you'd just said, 'It was my choice.' You were talking to yourself."

"Exactly. I was thinking how much I wanted to be in *Pinocchio,* and it was my choice not to be. Because I didn't pursue it after I missed the audition."

"Now, Abby, Miss Small will be coming back to do the show. I'm asking if you'll stand in for her for the first dress rehearsal tonight. We have two more weeks before opening night, by which time she'll be back. I hope I haven't raised your expectations." Joy looked concerned.

"Perfect!" exclaimed Abby. "I'm sure I'd die of stage fright if there was an audience. This way, I'll be involved and live to tell the tale."

Joy laughed happily. "Then it's a win-win situation. I'll leave the script on the kitchen table. The rehearsal is called for seven o'clock. Will you have time to ride Dancer and eat dinner before then? It'll be a late night."

Abby worked it out. "I'll pack some dinner. Then I can go straight to Wick Farm from Hogscroft. I'll have plenty of time." They were at the history classroom door.

"Thanks, Abby!" called Joy as she waved goodbye. "See you at seven! Ride carefully. I don't want to have to find a stand-in for my stand-in!"

Abby smiled and returned the wave. She wanted to be just like Mrs. Featherstone when she got old.

After school, Cody followed Abby's bike to Hogscroft. As usual, padding along the path in the woods beside the road, he listened intently for human noises coming from the Bad Man's den. Just to be sure, he detoured up through the woods and stared at the place where the Bad Man lived. He could see no activity. He could smell nothing new. But something was happening. He could sense it. Cody's ruff went up.

As intensely as Cody stared, another pair of eyes stared at Cody.

Abby tacked up Dancer in the Hogscroft barn, singing softly under her breath.

She had found the script, as promised, on the kitchen table. Abby had quickly gone through it as she gobbled up a snack, reading her lines out loud, and skimming the rest. It was a good script, Abby thought. Lots of action, bad guys, good guys, pathos, and a satisfying resolution. Joy had also left Abby a meaty sandwich for her dinner, with chocolate milk, a banana, and cookies separately wrapped up.

Dancer had become a cherished friend, she thought as she threw the saddle over the saddle pad and tightened the girth. He watched for her each day. She swore he'd tack himself up if he could.

"I've got sunshi-ine, on a cloudy day-ay. When it's cold out-si-i-ide, I've got the month of May-ay . . ."

Abby still could not get over it. She, Abby Malone, would be showing Dancer, the one and only Dancer, in a week and two days. Not just showing him, either. She'd be showing him in the Grand Invitational, against some of Canada's top riders. She didn't want to think of it. She'd get more nervous.

But what could go wrong? Abby wondered, fitting the bridle over Dancer's head. She had the best horse in the world. No other came close.

"Stop!" Abby chastised herself aloud. "That's such bad luck!" She rapped on the wooden stall door. "Knock on wood. Everything can go wrong! And at the same time, too. I could forget the course, I could panic and screw up Dancer's timing, Dancer could go lame. Anything might happen." Abby touched wood again. "Please, please, please let *bad* things not happen."

Today was a jumping day, and Abby was pleased when she led the muscular stallion into the paddock. The ground was neither too wet nor too dry. Just right. She'd already set up the jumps according to Hilary's diagram, and Abby hopped onto Dancer's back with a sense of cheerful anticipation.

Cody continued to watch the Bad Man's den. He saw him load the trunk of his moving machine. There were two big brown boxes and a digging tool.

The coyote was curious. He sensed that whatever this human was up to was not good. He waited.

Another creature waited nearby, attending carefully to the direction of the wind. Soon, he was joined by another of his species, then another. All eyes were on Cody.

Dancer's training session had gone remarkably well, so Abby left well enough alone, brushed the horse down, and biked the few minutes over to the theatre.

She was early. Nobody else had arrived, and Abby had the place to herself. She nervously opened the door into the dressing rooms under the stage and felt around for the light switch. It was to the right of the door. She cautiously turned on the lights and looked around.

There was a big open area in the middle. The cement floor was painted a rosy purple. There were vending machines at the end where you could get coffee, tea, or the most delicious-smelling hot chocolate.

On her right was a light-blue painted dressing table as long as the wall. There was a mirror above, with lights completely surrounding it. Green chairs were tucked under the table every three feet, all the way down the wall. Abby counted fifteen chairs.

On the yellow wall to her left was a series of six open doors, all different colours. Peeking into the first one, Abby reasoned that up to four people could occupy each room, based on the four chairs under the dressing table.

Abby hugged herself in sheer delight. She did a little dance of joy in the middle of the big room, then plunked herself down at the far end of the long table and opened her packed dinner. She searched for some change in her pocket, and jumped up again to get hot chocolate to drink with dinner.

As she waited for the machine to fill her cup, her eyes settled on a purple door to the left of the long dressing table. Where did it go? With hot chocolate in hand, Abby opened the door. Of course! The orchestra pit! This is how the musicians would get into the section below the seats in front of the stage. *Very clever*, she thought, closing the door.

Sitting down again, Abby bit into the sandwich that Joy had made for her. Joy made the best food, Abby concluded. Even a lowly sandwich became a work of art in her hands. Thick slabs of fresh, five-grain, buttered bread held thinly sliced cucumbers and tomatoes, with multiple thin slices of pastrami. Joy had spread mayonnaise on one side and Dijon mustard on the other, and sprinkled it liberally with freshly ground pepper. Abby took another bite. De-licious.

As she ate, she looked more closely at her surroundings. On the ceiling, right in the centre of the spacious hall, she noticed a large cut-out door. She contemplated what it could be. Perhaps a trap door, where an actor could either appear or disappear from the stage? She'd ask Joy.

The smell of the theatre was the best thing, Abby thought. She'd noticed it the day of the storm, and even though the theatre had been completely renovated since then, the smell remained. Greasepaint, dusty costumes, new stage sets, excitement. It was a living, breathing smell. It energized her. She loved just being here.

Abby flicked on the lights around her section of the long dressing table. She looked at herself as she chewed. Nice nose. Funny hairline. Freckles. Stark, unsettling green eyes.

Am I pretty? Not bad, but certainly not gorgeous. Abby finished her mouthful and wiped away the mayonnaise. She pouted, going for the model look she envied in the fashion magazines. Abby pulled her silky blond hair out of its elastic band and fluffed it up with her fingers. She struck a pose. *Any better?*

She turned around quickly.

"Hello?" she called loudly. "Hello? Is anybody there?"

Was it her imagination? Was somebody watching? She swore she'd heard a chuckle, but nobody was there.

Minutes passed. Raising her eyebrows at her own wild imagination, Abby finished her banana and started on the cookies. The chocolate milk was gone and, now that it had cooled sufficiently, she sipped the hot chocolate. Wow. It tasted as good as it smelled.

"Aren't you going to save me some?" asked a voice. Abby twirled around in a flash, knocking down her green chair as she stood.

"Who's that?"

"Ambrose."

Ambrose? Abby thought hard. *The ghost? Was he talking to me?*

"Yes, the ghost. I'm talking to you."

"No!" gasped Abby. "I don't believe it!"

Abby heard a deep sigh. "It's a problem. If people can't see something, they don't believe it exists, possibly because they're afraid."

"No. Not quite," said Abby, pretending to be calm. *Am I really talking to a ghost?* "I'm far more worried about a nasty person creeping up on me pretending to be a ghost. I'm all alone here. I hope you understand. I'm not challenging your reality, I'm checking for my own safety."

Ambrose Brown took his time responding. "I accept that."

"Good. So you are a real ghost?"

"Yes."

Wow. "May I ask where you are right now? So I can look at you and not somewhere else, and also to confirm that you are indeed a ghost?"

Casually leaning on the hot chocolate machine, right hand on his hip, Ambrose Brown became visible in degrees. First as a fog-like apparition, then filling in until he looked, for all the world, like a human being.

A handsome human being. He was of medium height and medium build. He was fit and trim, with a shock of blond hair rakishly hanging over his left eye. With his sparkling blue eyes and mischievous grin his face resembled an elf, or more precisely, a leprechaun.

His well-shaped athletic legs were clad in dark green tights. His long thin feet wore dark green, pointed slipper-like ankle-boots. A green tunic in a slightly lighter shade covered his body, and on his head he wore a jaunty green cap with a feather.

"Peter Pan?" asked Abby with delight.

"Robin Hood!" corrected Ambrose harshly.

"Excuse me, please," demurred Abby.

"Although I could use it for both, couldn't I?"

"Yes, you could." It seemed to Abby that they'd been friends for years. "If you had a bow and some arrows I'd have known it was Robin Hood, for sure."

"Then let me rectify the lack of a quiver at once." As the ghost spoke, a dark brown leather sack appeared, slung so that he could reach over his shoulder to pull out one of the dozen handmade arrows that it contained.

"Amazing!" Abby cried.

"Amazing, you say? Then look at this!"

The dressing room became a forest. A magical forest of multiple shades of green. Tree by tree it grew, until it became as dense and dark as Sherwood Forest.

"You're right. Mr. Brown, this is amazing."

"Call me Ambrose, my dear, everybody does. Mr. Brown was my father. Can't have that." The trees started to disappear as quickly as they had appeared. Abby stood, as before, at the long blue dressing table in the big yellow room.

"Ambrose, what's happening to you?"

"I'm changing. I'm an actor, after all. Guess who I am, and don't be too quick to jump to your conclusion, I warn you."

Abby studied the costume. Shakespearean, probably. An old man. A king, for sure, from the bejewelled crown that had just materialized. Ambrose's face had become jowly and saggy. His eyelids drooped and his lips looked purple with ill health. Veins crept all over his red, bulbous nose.

"You look altogether different."

"Isn't it wonderful?"

"You looked better before."

"For Robin Hood, yes, but an actor must be a chameleon if he wants to play different parts. You can't be vain. When a part requires ugly and old, you must become ugly and old."

"Which you've accomplished beautifully," Abby said, hoping it came across as a compliment.

"Enough chat!" Ambrose spoke regally. "Who am I?"

"Your Majesty," Abby said as she curtsied. "May your humble servant offer her guess without fear of decapitation?"

"Perhaps. We make no promises."

"Is Your Majesty King Henry VIII?"

"Correct! Excellent! How did you know?"

"Actually, I was waffling between King Lear and King John when I noticed the puffy sleeves."

"Muttonleg sleeves, yes. That was a good call. Otherwise, we would have proclaimed, 'Off with her head!'"

Abby laughed, delighted. Ambrose, meanwhile, was changing again. This time, he looked almost exactly like a large alley cat.

"Who are you now?" asked Abby. "Mistoffelees in *Cats?*"

Ambrose suddenly looked slightly alarmed. He opened his whiskered mouth and said, "People are here. See you later." And he was gone.

Abby was alone again. Her head was spinning. Was Ambrose real or had it been an incredible dream?

The door opened and Joy popped her head in. "Abby! I'm so glad you're here. Did you and Dancer have a good ride?"

Abby stared for a split second, then snapped back into reality. "The best!" Abby's face broke into a huge grin. "We're ready to kick some serious butt."

Joy pretended to be shocked. "Watch how you say things, Abby." She looked around the room. "Are you alone?"

"Don't I look alone?" Abby looked around. She wondered if Joy could see a man-sized cat.

"I thought I heard more than one person in here."

"Well, actually, I was practising my lines."

"Wonderful. How are you doing with them?" Joy asked.

Before Abby could answer, a loud chattering group of kids came clattering down the stairs, led by George Farrow, Lucy's grandfather.

"Abby! I didn't know you were in the play!" he enthused. "So glad you are! We've been having such fun. You'll love it."

"I'm standing in for the Blue-Winged Fairy, Mr. Farrow. And congratulations on getting the part of Geppetto."

"I'm trying my best, Abby, thank you. It's not easy teaching an old dog new tricks. Has Lucy arrived yet?"

At that moment, Lucy came hurtling down the stairs into the big room. "Abby, I heard! It's so great you're here! Maybe Margaret Small's flu will turn into some horribly dire virus so you can play the Fairy for the run!"

"Lucy," spoke Mr. Farrow sternly. "You must not wish ill on people."

"I know, but wouldn't it be fun to have Abby here all the time?"

Abby giggled, then covered her mouth. She didn't want Mr. Farrow to think she wished Margaret ill. "I have horrible stage fright, Lucy. I couldn't go on even if she dies."

"Who's dying?" asked Leslie, who came through the door panting. She thought she was late.

"Nobody's dying," said Abby. "I was just saying that—"

Lucy interjected. "Abby is a wimp. She's afraid to act in front of an audience."

Leslie looked empathetic. "I'm just the same, Abby. If I wasn't wearing a dog suit, I couldn't possibly be in the play."

"You're always so nice to people!" mocked Lucy humourously as she turned to get some hot chocolate from the machine. "You're no fun at all!"

Lucy walked smack into a tall person with the head of a fox.

"Ahhh!" she screamed.

"Gotcha!" laughed Sam. "Isn't it great? Orangeville Theatre lent it to us."

"It's perfect. Utterly perfect," said Leslie to her brother. "What's the rest of the fox costume like?"

"I'm just going to put it on. Your Trooper outfit is over there." Sam pointed to two long wardrobe racks that had been wheeled in.

Lucy wasted no time. She pushed past Leslie in her eagerness to try on her costumes. She was the townsperson who pushes a cart of cheese that gets overturned in the town scene, and she wore a partial donkey outfit in the carnival scene on Runaway Island.

"Abby! Come quick!" Lucy called, holding up a sheer blue sparkly dress with wings attached. "The Blue-Winged Fairy!"

Abby gasped. *Lucky I'm only here for two rehearsals*, she thought. *I'd never go out in public wearing that.*

13
THE SECRET OF AMBROSE BROWN

ABBY WAS ENTHRALLED. The people she went to school with and had known all her life had become different people altogether. The change occurred, she reflected, as they stepped into their costumes. Within minutes, Sam was slinking along sneakily as the Sly Fox. Leslie was so much like a dog that she was almost scratching her ears with her back leg. Mr. Farrow, even, had become a humble carpenter in his demeanor, cap in hand.

On stage, as scene followed scene, Abby felt transported into the world of the story.

Because this was her first rehearsal, everybody helped her. She was pushed on stage at every cue, and when she forgot what to say, someone would invariably prompt her.

Even so, the magic of the theatre began to possess her. *This is what it is all about,* she thought. *This is why Ambrose Brown became an actor.*

Cody waited outside the theatre. The Bad Man had been here in his moving machine for a long time. Now he got out of the machine and opened the trunk at the rear.

Cody's ruff bristled. Nothing bad would happen to his Abby.

The little coyote detected movement behind him. He froze as he realized that he had made the hunter's worst mistake. He hadn't noticed that he himself was being hunted.

Whipping around, Cody caught shadowy movements for a fleeting second. Now, all was still. He was not fooled. There were probably five or six wild coyotes here, waiting for their chance to finish him off. He had trespassed in cubbing season.

Cody must make no more mistakes.

Joy Featherstone walked onto the stage between acts. The actors were waiting for notes on the first act. They'd had a break and were now sitting in the audience seats in excited, talkative groups.

"Attention, actors! For the first dress rehearsal, you all did remarkably well with your costumes. We'll work again with costumes before the opening, but tonight we see what works, what doesn't, and how we can improve, since costumes are a big part of this show. Robert and I are delighted with your competence and professionalism." There was a rustle throughout the house as people sat up taller.

"We've rarely had to stop the action, you're paying attention to your cues, and, for the most part, your lines are solid. Remember, we have less than two weeks before opening night. That's more than enough time, but most of you are new to this, and I promise you, the time will fly by."

"The great iron sculptor, Petr Baloun, has finished the giant dogfish ahead of schedule, and we are going to work with it in Act 2 this evening." There were gasps. Applause broke out.

"Nobody shall touch it except the people handling it and the actors in that scene, who are Pinocchio, Geppetto, and the Blue-Winged Fairy. Does everybody understand? We want nothing to go wrong." There were nods and sounds of agreement from the actors.

"All right! Places, please, for Act 2!" Joy smiled broadly and exited the stage. The actors jumped up to prepare for the next scene.

Sam's part was in the first act only, so he had changed back into his shirt and jeans, and was helping Abby with the details of the Blue-Winged Fairy's role. He guided her to the wing on stage left, pulled the rolled-up script out of his back pocket, and showed her the timing of her next entrance.

"At the end of Act 1, Pinocchio and Wickley have been rowed across the Truant Sea. At the top of Act 2, they're about to enter Runaway Island, where there's the big carnival scene. Some of the kids have already turned to donkeys. Get ready to enter when you see that Pinocchio has a tail and ears. The tail goes on first, then the ears. When he looks into the pond and sees his ears, move onto stage right there," Sam pointed. "Stand in front of that bush, on this side of Pinocchio. Got your lines?"

Abby nodded tensely. She didn't want to screw up. "Thanks, Sam. I'm remembering the story as we go along."

Sam gave her a quick hug. "Do you want me to stay?"

"No, I'm fine for now, thanks. Go watch from the seats, but come back after I exit. Oh! Which way do I exit?"

"Stage right. The other side. Don't worry, you'll be fine." Sam grinned and disappeared behind the folds of the curtains.

"Fine?" said a whisper in her ear. "You're great. You'll be on stage one day, mark my words."

"Ambrose?" asked Abby.

"Yes, it's me."

"Thanks for the encouragement."

"My pleasure. Your coyote is outside guarding us, Abby. He's a good animal."

"Yes, he is. He always protects me."

"He's protecting us all. I'll report back."

Ambrose was gone. Abby briefly wondered what he'd meant, then she turned all her attention to the stage. The scene had begun.

Cody crouched outside the theatre, quivering with fear, but biding his time. The Bad Man had finished digging holes and placing upright sticks all around the back of the theatre. A lot of them had been placed at the doors. Now, he was uncoiling a skinny, long white rope. He ran it from stick to stick, then fed it through his fingers until it reached his car.

Behind him, Cody could sense movement. He didn't look. He didn't need to. The moment was coming when the coyotes would converge on him. He was ready.

The Bad Man started the motor. He leaned out of his machine and made fire with a little stick. He put the fire to the end of the rope and watched it burn.

The wild coyotes came slowly, stealthily, quietly. Cody waited for just the right moment.

When they were almost upon him, Cody jumped up into the air and raced to the Bad Man's machine. Five howling coyotes followed, snapping and growling.

Owens was shocked. His eyes bulged. He pulled his legs into his car, preparing for a speedy getaway. Cody was too quick. He leapt into the car, over Owens' legs and out the passenger side window. Owens howled and raised his arms in alarm. The wild coyotes streamed into Owens' car. He hollered as they ripped and tore and panicked.

Cody watched as the leader and one other leapt out the window and headed back home in full flight.

Owens gunned the engine, pulled his door shut, then started to drive off as two more coyotes scrambled out the driver's side window. Realizing there was still one more inside the car, Owens slammed on his brakes. He jumped out, tattered and bloody, followed by the last coyote, who shot out of the car like a cannonball.

Owens had left his car in drive. It began to roll slowly down the theatre lane toward the road. Owens desperately stumbled after it as fast as he could. He reached the car door with outstretched fingers and awkwardly managed to pull himself in. He drove haltingly away, cursing bitterly.

Cody observed the flame as it ate the rope, inching closer and closer to the door where his Abby had entered the building.

He sniffed the air. He felt fear. He puzzled about how to make his fear go away.

The rope was now only six feet from the theatre door. The flame was moving faster, picking up momentum. Cody didn't like it.

He loped over to the flame. It was too hot to pick up. He grabbed the end of the white rope closest to the door and tugged it loose. With the rope in his mouth, still burning quickly, Cody ran toward the rusted water trough in the little paddock beside the barn. He dropped it in. There was a little sizzle as the flame was extinguished by dirty rainwater at the bottom.

His fear had gone. Darkness had fallen and all was well. He would lie down and wait for his Abby.

Act 2, scene 1, the carnival, went off as well as possible with twenty first-time actors adapting to their costumes. Act 2, scene 2, began with Geppetto searching the Truant Sea for Pinocchio. This was the giant dogfish scene. The huge iron beast opened his jaws to swallow Geppetto. Its razor-sharp teeth flashed, and it roared like an angry sea. Abby could barely repress a terrified squeal. She was expected to walk in there? Talk about suspension of disbelief!

"Abby," came a now-familiar whisper in her ear.

"Later, Ambrose! I'm about to go on!"

"You've got oodles of time. Pinocchio hasn't even swum out there yet."

"You're right. I'm just jumpy."

"Very understandable. Anyway, I'm reporting back. Cody led a pack of coyotes through Samuel Owens' car and then stopped the fuse from reaching the fireworks. Everything's fine."

Abby was stunned. "What did you say?"

"Later. Gotta go."

"Ambrose, I didn't understand a word you just said!"

But he was gone. Abby was momentarily dazed. Fireworks? Owens? Coyotes? Everything's fine?

She'd have to ask Ambrose later, because her entrance was coming up. What was her line? She fumbled in her pocket and pulled out the script. Abby knelt at a stage light and peered closely. Here it was:

"The Blue-Winged Fairy appears as they hug and dance in their joy at being reunited. She nods wisely, and says, 'Loving father, Geppetto. Brave little puppet, Pinocchio.'"

I can do that, Abby thought.

The next morning, Joy Featherstone and Robert Wick drove to Samuel Owens' mansion. It was ten o'clock.

"There were a lot of firecrackers," said Robert, eyes on the road. "Big ones, too. Would've made quite the racket."

"Go through this for me one more time, Robert. Why are we going to see Owens when we still have so much to do before the rehearsal this afternoon?" Joy was tired. They hadn't finished last night until after midnight. After they'd sent the actors home, they'd discussed wardrobe changes, lighting, sound effects, and production details until they were exhausted and could work no more. Everything must be perfect by opening night.

"Abby told us that Ambrose told her that Owens dug in firecrackers around the theatre and was going to set them off. With everybody in the theatre. And firecrackers were there. You have to admit it."

"Right. So we say to Samuel, 'A ghost told us that you were doing bad things last night.' Ambrose also told Abby that Cody and a pack of wild coyotes thwarted him. Do we mention that, too?"

"Come on, Joy, I'm not an idiot. I'm not going to get into details, I'm merely going to offer to sell him my upper field."

Joy rubbed her weary eyes. "Tell me why."

"He wanted to buy the whole property so he could look out his windows and see nothing but land that belonged to him, right?"

"Right. According to Gus LeFarge." Joy lay back in the seat and rested her head. "But the day the ghost scared him, he said he wanted to buy the farm to burn down the theatre."

"True, but that was all bluster. Hopefully he's forgotten all about that, and has gone back to his original goal. And the upper field is the only part of Wick Farm that he can see from his windows." Robert looked pleased with himself. "He can't see the barn."

"You jump to the conclusion that Owens will leave us alone if he owns the field."

"Yes, Joy, I do. He tried to scare us last night. You have to agree, if the firecrackers had gone off, the explosions would have scared the living daylights out of everybody."

"And you think he was trying to scare us into selling him Wick Farm?"

"Absolutely! His message being that if he could set fireworks he could do a lot more. Obviously we don't want to sell the whole thing, but we'll never miss that field. Am I making any sense?"

"Possibly. It's worth a try." She yawned.

Robert parked his truck beside Owens' Mercedes. He hustled to open Joy's door for her.

"Why are you so darned perky this morning?" she asked.

Robert winked and escorted her to the big wooden door. "Just watch me," he whispered confidently. He lifted the evil-looking brass eagle door knocker and knocked three times.

Within seconds, the door was opened by a small man with a stooped bearing.

"May I help you?" asked Walter importantly.

"Yes, thank you," answered Robert, adjusting his tie.

He'd dressed with care this morning. "We're here to see Samuel Owens."

Walter looked worried, all trace of bravado instantly gone. "I'm afraid that's not possible. Mr. Owens is with his doctor."

"Is he ill?"

"No, he's had another accident."

Robert shot Joy a look. Joy raised her eyebrows slightly.

Walter continued. "May I tell him who is calling on him? He will get in touch with you when he feels up to it."

Joy stepped forward, and spoke in a charming, persuasive manner. "I'm sure he'd like to see us now. We're dear old friends. We've come to visit him in his time of need." She leaned closer. "And you know, don't you, that he has very few friends. If you turn us away, he'll have no visitors at all, and I imagine he might not be happy about that."

Walter's face showed indecision. The woman was right, Walter thought. He'd never had visitors before, except Mrs. Casey, and she wasn't here very much at all anymore, and whenever he did see her she looked unhappy. Might Owens be upset with Walter if he didn't let them in?

Using his hesitation to their advantage, Joy bustled through the door. "I missed your name," she said.

"W . . . Walter," he stammered. "But I'm not sure he wants guests."

"Of course he does!" Joy brazened on. "Everybody needs a friend when they're down. Come, Robert, Walter is taking us to see dear Samuel."

Faced with this immovable force, Walter was totally defeated. In trepidation, he led them up the grand marble stairs to Owens' master bedroom.

The doctor was leaving.

"Walter, he'll need a home nurse twice a day to clean and rebandage those wounds. I've made arrangements, so expect someone at six this evening. Give him one of these antibiotic pills four times a day until they're finished." The young doctor handed Walter a large plastic pill bottle and hurried down the hall. He looked back and took in Robert and Joy. "Good morning," he said, and ran down the stairs. "I'll let myself out," he called over his shoulder, and the door slammed.

Robert looked at Joy and whispered, "He must be new around here. I've never seen him before."

"You'll probably never see him again, either. He was in an awful hurry to leave."

"Owens has that effect on people."

"Who's out there?" Owens bellowed from inside the room.

"Speak of the devil," murmured Joy.

"Walter! I don't want visitors! Walter!"

Joy put her hand on the shaking arm of the horrified man. "You go. We'll handle this," she said soothingly. "Don't worry, Walter, we're old friends. We understand his little moods." Walter clattered down the gracious, curving staircase and disappeared through a door.

"Get him, Tiger," said Robert to Joy as he opened the heavy door to the master suite.

Lying in a luxurious chocolate brown satin-shrouded king-sized bed, propped up with leopard skin-covered pillows of various sizes, with exotic animal skins covering the polished hardwood floor, was Samuel Owens. Bandages covered most of his face and head. The little skin that was visible around his eyes showed tips of red, swollen gashes. His hands were invisible under huge pads of white gauze. What was under the covers was anybody's guess.

"Are you all right?" asked Robert, looking pale himself. He hadn't expected this much damage.

"Walter! Walter!" Owens barked angrily. His voice was muffled by the bandages and could hardly be heard, which caused him further distress.

Joy pulled an ocelot footstool over to the bed and sat down. "I'll get him in a moment, Samuel. We just wanted to pop in to give you our best wishes. We'll be gone in one minute." Joy turned to look at Robert, who stood with his hands in his pockets near the door, anxious to leave. "Robert, why don't you tell Samuel your good news. By the looks of him, he could use some." Joy smiled kindly at the invalid.

"Yes. Yes, Joy. Good idea." Pulling himself together, Robert took one step closer to the bed. "I've decided to put my upper field on the market. You can see it from here," he said, indicating the large bay window with a sweep of his arm. "And since you were interested in buying my property before we went into the theatre business, I thought you should have first crack at it." Robert rocked back on his heels and waited for a response.

Owens finally spoke. "No agents."

Joy gave Robert a little nod.

"No agents," he agreed.

"Market value. Not a penny more."

Robert nodded. "Sounds fair to me."

"Deal. Let's do it now. Bring me that pad of paper." He looked at his Louis XIV mahogany scrolled desk by the window. Robert lifted the pad and a pen and brought them to the bed.

"Joy Drake, write this." Owens dictated.

Joy did as she was told, and after small changes in the wording, everyone was happy with the result.

"Now sign," he ordered Robert. Robert obliged.

Owens struggled to sit up. He tried unsuccessfully to hold the pen in his mitted hand. After three tries, Joy took pity on him.

"Samuel, sign it with your mouth." She placed the pen carefully between his teeth, and Owens signed the contract with an "X."

"Since it doesn't look like your signature, Samuel," said Joy, "We'll have to trust that you'll honour the agreement."

Owens glared at her. "Walter will witness it. Get the phone and dial the number of my banker. It's in the red book beside the phone. Look under 'B.'"

Robert did as he was told and brought the receiver to Owens. Joy held it to his ear.

"Tony, Owens . . . Fine . . . Robert Wick will be coming by in half an hour. Give him one hundred thousand dollars. Get the deed and a receipt and bring it to me before noon." Owens pushed away the receiver and Joy put it back in the cradle.

"Now get out," Owens growled. "You can see I'm in pain."

"One more thing, Samuel," said Joy with authority. Robert looked at her with shock. He was itching to get out of there.

"Does this purchase satisfy your need to own Wick Farm?"

"It does," replied Owens.

"And we'll have no more incidents?"

"What the hell do you mean by that?" he exploded angrily.

"Joy, let's go. The man's in pain." Robert appeared to be in pain himself.

"Not until Samuel here swears he won't cause us any more trouble." Joy made herself comfortable. She held the contract up in front of her, as if she was ready to tear it in two. "I'm prepared to wait."

Robert clamped his mouth shut.

Owens sighed. "You win, Joy. I promise, no more trouble. I have what I want now that Robert has sold me that upper field." His bloodshot eyes looked helplessly at Joy, then Robert. "Now, I need my rest."

Joy stood, taking Robert's hand. "Thank you, Samuel," she said. "I hope we can count on your word this time."

"Oh, yes, you can," he said feebly. "This time, I'm a beaten man."

Outside the mansion, Robert opened the car door for a grim Joy.

"What's the problem? The theatre is a hundred thousand dollars richer, and Owens is happy. He got what he wanted. He'll never bother us again."

"I can't help but think of Neville Chamberlain making a deal with Hitler before the war. Peace in our time. Hitler attacked anyway."

"Relax, Joy. Owens has no reason to wish the theatre harm now."

"I hope you're right, Robert."

"You were terrific in there, the way you got past the butler."

"And you looked like you were going to throw up."

Robert shot her a sideways glance as they turned onto the road. "I talk tough, but I'm not such a big shot, am I?" he said sheepishly.

Joy laughed. "I love you just the way you are." She kissed him on the cheek, and laughed again as he blushed scarlet.

Abby stretched happily and yawned. With her big toe she opened the drapes a crack. Sunlight streamed into her little bedroom under the eaves. Sam had driven her home in the red truck last night after the rehearsal. He'd put her bike on the flatbed with Cody. She'd recently earned her driver's licence, but her parents preferred that she didn't drive while they were gone.

Sam, she thought. Sam was wonderful. She closed her eyes and relived the kisses that they'd shared as he dropped her off. Goosebumps shivered down her spine. She could've stayed in the cab of that truck all night, held in Sam's gentle arms, kissing Sam's kissable lips. *Is that bad?* Abby wondered briefly. *At least I'm happy.* She grinned as she twisted her pyjama-clad legs out of her warm bed and sprang to a standing position.

Noticing the blue sparkles on her dressing table, Abby vividly recalled the strange events at the theatre the night before. As well as the firecrackers, there were coyote tracks everywhere, and there were signs that a car had had trouble getting out of the ruts beside the driveway.

Interesting, Abby mused as she brushed her teeth.

Later that afternoon Abby arrived at the theatre and headed straight for the shower. That morning Leggy had learned to drop her head comfortably while being lunged, and Dancer and she had had a wonderful hack. It had been an altogether satisfactory day so far, and Abby was feeling good.

Towelled dry and sitting at the dressing table ready to apply her Blue-Winged Fairy makeup, Abby sensed a presence. Her backbone prickled.

"Ambrose," she said nervously. "Tell me that's you."

"Today is the anniversary of my death," he solemnly stated.

"Really?"

"Yes. Twenty years ago today."

"I'm so sorry. What did you die of?"

Ambrose Brown slowly began to appear. Today, he looked like the Tin Woodsman from *The Wizard of Oz.*

"It would be romantic to say that I died of a broken heart," he said. "But I died from an overdose of sleeping pills."

Abby was dumbfounded. "You committed suicide?"

"I prefer not to put it like that. I had no intention of dying, I merely wanted attention." He began to pace as he spoke, clanging slightly when tin met tin. "I was in love with someone who didn't love me, couldn't love me the way I wanted. I foolishly imagined that he would find me dying. I envisioned it all. He would panic, get help, sit with me, hold my hand, fix me up, and ultimately realize how important I was to him." He stopped pacing and looked at Abby. His voice went flat. "It was a romantic notion. And deadly, as it turned out."

"Holy," said Abby under her breath. She wondered how to

take all this information. "Mr. Pierson says that suicide is the most selfish way to die."

Ambrose looked at her thoughtfully through his silver make-up. "It is. But I only knew that later, when I saw the devastation and guilt I'd caused. People I loved thought that they'd let me down. They worried endlessly that they should've seen the signs, that they should have done more for me, been nicer to me. But none of that was true. I was desperate to reach one special person, and managed to destroy myself and hurt everyone else around me."

"And you didn't think it would happen that way?"

"No! Otherwise I wouldn't have done it, now, would I?" he snapped.

"I don't mean to upset you, Ambrose. I guess I think it's only logical that people would be hurt by suicide."

"You're hard, Abby, very hard." Ambrose began to pace again. "Firstly, I didn't have *any* idea how much people cared about me. Secondly, my reasoning was skewed by a slight drinking problem. And thirdly, I had no intention of actually being successful. I thought I'd calculated exactly how many pills would make me sick enough to *look* like I'd tried, but not enough to do me in. I was wrong. So shoot me."

"Ambrose, stop pacing, please. I'm getting dizzy." Ambrose glared at her, but perched on the edge of the dressing table. "Thank you, that's much better." Abby stood and faced him. "I'm not hard, Ambrose. I'm really very sympathetic. My mother has a drinking problem, too. She doesn't always make good decisions when she's had a snoutful, so I understand, I really do. And I know it's horrible when your feelings are one-sided." She was thinking of Sam. "If you didn't mean to commit suicide, it's extremely sad that you shortened your life for nothing."

"Thanks, Abby," the ghost responded, softening.

"The person who you loved, who couldn't love you, was that person hurt, too?"

"Yes, indeed. I don't think he had any idea, though."

"Of what?"

"That it was his attention I was trying to get. I loved him with all my heart, still do, but I don't think he ever knew."

"Really? That's sad, too."

"No. I don't think it is. You see, if he knew he'd think it was his fault, and it wasn't. He was married. He couldn't become what he wasn't."

"You mean he was straight, and you weren't?"

"To put it bluntly, yes."

"You must have thought you had a chance, though. I mean, for you to love him so much, you must have had some encouragement."

Ambrose sighed. "The mind is a curious thing, Abby. We see what we want to see, we hear what we're hoping to hear. The one thing we all do well is fool ourselves." He tried to cross his legs, but the tin wouldn't accommodate the movement, and clanked loudly. "He was a dear friend, and treated me well. It was all in my head from there."

"Oh, Ambrose, it must have been awful for you. To be so desperately in love, with no chance of fulfillment."

"If I'd had more sense, I would have gone away. Made a new life for myself. But I didn't. And here I am."

"Why *are* you here, Ambrose?" asked Abby. Hoping not to offend him again, she quickly added, "I'm glad you are, but why are you?"

"To be near the one I love."

"The one you love is here?"

"It's been twenty years," Ambrose said, evading the question. He shook his head and smiled. "Twenty years of haunting this place. I'm getting tired. Maybe I'll be allowed to rest soon."

"Who decides that, Ambrose?"

"There's not a rule book, no matter what the occult 'experts' say. It drives me nuts, cuckoo, crazy in the head to hear what those crackpots say." Ambrose was on another rant. "As if they have any idea!"

"Ambrose, I'm sure you're right. Unless you happen to be dead yourself, how could you know how it is on the other side?" Abby felt she'd sufficiently appeased him. "Then how is it decided when a ghost gets to rest?"

"It's individual. Different in every circumstance. Each ghost decides for himself, on his own terms, for his own reasons."

"If it's up to you, then, what's the problem?"

"You make it sound so easy!" he flared. Immediately, he calmed. "I'll rest when I'm assured my love is happy. And the way it's looking now, that will be soon."

Abby was itching to ask the logical question, but she didn't want to pry, or seem too presumptuous. Ambrose had a mercurial temper.

Suddenly the answer came to her. "It's Robert Wick, isn't it?" she blurted out. "It's Robert Wick whom you love!"

Ambrose said simply, "Of course." And he disappeared.

14
The Homecoming

Abby continued to stare at the place where the Tin Woodsman had stood just seconds before. Robert Wick? This was heavy stuff. What would he think if he knew? How tragic, that Ambrose had mistakenly killed himself trying to make Robert love him.

Abby's thoughts were interrupted by the sound of footsteps on the stairs. She pulled herself together, turned back to the mirror, and began smoothing foundation makeup on her face.

"What are you doing here?" asked a chilly voice.

Abby looked at the mirror. It was Margaret Small. She turned. "Hello, Miss Small! Are you feeling better?"

"Yes, and I'm here for the rehearsal." Her eyes were bloodshot, and her nose was all stuffed up. Her voice sounded hoarse. She didn't look well.

Abby blushed. "Oh! Wonderful. I didn't know, so I came to stand in for you today."

Margaret continued to look down her nose at Abby. "So it would seem."

The woman was intentionally making Abby feel uncomfortable, and Abby knew it. She said, "I came because Mrs. Featherstone asked me to help you out, not because I'm trying to steal your role."

"That's not what I hear, Abby Malone."

Abby stood and faced Margaret Small. She was getting upset.

"I've heard that you're acting your heart out for Robert and Joy, who's living in your house, by the by. You want them to think you're better than me so they'll give you the part." Margaret spoke harshly. "I see your plan."

"I'm doing my best because it's more fun that way, and so the other actors have something to work with. So shoot me." She borrowed Ambrose's line. "But there's no great plan. I was your stand-in while you were sick, and that's all I ever expected to be."

"Good. So you can go."

"You're welcome! No thanks necessary! So glad to have been of assistance! Any time!" Abby was furious. She felt insulted and wronged. Gathering her things as fast as she could, she ignored the other actors who were streaming into the dressing room. She couldn't trust herself to speak.

"Hi, Abby! Hey, what's eating you?"

"You got here early again, Abby. Abby?"

"What's wrong with the Blue-Winged Fairy? She turned her tongue into a toad?"

Abby rushed up the stairs, pushing people aside until she was safely outside and alone. She hoisted her knapsack on her back and pedalled away from the theatre as fast as she could, shadowed reassuringly by Cody.

When Abby got home, she unlocked the kitchen door and threw her knapsack on the floor. By force of habit, she checked the answering machine. There were four messages.

She pressed PLAY and the first one began. "Abby! It's your dad. It's noon on Saturday. Your mother is doing so well that they're letting her go home next week. We should be arriving for dinner on Saturday night, so throw another couple of shrimps on the barbie. I love you, sweetheart. Say hello to Joy from us, and keep up the training. We can't wait to see you ride Dancer next Sunday. Joy told me that you're an actress, too! Hope you're having fun. Love from us both. Bye."

Abby wiped a tear from her eye. The sound of her father's voice created a lump in her throat. *What a baby I am,* she thought.

The second message began. "Abby, it's Hilary. Mom says you're doing great things with Dancer. I'm so excited. Sandy and I are coming home for the Invitational, so I'll call when we get in. See you next week. Bye for now."

The next one was Christine James, for Joy. "Hi, Mom. Just checking in. Call me about when you want to move over here. Hilary and Sandy are coming home next Friday night. I never see you anymore, you're so busy!"

When the hushed last voice began to play, Abby's ears pricked up. "Abby, it's Sam. What happened? Margaret Small says you ran out mad because she came back, but I know you wouldn't do that. I'm coming over after rehearsal."

Sam had been whispering. Abby guessed that he'd used the hall phone outside the dressing room, and he hadn't wanted anybody to hear. She looked at her watch. Two thirty. Rehearsals would've started by now.

Should she go back to the theatre and explain that she wasn't angry? But what would she say? That Margaret was insulting and rude? Abby slumped down at the table and rested her forehead on her arms. *The day had been perfect until now,* she thought.

She heard a scratch on the kitchen door.

"Cody," Abby said fondly as she opened the door for the worried little coyote. "You came to comfort me." She knelt down and rubbed behind his ears. He liked that. He rolled over onto his back for a tummy tickle, then stood and shook. His intense grey eyes stared at her.

"Yes, Cody, I feel much happier. You've cheered me up." Cody wagged his tail and put a paw up on Abby's knee. "Thanks, little guy."

On the floor beside them lay her knapsack. Abby pulled out the script. *There's no doubt about it,* pondered Abby. *I've become*

SHELLEY PETERSON

stagestruck. Margaret's right. I really want to act in this play. And if I'm honest with myself, I did want people to think I was better than her.

When did it happen? When did acting turn from a way to join the herd to something she felt bereft without?

One rehearsal! That was her whole acting resumé. Her entire experience.

Abby took the script over to the chair by the window and curled up her legs. Cody found a comfortable spot on the rug for a nap, and Abby began to read. She read very carefully this time, watching for clues to character development and relationships, exits and timing, suspense devices. She realized that there was a definite shape to the play. A beginning where you meet the main characters and get involved in their lives. The story buildup with gathering events and necessary tension. The ending that tied all the strings together.

Abby started reading all the parts aloud, stressing different words to get different effects. She tried accents on some of the characters, just for fun. She played with funny voices.

Cody slept, content to be with his Abby as she amused herself in an imaginary world.

That was the scene that Sam came upon when he looked through the pane in her door three hours later. He smiled, then caught her startled eye.

School was out. By Wednesday at noon, the teaching staff had had enough and declared that the summer recess was officially started. Caledon High was a beehive of activity as lockers were cleaned out, the lost and found box rummaged. Kids exchanged summer addresses and hugged their friends goodbye. The graduating class could be identified either by a triumphant look or a tear in the eye. Music was played loudly in the halls until angry teachers stopped it. Then it would start again down another hall.

Finally, hands over ears, the teachers conceded and packed their desks, ready for a well-earned, much-needed vacation.

Sam had offered to drive Abby home. Lucy had her grandfather's truck and other kids were going her way, too, but Abby wanted to bicycle home on this last day of school. Everybody was going to rehearsal. She felt totally left out again. She wanted to be alone.

Her parents would be home in three days. She was eager to see them after all the time they'd been away. Four days from now was the Grand Invitational. Shivers ran down her spine, and her stomach churned.

Today was Dancer's last jumping day before the event. It was very important that all went well. He needed perfect confidence going into the show.

As she cycled, Abby rode a practice course in her mind. She would concentrate on each jump, setting him up just right then leaving him alone to let him find his balance, look for the next jump and do it all over again. She practised keeping her heels down to retain the correct seat and keep her calf muscles tight. She reminded herself to focus ahead, over the jumps, and not to look at the ground. She remembered the tip she'd been told about water jumps. She'd ride it like it was five feet high, to get Dancer's arch wide enough for the twelve-foot spread.

Sam had been driving alongside her for several seconds before she saw him.

"What are you laughing at, Sam?"

"You! Are you in another world again?"

Abby grinned. "Actually, I'm riding Dancer over a course. Am I clearing the jumps?"

"I don't see any poles on the ground," answered Sam. "You'll start to worry me soon, Abby," he warned. "The last time, you were acting all the parts in *Pinocchio*."

"Well, stop creeping up on me, then," she said, laughing. "Are you going to rehearsal now?"

"Yes. Everybody wants you back. Margaret Small is horrible to people, and she's not nearly as good as you."

Abby considered this for a moment as she rode along beside Sam's truck. "That might be her problem, Sam. Maybe she's insecure. Be nice to her. Tell her she's fabulous. If she relaxed, she'd probably be a better Blue-Winged Fairy and become easier to live with."

"I'll try. And I'll tell Lucy. She's really bugged by her. She can't forgive her for saying you were a sore loser."

"She said I was a sore loser? It wasn't a contest!" Abby said, dismayed.

"Water under the bridge, Abby. Everybody knows the truth." Sam looked at the clock on his dashboard. "Are you free for a movie tonight? A bunch of us are going to the eight o'clock."

"Sure! Have fun at rehearsal, and see you later. Oh! What time?"

"I'll pick you up on the way back, around seven fifteen, and we'll get something quick to eat before the show." Sam waved out his window all the way down the road until he disappeared from view.

He did it again. Abby smiled. *He completely restole my heart.*

On Saturday afternoon when Abby finished riding Dancer, she started organizing things for the horse show. With great anticipation, she opened Hilary's polished oak tack box. She took out the contents, washed the insides, then started shaking out bandages and dusting off brushes. The box had not been opened in five years.

Abby considered what she'd need. Grooming tools. She put aside hoof-oil, a hoof-pick, curry, mane comb, stiff body brush, soft brush, and a towel for the final shine. She'd need a cooling sheet and perhaps a light blanket. Leg wraps and trailer boots. Spare reins, crop, chin chain, lead shank, halter. The halter, lead shank, boots, and cooler she placed in readiness for tomorrow's trailer ride. The other things she rearranged in the trunk.

Abby looked up and watched Dancer graze beside Henry. She made a wish. Crossing her fingers she said aloud, "Please let us win." Then she touched the wooden trunk in case she'd jinxed herself.

Tomorrow morning she'd bathe him and shine him up.

His mane had already been pulled short, ready to braid. His whiskers had been shaved and he had a new set of shoes. The cuts and scrapes from his pit adventure had healed well. He looked like he did in the old days when no horse could outjump him. He was a beautiful sight. Abby got goosebumps.

She began cleaning the tack. She scrubbed the bit and polished the brass strip on his headband. She got the stirrups cleaner than they'd ever been. The leather martingale, bridle, reins, girth, and saddle were soaped with linseed and carefully wiped down. She oiled her saddle, then placed it on the saddle-rack. Tomorrow, she would pack it all in the tack box.

Hilary's clothes were hanging on the tack hook in a dry-cleaner's bag. Jacket, breeches, white shirt, ratcatcher, black gloves, belt. Tall black boots stood polished on the floor under the clothes. Abby mentally checked the items off. She thought she was ready. Was she missing anything?

Hilary James walked in. "Abby! Got everything?"

Abby smiled. "Hey, Hilary! I think so, thanks to you. You're great to lend me all this. Still, I can't help thinking I've forgotten something."

"There's a lot to remember, isn't there?"

"I'm so excited about tomorrow. I hope I'll be able to sleep tonight."

Hilary smiled. "I know how you feel, but even if you don't get a wink it won't matter. You'll do beautifully, then sleep tomorrow night."

"You think so?"

"I know so." Hilary reached into her pocket. "I've got something for you to wear tomorrow. For good luck." The young woman opened her hand.

Abby's jaw dropped. "Oh, no! I couldn't wear that. What if I lose it?"

"You won't. I'll pin it on you myself so if it falls off, it's my fault."

Abby gazed at the antique fox-head pin with its ruby eyes. "You always wore that, didn't you, when you showed?" she said in awe.

"Every time. And it brought me luck. Every time."

When Abby cycled up her lane, she immediately saw her parents' car sitting in the turnaround. They were home! She parked her bike against the wall and raced into the house.

"Mom! Dad! Where are you?"

"In here, Abby! The living room!"

Abby turned down the hall and came to a halt. There were her parents, with Joy Featherstone, and Pete and Laura Pierson.

"I don't know who to hug first!" cried Abby. "I haven't seen you for a long time," she said to the Piersons.

Laura laughed merrily. "Hug your parents first, dear. We can wait."

Pete put his arm around his wife and smiled in agreement.

Abby embraced her parents at the same time. The three Malones held each other tight. "I missed you," Abby said through the lump in her throat.

"We missed you, too," said Liam.

"I love you, Abby," Fiona whispered. "I hope you'll forgive me. I know it's been horrible for you."

Abby hugged her even tighter. "I'm just glad you're home. We'll talk later."

Fiona looked at her daughter. So mature. "We sure will."

Abby turned to Pete and Laura with open arms. "Now it's our turn!" They all laughed and hugged.

To join the fun, Joy made the three-way hug into a four-way hug. Fiona and Liam circled them, joking about the group hugs and touchy-feely sensitivity training at the spa.

The doorbell rang. "Are there more people coming?" Abby asked her mother.

"Answer the door and you'll see," she answered.

Hilary, Sandy, Christine, and Rory stood on the porch.

"Come in!" said a very surprised Abby. "Hilary, you didn't tell me you were coming over!"

"I was sworn to secrecy, and you don't cross my grand-mother. She organized a Welcome Home surprise party for your parents."

"You'd think I'd be let in on that," said Abby, slightly confused.

"You would have been," piped up Joy, "if it wasn't also a Good Luck Tomorrow party for you."

Abby was deeply moved. "Thank you," was all she could say. She looked from face to face. Her mother, radiant and much younger-looking than when she'd left, dressed in a soft jade silk shirt with cream pants. Her father, handsome and charming, making everyone feel at home and comfortable. Laura Pierson, in a bright pink dress, the feisty, kindhearted, sweet old lady who loved a good laugh. Pete Pierson, who was always there for her through thick and thin. Hilary, her idol, who was allowing her to ride her magnificent stallion. Sandy, always sensible, humour-ous, and intelligent. Rory and Christine, both loyal friends and good people. Joy Featherstone, to whom Abby had grown truly close, with a moral compass pointing true north. These people were her support group, she realized. She felt extremely lucky to have them in her life.

There was a knock on the door. Abby's eyebrows raised.

Joy winked at her and said, "There's one more person coming to dinner, Abby. Open the door. Go ahead."

It was Sam. Abby looked back at Joy, whose face was crinkled up with sheer delight, and gave her the thumbs-up. "Thanks," she mouthed across the noisy room. She opened the door and gave Sam a hug.

"For you," he said shyly, and handed her a small rectangular box.

"Can I open it now?" Abby asked.

"Sure. I hope they're the right thing. They're for good luck."

Abby ripped off the paper and lifted the lid, revealing a pair of black leather riding gloves. She gasped. "They're fabulous!" She tried them on. "They fit like a glove!" She laughed and modelled the gloves for everyone.

"Thanks, Sam. I'll wear them tomorrow. I love them."

"Dinner is served!" called Joy from the dining room. "Come sit down. Your places are marked. Come, come, before dinner gets cold!"

Through the kitchen door snuck Robert Wick, holding his forefinger to his lips. He kept out of sight behind Joy as she hustled around arranging dinner. Everyone had trouble not laughing aloud and spoiling the fun.

"Throw another place on the table," he finally shouted. "I'm not missing this party."

Joy spun around and faced him, grinning from ear to ear. "You said you were busy tonight! Who put you up to this, you old goat?" she cried.

"Guilty!" admitted Rory, delighted with the game.

"There's enough to go around, isn't there, Joy?"

"Even if I go hungry myself, I'd never turn you away." Joy wiped her hands on her apron and kissed him right on the lips.

This caused a great uproar. Hoots and applause filled the room as Joy and Robert continued their embrace.

The twelve dear friends sat down to a delicious, home-cooked meal. There was no shortage of conversation as plates were passed and appetites were sated. A happy glow filled every heart.

An angry man observed the scene through the dining room window. *This confirms it,* seethed Samuel Owens. *They're all in it together. The Caseys, the Malones, the Jameses. And Robert Wick. They think they can appease me by throwing me a crumb. I'll show them. I'll show them all.*

Another pair of eyes, these ones steel grey, kept watch over the intruder. Prepared to fight tooth and nail to protect his loved ones, Cody bristled and snarled softly. One false move, and he'd be there.

Owens slunk away as stealthily as is possible on crutches. Halfway down the lane, he whistled loudly. With the car's headlights off, Walter, hunched down in the driver's seat, rolled the Mercedes in neutral to meet him. Walter jumped out and silently opened the back door to usher in his boss.

"Get out of here fast," Owens barked to the cringing manservant. "This place makes me sick to my stomach."

Cody watched them go.

15

THE GRAND INVITATIONAL

SUNDAY FINALLY DAWNED. As she'd expected, Abby hadn't slept a wink. She'd spent the night practising every possible combination of jumps. She'd imagined every scary unexpected angle, and sorted out how to ride it. She'd used her leg aids, asked for leads, kept her pace. Again and again, she'd chastised herself for not sleeping, repositioning herself in her effort to slumber, removing blankets only to shiver and pull them on again. It had been a very long night.

Through the paned window over her bed, Abby watched the sun come up over the front field. It was pink and gorgeous. Shadows receded, taking with them the gloom of night and revealing a world filled with rosy light.

Abby remembered what Hilary had told her. She'd ride today and get a good sleep tonight. Lack of sleep never killed anybody. That's what Pete Pierson said.

Abby felt horrible. Her head was full of cotton, her stomach in knots. The last thing she wanted to do was get out of bed. Her whole body seemed leaden. Gravity took hold of each of her bones, pulling her into the mattress. Could she call in sick? Fake an injury?

No. She groaned and jammed the pillow over her head. No, she couldn't. Everyone had made such a fuss over her the night before. She'd be embarrassed for her whole life if she wimped out.

Slowly she crawled out from under the covers. Without bothering to get dressed, Abby stumbled downstairs for orange juice.

Through the window on the landing, she saw Dancer grazing with Moonie and Leggy. "No!" she groaned. "Not again! And not today!" Visions of Owens shooting him as he ran home popped into her mind. Or Dancer caught in a trap.

She ran outside barefoot in her white cotton pyjamas, hurdling the fence to save the time it would take to undo the latch. She called him. "Dancer, come here!" He looked at the fence, thinking of bolting. He looked at Abby, running through the field. He made his decision. Casually, he sat back and lifted his front legs over the four-rail fence, following through with a kick of his hind legs. For good measure, he gaily bucked before sailing away.

"No, no, no, no, no!" muttered Abby. She opened the gate and ran for Moonie. Winding her fingers through Moonie's mane, she jumped up and pulled herself onto the surprised mare's back. "Let's go!" she urged.

Moonie snorted, then put herself into gear. She trotted out the gate, then picked up a canter as they turned right onto the gravel road. Abby looked back to see a panicking Leggy. She'd been grazing when her mother went through the gate, and now she raced back and forth looking for a way out. Finally, in desperation, the young mare leapt the fence. It took Abby's breath away. *She's just like Dancer,* she thought. *She jumps like her old man.*

Cody followed Leggy, completing the unusual procession. Dancer galloped ahead along the road. Moonie and Abby were close behind. Abby was determined to keep him from cutting into Owens' woods, the path he'd normally take. As the entrance to the path neared, Abby squeezed Moonie's sides with her bare heels and steered him away. Luckily, Leggy flanked them on the inside, preventing Dancer from changing course and doubling back.

Bareback riding requires constant use of the leg muscles, and Abby's legs were getting tired. They turned up the road. Hogscroft was coming up on the right. Dancer picked up a burst of speed and cut up the lane. He was home.

"Whew, Moonie," Abby said with relief. She stretched her legs and wiggled her ankles and feet. Not trusting that Dancer would stay, she rode Moonie, with Leggy at her side, up the lane to the house. Christine was at the window, phone in hand. She waved with a large motion when she saw Abby. She put down the phone and opened the door.

"Abby! That was your father. He's on his way with Moonie's tack."

"He saw us leave?"

"Yes, he did."

Hilary James rushed out with a pair of rubber riding boots. "I got dressed the minute I heard. Here, wear these on the ride home. Do you want some pants, too?"

"Thanks, but there's no time. I guess I look pretty funny in my pyjamas."

Hilary nodded, giggling. "You sure as heck do."

"How'd he get out, Hilary? Was the electricity off?"

"The electric fence wire kept him in for a while, but I guess he figured he could clear it without getting zapped!" As she ran to the barn she called over her shoulder, "Abby, I'll look after bathing Dancer, you go get ready, and we'll load at eleven. Okay?"

"Okay. Thanks, Hilary! I'll be back in time to braid him." Abby patted her mare's sweating neck. "Good girl, Moonie. Just like herding Mr. Pierson's cows!"

Liam arrived within minutes. Without a word, he put the saddle over Moonie's back and tightened the girth. Abby yelled goodbye to Hilary and Christine as Liam gave her a leg up. Leggy followed Moonie down the drive along the road toward the

Malones' farm. A silvery flash in the bushes assured her that Cody was with them.

"That was quite the stunt, Abby my girl," said Liam sternly through the rolled-down truck window. "You might have gotten hurt. Why didn't you call me? I would've helped." He drove slowly beside them as they walked.

Abby was stunned. "I didn't think of it, Dad. It was an emergency. If Dancer had gone home his usual way along through the path, Owens would've killed him if he saw him, no questions asked."

"I could've achieved the same results with my truck, and you wouldn't have risked breaking your leg or cracking your skull. That was foolish, Abby. Plus, you galloped an unfit pregnant mare. You put Moonie's unborn foal at risk. And Leggy might have pulled something or gotten a shin splint, running hard up the road with her undeveloped joints."

Abby's head was hanging. "I didn't think of all that, Dad." She felt bad. "But I had to solve the problem. And I'm used to solving problems on my own. I didn't even think of calling for help. That's the truth."

Now it was Liam's turn to feel bad. "I'm sorry, Abby. Of course that's true. We've been away for almost two months. I'm sorry." Liam searched for a way to cheer his daughter. "I was worried sick when I saw what was happening. That's why I sound so cross." He smiled warmly at Abby. "And anyway, nothing bad happened, so we're all right. It all worked out. Mission accomplished."

Abby smiled back, relieved that she was out of trouble. "Did you see Leggy jump, Dad?"

Liam laughed. "Like a deer, Abby. Like a deer. She's a good one, all right. Just like her father."

"She'll be a good one if she turns out like her mother, Dad. Moonie's a great girl." Abby thought of the expert way the mare guided Dancer away from the path.

Liam nodded. "That's the only way to breed them. Good stock on both sides, or you risk the weak genes coming out in the foal."

Liam got home first and waited to help Abby with the horses. They walked up to the house in good spirits, and smelled bacon as they came through the kitchen door. Abby grinned. She was ready for the task ahead.

The show grounds were busy. Spectators had come out in full force to watch the spectacle and enjoy the beautiful, warm, sunny day. Abby and her parents followed the Hogscroft truck and trailer past rows of temporary stalls and tack shops and food stalls. There was no shortage of activity. A young man at the gate looked at their pass and directed them to their parking spot. Liam pulled up beside the rig and stopped.

"Abby!" called Hilary. "If you go in and untie Dancer, I'll put down the ramp."

"Okay," Abby called. She opened the small door at the front of the trailer and climbed up. She patted Dancer's head. "There's a boy. Did you have a good ride over?" He gently butted her with his nose. "Good, I'm glad. Today we have a job to do, Dancer. Let's go get 'em."

Abby pulled the rope through the loop. "Ready!" she called to Hilary, who slowly dropped the ramp to the ground and un-hitched the stall guard at the stallion's rear. They backed the great horse off the trailer.

Dancer's head came up. His nostrils filled with familiar smells. He arched his neck proudly and blew through his nose. His front right hoof pawed the ground, and he spun around, challenging any takers.

Christine and Hilary laughed. Christine said, "Just like always, right, Mousie? He's ready."

Hilary nodded and laughed. "Hang on to your hat, Abby!

Dancer's back!" Hilary felt proud of her gorgeous horse, and loved the way people were throwing admiring glances his way.

"Okay, folks, let's get Dancer settled," said Liam, taking charge. "Then we can figure out how to get ourselves organized."

"Look!" exclaimed Abby. "Over there. The Piersons are here." They all looked to see where she was pointing. Pete's new green sedan was parked half a field away in a row of cars. Pete was gallantly helping Laura out of the passenger's side. She wore a brilliant ensemble of yellows, pinks, and bright blues. Just as her large pink sunhat lifted with a gust of wind, Pete grabbed it and slammed it onto her head.

Fiona chuckled and said, "I'll go with them. I'll meet you at stall thirty-three." She strode across the field turned parking lot, happy to have a chance to visit with the Piersons while the others dealt with the details of the show.

Two hours later, Abby was on Dancer's back, surveying her competition. Her personal cheering section was settled in the stands. Liam had managed to secure her the number "97," the same number that Mousie had always worn when she competed. Abby checked that the string was tied properly. Even though the day was heating up, Abby shivered with nerves. She forced her mouth shut to stop her teeth from chattering.

They'd drawn their places. Ian Millar was going first on his newest champion, Beaverbrook. Jay Hayes was next on the brilliant Raven. Chris Pratt had pulled the gallant Davos out of retirement, and Jill Henselwood was riding Leicester Square. Dancer and Abby were the last of eighteen entries.

Abby became more and more uneasy. What was she doing here? She couldn't be more outclassed. *What are they all thinking about me?* she wondered. *I should have a sign on my back, "Dancer was invited, that's why I'm here."*

Over there was Beth Underhill and the great Monopoly. There was Ainsley Vince. Gayle Greenough. Mac Cone. Hugh Graham with Secret Agent. Jennifer Foster with Zeus. Lisa Carlsen came back from Edmonton for the show, and the Spruce Meadows contingent was highly visible, with Jonathon Asselin and John Pearce on their powerful mounts. Mario DesLaurier and Nightingale trucked in from Quebec with hopes of winning the coveted Grand Invitational Trophy.

Not only was the competition scary, the stands were filling with Canada's riding elite. Abby spotted Jimmy Day and Torchy Miller, Olympic team medal winners. Further along sat the Gayford family, and she was sure she saw Jim Elder and his brother Norman. The famous Major Gutowski, coach of Canada's winning team in the sixties, perched on a seat in all his stiff-backed military elegance.

Holy, thought Abby as her stomach lurched, *I'm going to crash and burn in front of all the horse greats in Canada. I won't even remember the course.*

The rules of the Grand Invitational were simple. The ride with the best time and the fewest faults would win. Each knocked-down rail counted as four faults. If a horse refused to jump, four faults were added. Two refusals, and the horse and rider would be eliminated. There was a prescribed time in which the course should be completed, and each second over that time was one-quarter of a fault. Horses that jumped clean within the time would jump again in a jump-off.

The caller ran into the warm-up ring. "First horse, please. Ian Millar, please, at the gate." As Abby watched, Beaverbrook lifted his head delicately and trotted through the entrance, tail swishing, head high.

Abby observed his ride very carefully. She had a lot to learn from the way this man rode, and she wasn't going to miss the opportunity. She noticed the way he slowed before a tight turn, and the way he set up his mount for the first oxer. He kept his head up and his hands still throughout his ride. It was almost like he was merely a passenger, doing nothing. *The art of concealing art,* thought Abby. He made it look so easy. Abby wasn't fooled.

But suddenly the crowd groaned. Beaverbrook had landed in the water jump. That was four faults. His back hooves slid on the slippery bottom and he struggled to right himself. Shaken, the horse lost confidence as he came into the triple combination. He knocked over a rail, but landed well, and expertly cleared the second and third jumps in the obstacle, thrilling the crowd.

Abby could feel the release of tension in the riders around her. Hugh Graham, sitting next to her on Secret Agent, breathed out. Ian Millar was the man to beat, and he'd just raised all their hopes by racking up eight faults.

Ian and Beaverbrook finished the course without further faults. Always a gentleman, Ian Millar patted his horse and waved to the crowd, smiling as he exited the ring.

Raven snorted and twisted to the starting gate. He bucked in anticipation of his solo in the spotlight as the crowd laughed with pleasure. He was Jay Hayes's feisty gelding, and named appropriately. Black as the bird, and seeming to fly, he was brilliant and keen, quick and accurate. Jump after jump, he flew and soared, defying gravity.

Abby checked the timer. He was speeding through this course in a time that few could touch. Abby wasn't even going to try. She would have to go for a clean round.

Raven made too tight a turn and found himself face to face with a five-and-a-half-foot jump. He crashed through the wide oxer, leaving bars scattered like pick-up sticks. Legs stinging with pain, the horse hopped and danced. Jay faced him at the last jump, a multicoloured creation that looked like a flight of stairs. He bounced gamely toward it, then had second thoughts, and slid to a halt inches away. They could have another go at it. Jay checked his horse's legs, decided that no further damage would be done, and faced it again. Raven cleared it easily. The crowd roared its approval as he doffed his hat, patted his horse's neck, and left the ring.

As riding hero followed riding hero, Abby became more and more demoralized. She realized the difficulty of the course, and how inadequate she was. If the big riders were having this much trouble, what chance did Abby have? How could she even imagine herself to be in this league? By the time the tenth horse had finished, only Mario DesLaurier and Kim Kirton had gone clean, and they had overtime faults. Hugh Graham was up next.

Abby noticed each rider's different style. She wondered if the rider adapted his style to the horse, or if the horse conformed to the rider's style. She knew that Moonie liked her to have a more forward seat than Dancer, and Abby rode that way to please her. And Dancer was offended if she gave him too clumsy a cue. He liked her to be subtle, and so she tried to ride him very quietly.

Hugh rode in with gusto and courage, and Abby was sure that the horses who liked his style would do anything for him. Secret Agent was jumping like a superhero, snorting and prancing around the course easily. They got into trouble in the middle of the triple combination jump. Coming fast out of the water jump, he'd jumped big over the first upright and landed too close to the second upright to take the necessary stride. He bounced with great strength and amazingly cleared the top rail. But he couldn't get organized in time for the third jump in the combination, and the rails came down. Secret Agent was rattled and knocked the next one down, too.

Dancer was calm. He knew what he was here to do, and Abby sensed that he was preserving his energy. Either that, or he was too tired from his morning's shenanigans to move. Abby prayed for the former as she repetitively memorized the course, getting more and more uneasy.

Beth Underhill rode her big black horse, Monopoly, to the starting gate. He'd been retired, like Dancer, and this was his farewell tour.

Abby was up next. She was covered with goosebumps and could hardly breathe for the huge weight that seemed to press on her chest. Her toes and fingers were numb. How could she go in like this? She'd fall off for sure. Beth and Monopoly cantered brilliantly around, but Abby wasn't concentrating. She heard the crowd cheer, but she couldn't tell what had happened. She wasn't keeping score anymore.

Absently, she patted Dancer's glistening chestnut neck and felt the great strength beneath his coat. He nickered softly, then blew through his nostrils. *He's trying to reassure me,* thought Abby, and a tear came unbidden to her eye. She was moved by the great horse's sensitivity. *But it's a lost cause. I can't do it. I can't go in there.*

Dancer somehow knew that his moment was nigh. He slowly began to perform dressage on the spot. Exercising each muscle, he crouched and lifted, arched and stretched, extended and compressed. Abby sat still as he warmed up in this strange but effective way. *Hilary never told me about this,* she mused with detachment. Her mind was miles away.

"Dancer, please! To the gate!" The voice sounded muted and distant.

In a state of cold agitation, and with the sense that her mind was not connected to her body, Abby allowed Dancer to do as he was told. Abby couldn't move, let alone direct him. She was in another zone.

As Beth Underhill rode out of the ring to loud applause, Dancer trotted in. Vaguely, Abby heard the crowd recognize the retired legend. Her vision blurred, and she had the delayed feeling that she was slowly tumbling off. She wasn't breathing, wasn't present, wasn't coherent. All she knew was that she was blacking out.

Dancer jumped straight up in the air and landed exactly where he'd started, shifting his weight slightly to keep himself under Abby. He tossed his head and whinnied loudly. Shaking his body as if he'd been through a rainstorm, Dancer managed to wake Abby from her frozen terror.

He snorted impatiently and stamped his foot. He neighed angrily. "Yes, Dancer, I hear you," Abby rasped, struggling to get herself together. She took a deep breath. In. Out. Another. In. Out. She took hold of the reins and gripped with her legs.

Dancer reared up and thrashed with his forelegs, whinnying his deep, fulsome noise. He was the king of all, he seemed to trumpet.

Her body racked with nerves, Abby cantered Dancer through the starting gate. She clenched her teeth to keep them from rattling. She swallowed her bile and willed herself not to vomit. Blinking hard, she tried to focus on the first jump. "Let's go, let's flow," she chanted, struggling to clear her head as Dancer reduced his stride to take off at the perfect distance. Abby's body reacted automatically and followed him through.

Abby remembered where to go next, and headed Dancer toward jump number two. She was still in dreamland. They skimmed over the huge hedge and Abby counted absently, "Land, one, two, three, four," and they lifted again over a rainbow-shaped jump of many colours. "Land, one, two, three, four, five." They turned the corner of the ring, hugging the fence to get in straight to the broad oxer.

Abby awoke from her stupor. Immensely grateful that the mighty horse had carried her this far, she spoke to him through clenched teeth. "I'm not going to let you down, Dancer."

Her eyes were focused now, her brain intact. The feeling returned to her legs. Abby blinked and licked her lips. She felt resolve and courage well up in her heart along with the desire to win. This was Dancer's show, and she had almost blown it. She was determined to let him shine.

The oxer looked huge to Abby, but Dancer continued toward it with confidence, head up and eager. She looked over the jump through his delicately pointed ears. "If you can do it, I can do it," she muttered. Three, two, one. Liftoff. Dancer's muscled haunches sprang with great power. His front knees tucked into his chest, and his neck lengthened gracefully as he straightened his head. Abby knew how beautiful he must look.

She was riding well. Pure joy filled her chest.

They were quickly coming to the water jump. "Head up," muttered Abby, remembering the tip her father had given her. "Head up, heels down, sit back." She rode into it imagining a five-foot-tall jump. Dancer flew over the water and landed safely on the other side. On they cantered to the triple combination, the jump that had caused the most problems for this experienced group of riders.

Abby felt Dancer's excitement. "Easy, big boy," she said as she sat up slightly. Abby made the decision to let him set his speed. It was faster than she would've chosen, but he'd been right so far. Plus she didn't want to fight him so close to the three big obstacles. At the third to last stride, the intelligent stallion slowed considerably and organized himself perfectly.

Over the first jump, land, then a stride. Over the second jump, land, stride, stride. Over the third, and land. They'd done it. They'd cleared the triple!

Wow. Abby grinned broadly. *Holy. What a horse.* She focused ahead. They weren't done yet. Four difficult jumps remained.

Up in the stands, Hilary James sat rigid. Every muscle in her body, every fibre of her brain was involved in Dancer's ride. She'd been alarmed when she saw Dancer carry in Abby's unresponsive body. Abby was in shock, and Hilary could hardly watch, but as Abby gained control, Hilary started feeling better. Now, Hilary was jumping each jump with Dancer, counting the strides aloud. Mousie James was riding again.

Sandy Casey sat on her left. He remembered the first time he'd seen Hilary riding Dancer. It had been at the Queen's Exhibition in the Coliseum, five years earlier. They'd been a spectacular team. He took her hand in his and gave it a squeeze.

Christine sat on Hilary's right. Sympathetic and supportive, she sat with her arm firmly around her daughter's shoulders. Sitting beside Christine was Rory. He marvelled at Dancer's incredible strength and beauty, and noted the difference Abby's training had made in the scruffy, ill-mannered beast that had been jumping the farm's fences only months before. Liam and Fiona held hands, breathless, eyes on their daughter. Liam nodded and urged her on. Fiona sat quietly with tears of admiration glistening on her cheeks.

Pete Pierson's arms surrounded Laura as she buried her head in his chest, her eyes securely shut. Her lips moved as she said a prayer that Abby would not get hurt. Pete watched Abby carefully. She was allowing Dancer to clear the big jumps by leaving him alone, and he admired her restraint. It was rare for a young, inexperienced rider to have the wisdom that Abby was demonstrating.

Joy Featherstone and Robert Wick had slid into the stands behind Christine and Rory just in time for the start of the show. They sat slack-jawed, in awe of this incredible combination of talent and determination. Sam and Leslie Morris had brought Lucy with them. The teenagers huddled together silently, eyes riveted. This was intense.

Each face in the stands was intent on Abby and Dancer's progress through the course. Not only were they clearing each fence, but their time was looking good.

Another face in the stands wore an altogether different expression. Samuel Owens, bandages off but still using a cane, glowered through the coyote scratches. He would put a stop to this and he knew how to do it. Pushing himself up onto his feet, and clutching his cane, Owens made his way down to the judges' booth on the other side of the stadium.

Abby concentrated on the job ahead. The optical illusion was next. This jump fanned out, making the ground line completely off-angle from the top rail. The width was deceptive. If you went strictly for the top rail, you might step on the bottom rail and tumble it down. If you rode to the centre rail, you came in crooked and risked ticking the angled top rail with a back hoof.

Abby decided to ride straight to the top rail. Dancer noticed the illusion and slowed. Abby let him figure it out. They cantered on the spot for a stride, then Dancer surged ahead. He took off well ahead of the jump, and sprang a foot over it. Abby was thrown slightly back with the unexpected enormity of the action, but grabbed his mane and regained her balance as quickly as she'd lost it, taking care to leave his mouth unjerked.

They landed too long. They could take either four extra-small strides or three extra-long ones before they got to the wall.

Head up, ears forward, hind end in gear, Dancer hopped straight-legged. Four, three, two, one. Up they sprang, over the wall with its precariously balanced top bricks. Clear! Land, one, two, three, four, five, turning tightly all the way, into the tall yellow and white vertical. Over they went, Dancer tucking his hind legs sideways to avoid the top rail. He then gently landed, switched his leads, and turned right. Now they were facing the last obstacle.

Abby noticed that Dancer was getting tired. His sides were heaving, and his strides were less springy. He was going too fast, reasoning wrongly that speed would help him clear the wide, colourful steps that loomed ahead. For the first time in their short riding history, Abby sat back and forced him to change his speed. He resisted, throwing his head up and down.

She spoke to him. "Steady, Dancer, we're almost home."

The stallion relaxed, and Abby released her pull. He steadied in time to take the last two strides before his mighty leap. Upon safely landing, the stallion bucked high in the air, and swished his tail mightily. Head down, nose straight out, Dancer raced through the time gate, four seconds under time, and clean.

They'd won. Abby punched the air with her fist and leaned over Dancer's neck, hugging him with all her remaining strength. "Dancer, you did it! Dancer! You won!" Tears flowed down her cheeks.

Up he reared, bellowing his victory. He walked around on his hind legs pawing the air. Sweat dripped from his flanks and neck. As the crowd stood roaring with approval and clapping wildly, Dancer lightly dropped his front feet to the ground, and bowed deeply to his audience. His nose touched the ground. He stayed in that position for five full seconds before he stood up. He tossed his head and walked proudly out of the ring, huffing to get his breath.

There was only one dry eye in the house, and it belonged to the man with the scratched face in the judges' booth.

As soon as they were out of the ring, Abby took her feet out of the stirrups and dismounted. Dancer's sleek chestnut coat was drenched. His eyes showed white, and his nostrils were flared and so red that they appeared in danger of bleeding. Abby feared the exertion had been too much, so soon after his injury.

His sides were heaving. She loosened the girth, ran up the stirrups, unbuckled the chin strap and nose band on his bridle, and began to walk him toward his stall. He held his head low to allow more oxygen to enter his lungs, and plodded rather than walked. He'd used every ounce of his energy.

Every rider she passed gave her the thumbs-up, or a pat on the back. "Congratulations!" called Chris Pratt from across the paddock. "Well done!" yelled Hugh Graham. Ricky Thompson winked and said, "Not bad for a girl!"

Abby laughed and graciously accepted the good wishes, but she was more concerned about Dancer as they neared the stabling facilities.

Hilary James stood waiting at the stall. Her radiant smile faded as she noticed Dancer's condition. She threw open the tack box, producing towels and the warmest blanket. Hilary ran to Dancer and pulled off the saddle as they walked. She replaced his bridle with his halter.

Without saying a word, the two young women rubbed Dancer down, blanketed him, and kept him walking. Slowly, his breathing returned to normal. Hilary allowed him a small drink of water, then took away the bucket to prevent him from colicking.

Finally, after they'd walked him for fifteen minutes, Hilary said, "He'll be fine now, Abby." They put him in his stall and watched.

"Maybe it was too soon," said Abby. "I hope I didn't hurt him."

Hilary was stern. "We were all in it together, Abby. You, me, even the vet said he was fine to go. He hasn't been in the ring for five years. Maybe there was more stress than we counted on."

Abby shook her head. "There was certainly more than I'd counted on. I froze out there. Dancer shook me out of it."

Hilary smiled. "I saw. But you came back, Abby. You rode that course better than I ever did."

"You're crazy, Hilary. Dancer did it all. Every bit of it, unt the last fence."

"You knew when to leave him alone. I'm impressed."

Liam Malone came running up to the girls, out of breath "They've disqualified you!" he said to Abby. "They're giving th trophy and prize money to the second-place rider. They need jump-off to determine who that is because the next three horse have equal faults."

Abby couldn't believe her ears. "Disqualified?" she aske "For what?"

Liam's mouth became a hard thin line. "For riding a sta lion. You're under eighteen years of age."

Abby's hands shot to her mouth. Her eyes widened.

Hilary James looked directly at Liam. "Who made th complaint?"

"Three guesses."

16

MOUSIE RIDES AGAIN

PETE PIERSON WENT STRAIGHT to the judges' booth. It was crammed with irate people. Two women and a man, all in their fifties, sat behind a table. Laid out in front of them was Dancer's application form. Behind them stood a smiling Samuel Owens, leaning on his cane. The judges were trying unsuccessfully to stem the flood of complaints about Abby's elimination.

Pete elbowed to the head of the line and stood tall. He had a dignified air under normal circumstances, but now he appeared imposing. He had their attention.

"You accepted her application," he projected over the din, pointing at the form. "Her age was honestly acknowledged. It's right there in front of you. If you were going to disqualify her, you should have done so before."

The judges knew he had a point. They looked at each other. After a moment, one of the women spoke. "Of course you're right. It was an oversight."

Owens quickly spoke up. "Everyone knows the rules, Pierson. A person under eighteen years of age can't ride a stallion on any showgrounds in Canada. It was Abby Malone's responsibility in this case to adhere to the rules. She disregarded them at her per—" His grin had an ominous look to it.

"This exhibition has its own set of rules," said Pete. "And you all know it. Horses are invited at your whim, and many regulations are waived. Plus, there was no rule book sent out." Pete glared directly at Owens as he spoke. The noisy people in the booth went silent. He shifted his glare to the judges and continued. "You invited Dancer, you accepted him with Abby as the designated rider, and she won fair and square. End of story." Applause and murmurs of assent filled the tiny room.

The judges huddled.

The male judge rose to his feet. "The judges need to confer. We will announce our decision within the hour. Would everyone please leave the booth. Our decision will be final."

Pete nodded. "I've said my piece. I trust you were listening." The tall old man with ramrod posture turned to leave the booth. "I'll await your decision outside." Once out of the booth, Pete stood within sight of the judges right outside the door. He wasn't moving.

People quietly left the booth, unsure of the outcome. Until now, Pete had been too intent on getting his point across to notice who the people were. They were the other riders, here to support the girl who they knew had won.

Pete nodded his approval. "You're good competitors, all of you," he said so all could hear. "And good sports. Thank you."

Ian Millar spoke. "Abby Malone won the class. You're right about the rules. We all know that."

Kim Kirton nodded in agreement. "That's why I'm here. Sandstorm hasn't competed in four years, and he was invited. He wouldn't qualify for an A-circuit show right now."

Their conversation was interrupted by yelling in the booth.

"I'm bloody well not leaving this room until I'm sure that Dancer is disqualified!" Samuel Owens barked.

"Sir," said the man. "Everyone must leave the booth!"

"I am the past president of the Canadian Equestrian Federation. You can't make me leave. And I contribute tens of thousands of dollars yearly to the Olympic Equestrian team."

Pete walked in. "Samuel Owens, smarten up or they'll call security."

The judges whispered to each other.

"Excuse us," said one woman. "Of course you can stay, Mr. Owens." She looked at Pete. "Now, if you'll kindly let us make our decision?"

One half hour later, the announcement was made over the loud speakers. A woman's voice was heard throughout the park.

"After extensive review of the situation, the judges have decided to proceed with the jump-off. Dancer and Abby Malone have been eliminated."

There was a great disturbance in the crowd, and much discussion. No one seemed happy with this result.

Pete, who hadn't left his post outside the booth, walked in. The judges cringed.

Owens beamed. "The decision is final, Pierson, you know that. Go away or they'll call security."

"I have one question," said Pete calmly. "May I?"

The man said, "If it's a quick one. We must get going or we'll lose the crowd."

"Don't worry about that, you've already lost them," said Pete with a glance at Owens. "This is my question. Who's disqualified, Dancer or Abby Malone?"

"Actually, that's a valid question," said one of the women.

The other woman spoke. "Abby Malone is disqualified because she's underage to ride a stallion. Dancer was invited to compete and has broken no rules." She looked at her fellow judges for approval. They both nodded.

"Then Dancer can compete in the jump-off?"

"Ridiculous!" sputtered Owens. "I never heard such nonsense!"

The judges, weary of the whole situation, looked at each

other in dismay. "Is there a rider?" asked a woman judge. "Of proper age?"

"Yes." Pete was going out on a limb.

"Name and age?"

"Hilary James, age twenty-two."

Samuel Owens turned purple. Veins throbbed at his temples and he gasped for air as the judges whispered among themselves.

"Dancer can compete in the jump-off with a rider over the age of eighteen," the man said as he sank down in his chair. "Now, everybody out. I've got a terrible headache. I hope everyone is happy."

"I'm not happy! And I'm not leaving!" yelled Owens in a croaking voice. "This whole thing is preposterous!"

"Call security," said the male judge.

The jumps were set up. The course designer chose four of the most confusing and challenging of his creations and placed them where the skill of the horse and rider would be tested to the maximum. He introduced two surprises as well. These were permanent fixtures in the paddock, but not generally used for jumpers. The horse with the fewest faults and the fastest time would be the winner.

Four competitors walked the course. They'd drawn their places. Mario Deslaurier was going first, Kim Kirton was second, Hilary James was third, and Beth Underhill would be showing last.

While Hilary was in the ring planning strategy, Abby held Dancer's reins in the warm-up area. An hour and a half had passed since his trip around the jumps. He'd been rubbed and wrapped and walked and rested. The fire had returned to his eyes. He'd had a big drink of water and a flake of hay.

"You'll be great, Dancer," Abby whispered. "There are only

four jumps, a drop, and a bridge. They're tricky, so be careful. This is all about brains, and you've got lots."

Dancer rubbed his head on her shirt. The moment the announcement was made, Hilary and Abby had exchanged clothes. Hilary now wore the somewhat sweaty riding habit, and Abby was wearing Hilary's outfit, down to her shoes, which were a bit loose.

"You'll have to look after Hilary, Dancer, like you looked after me. She hasn't ridden in ages."

Minutes later, Hilary was up on Dancer, watching Mario DesLaurier navigate Nightingale around the course. He had no trouble with the fan jump or the triple combination. He headed to the picturesque wooden bridge that stood before the four-foot drop. Show jumpers rarely see such things, and Nightingale was no exception. His ears were pinned as they approached it, and his tail swished. He didn't want anything to do with either the bridge or the drop. He stopped. Mario urged him with his legs, then his spurs. Finally, he smacked him sharply with his crop. Nightingale leapt forward in surprise, which got him halfway over the bridge, but then he skidded to a halt at the drop. No way was he taking another step. He was whistled out. Hilary shook her head in sympathy. "Dancer, don't watch."

She wondered again what she'd gotten herself into. This wasn't just crazy. This was lunatic. She prayed that her leg muscles would hold out for as long as she needed, and that her body would remember to follow Dancer's motion over the jumps, neither anticipating nor being left behind. It had been a long time since she'd schooled over high jumps. Her brain would be fine, but her muscle memory was rusty. Hilary patted Dancer's neck and murmured, "It's a long shot, boy, but we're in it now."

She nodded hello to Mario as he grimly left the ring and watched Kim Kirton ride in on Sandstorm.

Kim was determined and brave. Sandstorm looked fit and ready. They cantered fast through the gate and took the fan jump head-on, clearing it by a foot. Sandstorm took on speed around the corner and scrambled toward the triple combination. Kim gathered him up in time and they made a perfect job of it. The crowd was breathless. The bridge was no trouble, and the drop was a breeze. It looked like Kim and Sandstorm were the ones to beat. Tearing around the tight turn, Sandstorm scrambled again. He lifted in time and cleared the wall, but on their descent his back hoof kicked out and knocked off a brick. The crowd groaned in sympathy. The strange-looking yellow jump had been placed in front of the water, and Kim and Sandstorm rode at it with confidence, landing a good foot clear. They left the ring with four faults and an unbeatable time.

They don't call her the Queen of Speed for nothing, thought Hilary.

She felt a hand grab her leg. She looked down into Abby's intense face.

"Good luck, Hilary, and don't forget to breathe!" She patted Dancer's neck. "Get 'em, boy!" Abby stepped away to let them pass.

Dancer pranced on the spot, muscular neck arched and haunches coiled. His smooth chestnut coat gleamed in the sun. Abby's appreciative eyes followed him into the ring as she stepped over to the fence to watch.

Hilary cantered him through the starting gate at a good pace. Abby knew they were going faster than they looked, because Dancer's stride was extra long. Dancer powerfully soared up and over the optical illusion and tightly turned the corner toward the triple combination. Hilary hung on as tightly as she could, correcting her balance after the turn. Dancer's sinewy muscles flexed with each stride, and his coat shimmered with good health. His intelligent eyes were fierce with determination as he figured out his distances.

Hilary was doing incredibly well, Abby thought. Her legs looked slightly wobbly, but her position was correct. She was smiling, Abby noticed. But what was this? Tears were coming from Hilary's eyes! Abby understood, and wiped a tear from her own eye. *I sure hope emotion doesn't overpower her,* Abby thought.

Dancer lifted and flew over the first of the jumps in the combination. Hilary grabbed his mane and flopped onto his back. Land, one. The second jump. She lost a stirrup. Land, one. The third. *Well done!* Hilary pushed her hat back into place and adjusted her feet and reins as they made their way to the arched wooden bridge and then the drop.

Abby felt a cold nose in the palm of her hand. "Cody! What are you doing here?" she asked her pet. He must have hidden himself in the horse-trailer. He wasn't in the truck, she'd checked. He merely stared into her eyes with a panicked look and whined. Abby was alarmed. Cody never allowed himself to be seen unless there was a very good reason.

Abby looked up to see Dancer canter over the bridge as though he did it every day. He sprang with a huge leap down the drop, closing the distance to the wall.

Cody whined again. He urgently pulled her hand with his mouth. *Something must be very wrong.* Abby let herself be led by Cody. He was taking her, as fast as she could go, behind the callboard.

At a run, she turned her head to see that Dancer was cleanly over the wall. He was turning toward the yellow jump and moving well. He was sitting back on his haunches, preparing to jump when Abby bumped hard into someone and knocked him over. It was Samuel Owens. The crowd was cheering madly and Cody was nowhere to be seen.

"I'm so sorry, Mr. Owens! I wasn't looking where I was going!"

"You idiot! You see what you've done?" Owens was shaking with rage. Abby tried to help him up, but he violently shooed her away. "Get away from me you imbecile! You assaulted me, and that's something I'll not forget!" He was standing up as he spoke, holding his cane in one hand and dusting himself off with the other.

"I'm sorry," said Abby fearfully. "Can I do anything to help?"

"Yes, you can." Owens seemed suddenly pleasant. Then his face darkened, and he screamed, "You can remove yourself from my sight! Permanently!" He lifted his cane to hit her, then thought better of it and, shaking with rage, carefully lowered it to the ground.

Something in his manner struck Abby as suspicious. Owens was guarding his cane. He glanced at it, nervously, then glanced back at Abby.

Abby took a good look at the metal cane. With horrifying clarity, Abby sensed that Samuel Owens' cane was something more than a cane. The elaborate detail might hide a small trigger under the handle, and it looked like there were two view-finders down the shaft. His cane could very well be a cleverly adapted gun.

Why was Owens hiding behind the call-board?

Abby's mind raced. She backed away from the angry man, not wanting to risk being shot. She glanced over her shoulder.

Hilary and Dancer were trotting out of the ring. Abby knew by Dancer's posture and Hilary's relieved smile that they'd done well. There was only one more contestant.

Pete Pierson would know what to do. And he was standing with Hilary James and Dancer in the warm-up ring. With a last glance at the furious Owens, Abby turned tail and fled.

"Mr. Pierson!" she shouted.

The wonderful old man looked at her. "Abby!" His hand

dropped from patting Dancer's neck. He strode toward her, limping from his arthritic hip. "What's wrong?"

Abby was panting, her chest constricted with fear. "Samuel Owens is behind the call-board with a cane that's probably a rifle. Cody brought me over there while Hilary was riding, and I bumped into him by mistake and knocked him over. He's furious, and I don't know what to do."

Pete stared into Abby's eyes, trying to make sense of all she said. He knew Samuel Owens too well. He trusted Abby. He'd seen Cody in action. He had no doubts that what she said was true. They had no time to lose.

Pete spoke sharply to Hilary. "Take Dancer away from here. Keep lots of people around you. Don't ask questions." Hilary's smile dropped.

Taking Abby by the arm and leaving Hilary astounded, Pete walked quickly toward the public telephone beside the registration office. Pete hurried into the office and told the woman, "Get security! There's been a disturbance behind the call-board in the warm-up ring. An older man with a weapon."

Reaching the phone, he dialed 9-1-1. He called for the police to come, with a special request for the chief, Mack Jones. Abby saw five security men run toward the call-board.

Call completed, Pete and Abby watched as Samuel Owens was taken by force to the security building. Even from a distance, they could see that he was livid.

"It'll buy us some time until the police get here," said Pete. "Go tell Hilary that she can come back to the warm-up ring. They'll be awarding prizes within minutes. I'll head over to security to keep an eye on things."

Abby ran, looking for Dancer. She raced through the stalls, but he wasn't there. She tore around the practice field and didn't see him. Finally she spotted Hilary holding the tall, elegant stallion's reins behind the row of women's lavatories.

"Good thinking!" Abby called. "He'll never look here."

Hilary's face wore a shocked expression. "Who'll never look here? What's going on, Abby?"

"It's all right now. Bring him back to the warm-up ring. Security has Owens with them, so it's safe to come out of hiding. It looks like he might have tried to shoot Dancer with his cane."

"With his what?"

Abby snorted. "I'm not sure, but I think his cane is really a gun."

"Are you sure?" asked Hilary.

"No, but with Owens I don't want to assume innocence."

Hilary shuddered. "You're right."

They got to the warm-up ring just as the competitors were being called in. Abby gave Hilary a leg up. Hilary looked down at Abby and said, "This puts it all in perspective, doesn't it?"

Abby knew what she meant. She stood and watched the four horses with their riders walk away. Whether Dancer won the trophy wasn't important any more. He was alive.

The horses lined up. The judges walked out into the middle of the show ring. One woman carried colourful ribbons. The other had a wool cooler over her arm. The man carried a large silver trophy that flashed and shone in the sunlight.

The male judge held a microphone. Shifting the trophy to his left hip, he announced, "Thank you for coming out today. As you know, all proceeds go to support the Canadian Olympic effort. Now, I have the honour of presenting the results."

"The sixth-place ribbon belongs to Lisa Carlsen riding Thatcher." Lisa calmly rode up to the judges and graciously smiled to the crowd as they applauded. "Fifth place goes to Ainsley Vince on Colour Blind." Ainsley's mare kicked out at Thatcher as she passed, but didn't connect. "Fourth place goes to Mario DesLaurier on Nightingale." The crowd continued clapping as Mario rode up. The woman judge clipped the yellow ribbon on his bridle and he walked back to the line, nodding and waving to the crowd.

"Third place goes to Beth Underhill on Monopoly." Horse and rider trotted to the judge with the ribbons. The judge attempted to clip it on, but Monopoly shied away. Laughing, Beth reached out and accepted the white ribbon in her hand. The applause continued.

"Second place goes to Kim Kirton on Sandstorm." The applause got stronger as Kim and her fiery mount collected their blue second-place ribbon.

"The winners of the Grand Invitational are Hilary James and Dancer!" The crowd rose to their feet. The entire audience stood in thunderous applause.

Dancer, the ultimate showman, walked on his hind legs, bellowing his victorious return. He landed lightly, then wedged his muzzle into the middle of the trophy. He lifted the silver vase high in the air, and proceeded to parade around the ring, trophy firmly encasing his upturned nose.

People could not believe their eyes. Hilary laughed so hard she was in danger of losing her balance. Dancer had created another story for people to recount for years to come.

The playful stallion returned to the judges, and very carefully placed the trophy back in the male judge's outstretched hands. He allowed one woman to clip on his red ribbon. The other judge draped the cooler over his rump. It was deep blue with gold letters reading, "The Grand Invitational."

Abby's hands hurt from clapping so loudly and for so long. Her face ached from smiling. She was surprised when Hilary dismounted and took the microphone from the startled judge.

"Thank you very much." Hilary spoke clearly and slowly so that everyone could hear. Her voice echoed throughout the stands. "Dancer will keep the ribbon and the cooler, but I'm sure you'll all agree that the trophy and the prize money belong to

Abby Malone, the rider who had already won the Grand Invitational before the jump-off!"

The crowd rose to their feet again, noisily approving of Hilary's generous gesture. Beth, Mario, Lisa, Ainsley, and Kim dropped their reins and clapped until their horses needed controlling. The riders came into the ring, applauding, and forcefully escorted an embarrassed Abby Malone with them.

Abby walked into the middle of the show ring in Hilary's ill-fitting shoes. She felt proud.

The male judge handed her the trophy, understanding that he had no choice but to go with the crowd. He shook her hand warmly.

Abby carried the trophy to Dancer and Hilary. She put it on the ground and gave Hilary an enormous hug. The two girls hugged and jumped in a circle, to another great outburst of applause from the people in the stands.

Not to be upstaged, Dancer picked up the trophy again with his nose and comically began to exit the ring at a trot. Abby and Hilary chased him out, followed by the other horses and their exuberant riders.

This was a show to remember.

Abby and Hilary were happily getting Dancer packed up and ready to leave, still laughing about his antics with the cup, when a grim-faced Pete arrived at the stall.

"They let him go," he said. "There's no sign of a cane."

17

STAGESTRUCK

IT WAS WEDNESDAY AFTERNOON. Abby Malone sat on her porch rubbing Cody's ears. The Invitational was over and she had nothing to do.

All her friends were deeply involved with *Pinocchio*. Tomorrow was opening night. Rehearsals had intensified all week as the opening loomed. There was one rehearsal this afternoon, and another tonight. Tomorrow, they'd perform in front of a small, live audience in the afternoon, before the big event.

Joy had moved in with Christine and Rory. Abby missed her. Hilary and Sandy were working in Toronto at the museum. Abby missed them, too.

Moonie was unable to do much more than light work in her present condition. Leggy's training took only an hour a day, which Abby did every morning, and Dancer was resting this week, tired but content. He grazed alongside Henry, making no move to leave his field.

The chief of police had talked to Abby after the Invitational. Mack Jones assured her that he believed what she'd told him, but so far the police hadn't been able to find the cane. Owens denied owning such a weapon, and complained that Abby had made it all up and that the security people had handled him roughly. He was calling his lawyers. The police had put surveillance on Dancer, however, on the strength of Abby's statement. A bored young officer sat in a marked car at the end of the

Hogscroft lane, reading and doing crossword puzzles.

Abby sighed. Cody put his paw on her knee.

"Thanks, Cody. You're right, I need cheering up." She looked out into the field and studied her mares. Moonie, sleek and healthy, grazed diligently, missing no blade of grass in her path. She had an elegant line and a lovely face. Her glossy, dark bay body and long black legs cut a fine silhouette.

Beside her, the spunky Moon Dancer lifted her head and looked alertly around. Abby smiled. "You're a troublemaker, Leggy," she said aloud. The two-year-old was well built with a deep chest, short back, graceful neck, and long legs. Her chestnut coat glimmered in the afternoon sun. The star on her forehead was the only white she sported.

Robert Wick's truck drove up the lane. Abby waved hello, then realized the driver was Joy Featherstone.

Joy caught sight of her and slammed on the brakes, spraying gravel.

Abby rose from the steps. This was unusual behaviour. "Mrs. Featherstone!" she called, running to the driver's side window. "Is anything wrong?"

Joy smiled. "Nothing, now that I've found you. I really hope you can do us another favour."

Abby blinked. "A favour? Sure. Whatever you want."

"Are you busy this afternoon?"

"No. I'm bored to death."

"Wonderful! Hop in the truck. You're the Blue-Winged Fairy!"

After hurriedly leaving a note for her mom, Abby climbed into the truck beside Joy. On the way to the theatre, Joy explained the situation.

"How did it happen, Mrs. Featherstone?"

"Nobody was anywhere near, but Margaret Small insist that she was pushed."

"Pushed?"

"Yes. And a firm push. Enough to send her over the lip and down the stairs next to the orchestra pit."

"She was lucky she didn't fall down there," said Abby.

"You better believe it. She would've had more than a sprained ankle and a broken wrist."

"Poor woman." Abby shook her head and grimaced. "When did it happen?"

"This afternoon, just before she made her first entrance."

"And nobody saw?"

"No. Everyone was either on stage, backstage, or in their place, waiting to go on. Robert and I were talking to the lighting man. That's the odd thing, Abby. Nobody was there to push her, not that anybody would. No matter how much she riled people."

Abby tried to squelch the joyful feelings bubbling up inside her chest. It was a painful accident, and she should appear sympathetic. She didn't want Mrs. Featherstone to think her callous.

"Well, aren't you happy to be back in the play?" Joy asked.

Abby's smile broke loose. "Yes!" she emphasized. "I'm absolutely, positively, one hundred percent happy!"

"That's good," Joy said. "Because you have a lot to catch up on in a very short time."

"I won't let you down."

Opening night. It was Thursday evening at five minutes to seven. Abby nervously completed her makeup. Dusting the blue sprinkles over her face and arms, careful not to get them in her eyes, she wondered at her compulsion to be early. Nobody else had arrived.

She had indeed worked night and day to get herself prepared. After the two rehearsals the day before, Abby had gone home and studied the play with fierce concentration. Analyzing characters and their relationships to other characters, making note of action and reaction, charting the story development, Abby worked late into the night. Finally at three o'clock in the morning, lines solid and entrances nailed, she'd fallen asleep in a heap on her bed. At four she'd awoken to get into her night gown and brush her teeth.

That morning before the final dress rehearsal, after going over her lines for the umpteenth time, Abby had written opening night notes to every actor in the show. She'd found greeting cards with a picture of an open-mouthed shark on the front. It seemed as close as she'd get to a dogfish. Inside were the words, "Bite Me!"

She'd added, "If you're not a brilliant Geppetto," to the one for Mr. Farrow, and "If you remember your lines," on Lucy's, who didn't have any. Abby had come up with appropriate comments for all the actors, but her favourite was Sam's. After the "Bite Me!", she'd written, "But not too hard, you foxy thing." She hoped to watch his face when he opened it.

Abby had placed the cards on the actors' dressing tables, and pinned them to the costumes of those who used the big dressing room.

A rustle of air, then a sneeze, snapped her to attention. Ambrose Brown materialized behind her, dressed as a liveried footman with a powdered wig. He sneezed again. "I'll never get used to the powder," he snorted with a snobby-sounding English accent.

"Can't you just wear a white wig?" asked Abby.

"It would never do. It wouldn't be authentic. I couldn't feel the part. An actor must walk the walk if he wants to talk the talk. Ah . . . ah . . . ah . . . choo!"

"Or sneeze the sneeze," Abby added.

"Don't be impertinent. There's a lot you have to learn about the profession, and you're lucky that I take the time to teach you." He strutted like a peacock.

"Where have you been, Ambrose? I've been back since yesterday, and I haven't seen you 'til now."

"I'm not at your beck and call, I'll have you know," he said down his nose.

"I'm not sure I like you very much in this role," said Abby.

"Quite as it should be! Pompous is good, as a footman for the King of England." He took another haughty step, then relaxed. "But I'm tired of it myself." He dropped the accent and slowly dissolved into an ordinary man, wearing a white shirt and pleated pants. "So I'll step outside the character and into myself. At least for as long as I wish."

Abby smiled. "Much better. It's nice to see you."

"And nice to have you back. That Margaret woman was driving us all bananas."

"What a nasty fall."

Ambrose lifted his eyebrows. "Yes, wasn't it? Timely, too. Any later and you wouldn't have had any rehearsal time. Hardly enough as it is."

"Ambrose, do I get the feeling you might have had something to do with her fall?"

"How could you even suggest such a thing!" He paused dramatically. "I had *everything* to do with her fall!"

"Ambrose!" exclaimed Abby.

"Later, my dear, we've got company."

It was seven o'clock. The cast was arriving.

Everyone was nervous. Laughter was high-pitched, chatter was constant. People fretted over last-minute costume alterations, hairpieces, masks. Makeup was borrowed and powder was spilled. Squeals went up as actors opened first-night gifts and cards, followed by hugs and kisses, and in rare cases, tears.

No one dared mention any line from *Macbeth*, called "the Scottish play" in lieu of saying the title aloud. It was bad luck. But you couldn't talk about good luck either. "Merde" or "break a leg" wouldn't tempt the gods of the theatre the way "good luck" would. A person couldn't whistle without having to leave the room, turn around three times, then knock on the door and beg forgiveness.

Abby enjoyed every second.

There were fifteen minutes left before the show would begin. Because she was dressed and ready, Abby went up to the stage. She wanted to be alone, to get away from all the frantic energy in the dressing room.

It was dark behind the curtain. Little guide-lights lit the off-stage steps, and the set was marked with glow-tape to avoid stumbles during scene changes. Abby breathed in the backstage air with all its tension and paint and wood and dust. Pure delight filled her body. *It feels like home,* Abby thought. I belong here.

Abby stretched her arms over her head, then bent over and touched her fingers to the floor. She shook the tension out of her hands and rotated her shoulders. She shook out her legs and stretched her feet. She put her hands on her hips and twisted her body at her waist, back and forth. Then she stood, legs slightly apart, eyes closed, and felt the floor under her feet. She let the solidness of it steady her and give her the comfort of her own gravity. She took deep breaths from her diaphragm and felt the calmness seep throughout her body.

Abby was ready. She smiled, all alone behind the curtain. There was one more thing she wanted to do, and that was to see the audience come in. She'd been told that a peephole existed somewhere in the heavy new purple curtain on stage right.

Searching fruitlessly through yards of velvet fabric, Abby thought the peephole might be another actors' tale. Then she found it.

She peeked through. The theatre was filling up. The ushers read ticket stubs, pointed down aisles, and handed people programs. The orchestra was warming up, which gave a strange sort of musical background to the proceedings, almost like a pre–Act 1. Row after row became seated as she watched.

Pete Pierson looked handsome in his suit and tie, and Laura was flushed with excitement. She loved the theatre, and she'd had her hair done for the occasion. She wore a delightful confection of yellow, and Abby thought she'd never looked so lovely.

Many of Abby's neighbours were there, as were friends and family of the other actors. It was a cheerful crowd. They looked ready to be entertained, which seemed like a good sign.

Abby spotted her parents walking down the stage-right aisle. Liam and Fiona Malone's seats were very close to the front. Abby vowed not to let their anxious faces distract her.

She began to feel nervous again. She'd only been at four rehearsals. Five if you counted the one from which Margaret had banished her. That wasn't nearly enough. And all these people would be watching.

"Get a grip," she murmured softly, scolding herself. "Don't get all crazy and freeze like you did at the Invitational. Dancer's not here to save your bacon." She wondered if she was already crazy, talking to herself like she was another person.

She knew her lines, which thankfully were few. She knew her cues.

Abby closed her eyes, crossed her fingers and toes, and made a wish. "Please let the show be a howling success. For Mr. Wick, whose dream should come true, and for Mrs. Featherstone, who is among the great people on this earth. And for me, because it's my wish." Just in case, she knocked on wood, reaching down and rapping on the hardwood floor.

The house lights began to dim.

"Holy!" muttered Abby, hiking up her blue crinoline and overskirts. She hurried downstairs just as the stage manager began her speech.

Cody found a good watching place behind the building, and waited. From here the small coyote could see every movement around the old barn. His instincts were sparking. Something was about to happen, and he would be prepared. His Abby was inside. Cody would keep her safe. That was his job.

After the stage manager's speech, Robert Wick spoke. "Just a word," he said with dignity. "You are terrific, every one of you. You'll make me very proud tonight. It's just like the old days. Thank you, all." Emotionally, Robert stepped aside and indicated with a nod that Joy Featherstone would speak next.

"Go out there and have fun," Joy said with a bright smile. "The work is done. It's time to play." Her eyes quickly scanned her notes. "Just give it lots of energy in the first scene. The rest will follow. Go! Now! Places please! This is for you!" Joy clapped her hands and laughed. All the actors clapped, too, eyes bright and faces eager. Joy's words had hit them. They were going to go out on stage and have a good time.

At the stroke of eight that evening, the massive purple curtain rose on the humble shop where Geppetto was carving a wooden puppet. Abby watched from the wing, stage right. Mr. Farrow's hands were shaking as he carved the last details, but his voice was strong as he told his dog Trooper about his desire to have a little boy of his own. Trooper, played by Leslie, scratched her ear with her hind leg and cocked her head attentively.

Abby covered her mouth with her hand and smiled. It was working. The play was coming alive. Geppetto, not Mr. Farrow, was speaking in a moderated Italian accent. Trooper, not Leslie, was loyally listening to her master. The sets were convincing, the lighting subtle.

It was magic.

Abby made her entrance as the Blue-Winged Fairy. She had no lines in this scene, but her appearance must convey kindness, goodwill, and authority. When she raised her wand to give life to the inanimate puppet, Abby felt the power, the goodness, the

246

righteousness of the act. She was in the moment, in a way that felt so right she had no doubt that it had been perfect.

Moment over, she wafted off the stage.

"Lovely, lovely, lovely, Abby. Keep in the groove." It was Ambrose, and Abby knew she wasn't to reply. There were others around.

Cody watched closely as Samuel Owens parked his car behind the theatre. He had backed into exactly the same position as before.

Owens got out and lifted a heavy sack from the back seat. Cody's nose quivered. Food! Fresh red meat! Owens crept around the theatre, silently placing chunks of irresistible raw flesh in a circle, about a hundred feet out.

When he was back at his car, Cody crept closer to sniff one. He drooled with a great desire to gobble it up. He sniffed the hunk of meat again. There was something strange about the smell. He crept back to his hiding place without touching the meat.

Cody waited. Something was going to happen. He knew it was only a matter of time.

It was the nose-growing scene. Abby went over her lines quickly as the moment for her entrance approached. She followed the action closely. The Sly Fox exchanges a ticket to Runaway Island for Pinocchio's school book; the book that Geppetto had bought in exchange for his only warm coat.

The Fairy enters and asks Pinocchio, "Why are you not going to school like Geppetto thinks?"

Pinocchio answers, "But I am, Blue-Winged Fairy! I'm helping my friend to find his way first, then I'm going straight to school!"

Pinocchio's nose begins to grow. It grows longer and longer until it's a foot long.

"What's wrong with my nose?" Pinocchio cries in great distress.

"Your nose will grow until you tell the truth."

"Help me! Help me, Blue-Winged Fairy!"

"Only the truth can save you, Pinocchio."

"Okay, okay. I lied! I'll go to school, I promise! I was going with the other boys to Runaway Island. The Fox said that's where real boys go! But now I won't. I'm going to go to school."

The Blue-Winged Fairy believes him. She takes pity on the puppet and shrinks his nose back to normal size. She shows her pleasure as he dutifully heads for school.

The Blue-Winged Fairy exits the stage as Wickley, the bad boy, appears in the schoolyard to entice Pinocchio away from school to Runaway Island.

Abby breathed deeply. It had gone well. She had no more scenes until after the intermission.

When the doors opened at intermission, Cody scanned the crowd for his Abby. Samuel Owens had been preparing his equipment, but now Cody watched him slide down below the windows in his car to become invisible to the crowds of people streaming outside to stretch their legs.

Some smoked. Some got drinks. But all of them chatted noisily. Cody knew that these humans were happy about whatever they were doing inside the big old barn. The place where his Abby remained.

Fifteen minutes later, the people began to re-enter the theatre. The second act was about to begin.

Samuel Owens' head appeared. Cody shifted his position. He was patient.

The second act began on time.

The curtain rises on an extravagant, colourful carnival scene, with jugglers, acrobats, candy carts, and gambling games. Shifty dealers lure boys into card games. All the boys are yelling and eating candy. Some boys have donkey tails. Others have tails and ears. Some are total donkeys, fur and all.

Pinocchio has grown a tail and ears, but doesn't know it until he goes to the pond for a drink of water and sees his reflection. He is horrified and begins to cry. "What will Geppetto say?" he wails.

The Blue-Winged Fairy appears. "Pinocchio, it's me, the Blue-Winged Fairy."

"Oh, Blue-Winged Fairy, help me, please. I've been bad, and I want so much to be good, but I don't know how. What should I do?"

"You should leave this place and go back to school. It's not good for you. The boys are so selfish that they're turning into donkeys, as you well see. And so are you."

"But how can I go to school looking like this?" Pinocchio grabs his tail and pulls it. He takes an ear in each hand and tugs. They don't come off.

"I can help, but you must promise me something."

"Anything, anything at all!"

"Will you keep your promise this time?"

Pinocchio looks sheepish. "Yes. I promise I will."

"Then you must go to the Truant Sea and find Geppetto. He is heartbroken. He searches for you endlessly. He thinks you're lost at sea."

"I'll do it!" cries Pinocchio. "I'll go right now!"

As the audience watches, The Blue-Winged Fairy magically removes his tail and ears with a wave of her wand. She winks, then disappears, tail and ears hidden in a convenient pocket in her billowing blue skirt.

Each actor removes a cart or a table or a piece of scenery as they go. The lights change. The boisterous carnival is replaced in seconds by an angry sea, with Geppetto rowing a boat through huge waves created by offstage workers pulling and flapping stretches of green, blue, and grey fabric. The boat is on swivelling wheels, with a cut-out section at the bottom where Geppetto's feet create the movement.

"Pinocchio!" Geppetto hollers mournfully. "Pinocchio! I'm here to save you!" The old man looks exhausted. The wind howls and the ocean roars.

"Pinocchio!" Geppetto calls. He's a beaten man, rowing against the waves.

He is unaware of a giant dogfish stealthily moving up behind him. The giant predator opens its fearsome jaws.

Pinocchio appears on the bank. Seeing Geppetto about to be consumed, he jumps headlong into the raging sea and swims toward him, dodging waves and breathing hard.

"I'm here, Geppetto! I'm coming to save you!"

Just as he reaches the rowboat, the dogfish swallows them whole—Geppetto, Pinocchio, rowboat, and all.

The waves disappear as a painted scrim rolls down from above, hiding the mechanical dogfish. A huge interior mouth complete with tonsils and glottis covers the entire stage area. Geppetto and Pinocchio appear to be inside the dogfish with their ruined boat.

"Pinocchio, my brave little puppet!" Geppetto hugs Pinocchio.

"Father! I've been bad!" Pinocchio hugs him back, repentant.

"Never mind all that. It's so good to see you!" Geppetto heartily forgives him as he pats his back joyfully.

The Blue-Winged Fairy appears. She watches and approves, then fades away. This effect is achieved by lighting. Abby stands on a stool behind the scrim, which is translucent. She cannot be seen until a special light illuminates her. When the light fades, she disappears from view, leaving only the scrim, painted like the dogfish's mouth.

Pinocchio and Geppetto worry about how to escape. It looks

hopeless, but they have each other.

When the dogfish finally sleeps, he snores. Pinocchio and Geppetto time the snores and jump out of his mouth at the perfect second. They must swim for their lives, but Geppetto doesn't swim.

Pinocchio, because of his buoyant wooden body, drags Geppetto to the shore, where Trooper waits. Geppetto is unconscious.

The Blue-Winged Fairy appears on the beach.

"Pinocchio, you saved Geppetto's life."

"I've caused him nothing but grief! Will he live? Will he be all right?" Pinocchio looks with sadness at Geppetto's unmoving form.

"Yes, Pinocchio, Geppetto will be fine. Roll him onto his stomach."

Pinocchio does this, and says, "I love him more than anything on earth."

"That is why I'm here, Pinocchio. You have learned the most important lesson about being human. You've learned that loving and caring for someone else is more important than being selfish and doing only what you want.

"When Geppetto awakes, he will find a real boy sitting with him on this beach. Pinocchio, you have passed the test. You have earned the right to become a real boy."

With a grand wave of the Blue-Winged Fairy's wand, sparks fly and crackle.

Pinocchio ecstatically tests his arms and legs and feels his skin. Music plays while Geppetto wakes and realizes that his dream has come true. Pinocchio is a real boy. They dance and laugh and leap around the beach.

Outside the theatre, Cody watched as Samuel Owens laughed like a maniac. The coyote's ruff bristled. He howled softly.

"The grand finale!" Owens yelled. He chortled and hooted

and giggled as he prepared to light the fuse. His masterful plan would work like clockwork. He'd solved the coyote problem with poisoned meat. If they got past the bait, he was armed with a rifle and a handgun in the car.

He had doused the theatre with gasoline. The fuse split in three, to ensure there was no escape for the people inside. It ran from Owens' car to the stage door, the front door, and the side fire exit.

The theatre was full. Much, much better than the first dress rehearsal. The fireworks had been his rehearsal, too, he rationalized, even though it hadn't worked. Tonight would be the big one. Tonight would be Owens' final revenge.

The best part was that Dancer would be blown up, too, exactly ten minutes after the theatre. A bomb was rigged under a bushel of apples in the field beside the road, programmed to start ticking by remote control. Owens would have the pleasure of watching the demolition of the theatre, and then be able to arrive on time to witness the violent death of the one creature who had caused him more misery than any other on earth. Dancer would die. Owens cackled and hugged himself with glee.

Owens yelled at the theatre, "You mess with Samuel Owens at your own peril!" His voice screeched with excitement and shook with rage. "You hate me! Well, I hate you more! You're all a bunch of garbage! I'm doing the world a favour!" He giggled like a hyena as he waved the fire-starter over his head. It looked like a wild firefly zooming crazily in the dark.

Cody was unsure of what to do. The strong smell of fuel was everywhere. It hurt his nose and made water come from his eyes. The Bad Man was unstable. There was no way to know how he'd react to anything. But he must be stopped from hurting his Abby.

Cody crept closer.

Owens couldn't wait to see this stupid, haunted barn theatre explode before his very eyes, destroying all the people who'd thwarted him.

The Jameses, who'd laughed at him for years because he couldn't have Dancer. The Caseys, who'd fallen in with the Jameses. Even the beautiful Helena didn't want anything to do with him anymore, and she would die tonight with all the rest. The Malones with their brat Abby, who had that horrible coyote and had prevented him from shooting Dancer with his cane-gun, over which he'd gone to considerable trouble to have made. Robert Wick, who'd refused to sell him the farm, then insulted him by thinking a mere field would appease him. The Piersons, who butted their noses into his business. It was Pete who'd called security at the Invitational. Even his illegitimate daughter and her children, Sam and Leslie Morris, deserved to die. How dare she name that bastard after him! The insult!

With a triumphant wave of the fire-starter, Owens knelt to light the fuse. At the same time, he pressed the button on the small remote control that activated the bomb in the bushel of apples in Dancer and Henry's field. His body was racked with laughter as he imagined the horses happily eating apples, unaware that their last minutes on earth were nigh. "Kaboom!" he hollered. "Die Dancer! Die!"

Owens jumped into his car. His plan was to back up the hill to get a safe and complete view of the fire that would kill and maim the entire community, then drive the short distance to Hogscroft for the *pièce de résistance*. He longed to see the panicked survivors screaming and rushing out the doors, clothes and hair on fire. He wished he could see each one's personal agony. He giggled grotesquely.

A giant spark from the fizzing fuse flew free. It landed under Owens' car, where gasoline had splashed from one of the plastic containers. In seconds, the grass caught fire. Fuelled by the spilled fluid, the flames built quickly beneath the car.

Poom! Owens' car exploded into a thousand pieces.

Inside the theatre, the cast was taking their third curtain call. When the car exploded, the noise was deafening, even above the standing ovation and the music of the orchestra.

The huge bang was followed by the plinks and whaps and thuds of metal objects hitting the theatre. People froze, unable to make sense of it.

Ducking the flying debris, Cody raced to the fuse. This time, he knew exactly what to do and wasted no time. Where the single fuse divided into three, Cody grabbed the white cord in his mouth. Dragging and pulling, he managed to free it from the rocks that held it. He ran away from the theatre as fast as he could, while the single fuse burned closer and closer to his face. Up the hill, through the brush to the pond where he jumped right into the water without a pause. He swam until he was sure that every bit of that cord was soaked. He opened his sore jaws and dropped it.

On stage with the cast, Abby heard Ambrose speak directly into her ear. "Owens is dead, Abby. Your coyote took a lighted fuse to the pond over the hill. He saved all our lives. Well, not mine, I'm already dead. But the big horse is in danger. There's a bomb in a basket of apples."

Cody crawled out of the pond and shook himself off. Quickly, he loped to the crest of the hill. Hundreds of humans were streaming out of the theatre doors and moving themselves far from the building. Sirens pierced the air and flashing lights lit up the dark night. Cody had seen it all before when his own barn had burned down.

Risking human detection, the wet and exhausted coyote raced toward the theatre below. There was one more job to do. He must make sure his Abby was safe.

Abby ran out of the theatre and up the hill toward the pond where Ambrose told her Cody had gone. She must first find Cody, then rush to Dancer. "Cody!" she called, unsure of what to expect. *Was he blown up in the blast? Was he injured? Would she be able to find him in the dark?*

She moved as fast as her shaking legs would carry her, her mind running faster than her feet. Blue-Winged Fairy costume floating wildly and wand in hand, she tore through the brambles in the dark.

The small coyote saw her first. He ran to Abby and joyfully jumped up on her, whining his enduring love for her.

"Cody, oh, Cody!" Abby knelt to the ground and cuddled his soaking, trembling body to her chest. "Good boy, Cody."

Ambrose's warning about the horse left them no time to spare. "Dancer, Cody. Go to Dancer!"

Cody searched her face for clarity, then dashed away in the direction of Hogscroft. Abby lost sight of him in the crowd of frightened people rushing to their cars and firefighters hosing down the gasoline with chemicals. She followed as fast as she could.

Stumbling a little on the gravel in the dark, Abby ran down the road. What she'd find, she had no idea. She had even less idea of what she'd do when she got there. Panic gripped her chest as she breathed hard, exhausted, but fighting the need to rest.

A huge explosion split the air. It came from the direction of Hogscroft.

"No!" screamed Abby. "No!"

Abby willed her legs to keep sprinting along. Her heart pounded through her chest wall. Fear tingled in her every nerve. Her imagination created a bloody scene of scattered horse and coyote parts.

"Please, please!" Abby sobbed. "Please, no!" She prayed for a miracle as she pumped her leaden legs toward the farm.

Seconds later, Abby stood against the fence with heaving sides, her Blue-Winged Fairy costume torn and soaked with sweat. The horses ran to her. Dancer nuzzled her neck. Henry breathed into her face. Cody stood on his hind legs beside her, resting his front paws on her hips.

Fragments of brush and earth were everywhere. A bushel basket innocently rested against the fence down the hill. Apples were here and there, some half-eaten. It looked to Abby that the bushel had been kicked over, possibly by a horse impatient to get at all the apples, or maybe as a result of an argument between the two horses over the sweet fruit. However it had happened, the basket had been sent flying, the bomb had rolled into the trees and exploded far enough away to do no harm to the animals.

Abby hugged them all. Relief came flooding through all her senses. Slowly, she slipped to the ground as her body released its tension. She had no strength left.

EPILOGUE

WEDDING BELLS

AUGUST 15 WAS CHOSEN as the night of the double wedding because of the full moon. Laura Pierson strongly believed that it meant not only good luck but also good weather, which would make for a more pleasant event.

Hilary and Joy, the blushing brides, were allowed minimal intervention, and every detail was planned by Christine James, Fiona Malone, and Laura Pierson. Helena Casey had added her touches, too, and it was she who had suggested that the theatre would be the perfect place for the big event. The decorations were lavish and whimsical, the menu mouthwateringly tempting. It was designed to feel like a midsummer night's dream, and hundreds of friends and family and families of friends were invited to fill the seats.

Abby was a bridesmaid. Her silky, fair hair was smoothed back from her face in a low braid entwined with wide ribbons of rose, lavender, and soft ivy green. The colours were chosen to compliment the purples of the theatre decor and the opulent theme.

Her long, simple gown swept the ground, covering her ivy-green flat satin pumps. The sleeves were elbow length, and the neck was slightly scooped and sat open to her collarbones. The blended linen dress was rose, with a ruffle of lavender, a ruffle of rose, and a ruffle of green below the knees, creating a wave-like action when she walked. Abby loved the way she looked.

There were six bridesmaids and six ushers, three of each chosen by both couples. Two bridesmaids wore rose dresses, two wore lavender, and two wore the soft green.

Christine had pinned an elaborate corsage of lavender, pink roses, and baby ivy on the right shoulder of each of the bridesmaids' dresses. Not only did they look gorgeous, observed Abby, they smelled divine.

Being part of the wedding was a welcome diversion for Abby. Since the night of Samuel Owens' demise, she had been plagued with the image of his body hurtling through the air in the blast. She'd woken in the night several times, shocked and sweaty, imagining the horror if Owens' plan had been successful, if she and all the people she loved had been killed. If Dancer's body had been scattered to the four winds.

That night, Mack Jones had been on the spot almost immediately. He'd personally handled an anonymous call minutes before, and was already driving to the theatre, sirens blaring, when he'd heard the enormous explosion. He'd radioed for ambulances, firetrucks, and police backup. Mack had had no idea what he'd find, but the caller had mentioned Samuel Owens, The Stonewick Playhouse, and gasoline. That was more than enough. He knew it was a potential disaster, and he wasted no time.

The caller who warned the police turned out to be Owens' personal valet, Walter Poppins. The man had been cowering in his bedroom when he'd made the brave decision to get involved, consequences be damned. Walter also turned Owens' cane into police headquarters in Orangeville, which confirmed Abby's suspicions.

The weapon had been cleverly designed. It was crafted from silver, with ornate silver sculptings covering the handle. The trigger and target-finders were obscured by these scrollings, allowing it to pose as an elaborate but harmless cane. Walter

Poppins had retrieved it the day of the Invitational, on Owens' instructions, from the metal tubing that supported the call-board at the show grounds. Owens had simply slipped it down a hollow pole when security came running to hold him for questioning.

Helena Casey had grown fond of the meek, industrious Walter during her ill-fated courtship with Samuel Owens, and had hired him the morning after the explosion. He was happier than he'd ever been. Working for the temperamental and difficult Helena was challenging, but much preferable to the dark, dangerous environment of Owens' estate.

The bridesmaids and ushers were asked to assemble, three of each on stage right, three of each on stage left. The men wore grey morning jackets and striped pants. Their shirts were rose coloured, and their cravats were striped with rose, green, and lavender. Their boutonnieres were a single pink rose. Everyone said that the men looked extremely handsome, and the men were only too happy to agree.

Carrying luscious bouquets of roses, lavender, and trailing baby ivy, the women looked like they'd walked out of a painting by Degas. The stage was dark, the house lights dimming. The four-piece musical ensemble awaited instructions.

Abby's entire body tingled with expectation. It felt like opening night all over again. Abby smiled as she recalled the success of the show. Pinocchio had run for ten days with four matinees, and every house had been standing-room-only. Her Blue-Winged Fairy costume had been washed, mended, and pressed to perfection after the beating it took on opening night. The reviews had raved about the production, bringing eager and curious people from miles around.

Miss Iman, the supply teacher, had written a review for the local paper that singled out Abby Malone as a budding actress of singular presence and watchability. Abby never pretended that the comments didn't please her. She'd grown to love the theatre more with each performance. She'd delighted in finding new reactions, new thoughts, new moments in each show. Her portrayal had subtly grown with each performance, not so much that any other actor was thrown, but enough to fill Abby's need to complete her character.

After the positive reaction to Pinocchio, Joy and Robert were rapidly putting together a season of three plays for the coming winter, and, if all went well, a summer season of two more. Abby had already chosen her audition pieces and was working on a song with the help of her mother. Fiona had a beautiful voice and was quite proficient on the piano.

The theatre was dark. The oboe began a husky, haunting introduction to the first piece. It was "Never Tear Us Apart," INXS's proclamation of unwavering commitment. The oboe player put down his instrument and picked up a saxophone. The sax was joined by the violin, then the guitar, with the percussionist brushing on the snares. Six dozen tiny lights suddenly lit the floor of the stage, creating a dazzling runway.

The saxophone wailed its heartbreaking tones as the garden-painted backdrop lifted, revealing the two rows of bridesmaids and ushers as they entered from both sides of the stage.

Hilary had asked her best friend from McGill University to be her maid of honour. Maria Brinks was statuesque, with thick dark hair and an engagingly sweet smile. Sandy's best friend, Nick Mays, was enthusiastically paired with her.

Sandy's beautiful fourteen-year-old sister, Rosalyn, walked on with her proud father, Rory.

Abby held the arm of Luke Best, a very humourous person and Sandy's long-time friend. He told everyone that he was the "best" man.

Norma Dinniwell, Joy's great friend and soulmate since childhood, looked healthy and radiant. Beside her walked

Charlie Watson, Robert Wick's chum since the day they'd met in kindergarten.

Christine James was very pleased to be escorted by Pete Pierson, and Laura Pierson was cheerfully attended by Robert's brother, Daniel Wick.

Helena Casey was proudly escorted by George Farrow, who appeared amazed to have the blond beauty on his arm.

Maria and Nick led the way on stage left, followed by Rosalyn and Rory, and Abby and Luke.

Norma and Charlie headed the lineup on stage right, with Christine and Pete next, then Laura and Daniel. Helena and George followed, completing the party.

They were all sizes, ages, and postures, but the common feature was the happy smile worn by each person. There was a short pause in the music when the wedding party arrived in place on the stage.

The music ensemble dramatically began playing the wedding march.

Breaking with tradition, the two couples had choreographed a unique solution to the lack of fathers to give away the brides. Hilary and Sandy started their walk together from the back of the stage, heading downstage, slightly stage left. At the same time, step for step, Joy and Robert strolled forward to settle beside them, slightly stage right.

The grooms were in black tuxedos with snowy white shirts and bow ties. They stood on the outside with the brides in the centre.

Hilary's gown was creamy white satin, streamlined down to the ground, showing off her elegant, feminine shape. The back was cut low to her waist, and the neckline sat at her collarbones. In her upswept hair perched a glittering rhinestone tiara. A sheer lacy veil trailed from the tiara, billowing back and attaching to her tapered sleeves. The slit that ran up the back of her gown revealed more of the sheer lacy fabric.

Joy had chosen a three-piece ensemble of shades of cream. The floor-length skirt draped becomingly from her waist, flaring at the back to create a train. A silky camisole dipped to reveal a lace bodice beneath, and was completed with an open bolero jacket of the same fabric as the skirt. Joy had chosen not to wear a veil at all, but a small diamond tiara similar to Hilary's glinted in the lights through her freshly coiffed silver curls.

In the plush purple seats below sat the invited guests, whose attentive faces showed their appreciation of this magical service.

The two couples had agreed that the service be performed by the same clergyman who had married Rory and Christine five years earlier. They logically concluded that since that marriage had worked so well, why not duplicate, and triplicate, the success?

The local pastor slowly and with a great sense of occasion walked up the four stairs to the stage. He wore a white clerical collar, and a simple black suit covered his ample stomach. He carried a large, flat, black leather book.

As the couples walked to the lip of the stage, Ambrose Brown whispered in Abby's ear. "I'm going now, Abby. My vigil is complete. Robert will live the rest of his life happily, and I will finally get some rest. It was nice meeting you."

"I loved meeting you, Ambrose," said Abby as quietly as possible. "Will I ever see you again?" She moved her lips only slightly.

"You'll see me again, just not when you expect it. Will you miss me?"

"Of course I'll miss you! I've grown to adore you. And you've taught me so much."

"I'm glad you recognize that, Abby. Most youth are callow. You'll have a great career, if you work hard at it. Now, goodbye, and God bless."

Ambrose was gone. It wasn't like other times. Abby knew he was really gone, up to heaven or wherever spirits go to rest. She was happy that Ambrose was at peace at last, but she felt a great tug of loneliness in the pit of her stomach, and she wiped a tear from her eye.

"Are you all right?" asked Sandy's friend Luke, with a worried expression on his face. "And do you always talk to yourself?"

"Only when I feel like it," she answered sweetly, batting her eyelashes. She heard Ambrose laugh his approval.

The wedding march ended with the wedding party fanning out to create a semicircle behind the brides and grooms. The pastor, with his back to the congregation, stood erect and breathed deeply, taking a long dramatic pause before beginning his task. He importantly opened his mouth to speak.

There was a thunderous knocking at the side door fire exit, stage right. Everyone was startled. The pastor turned to look. The great disturbance continued, shattering the mood and alarming everyone in the theatre. It sounded like a battering ram.

Hilary James suddenly gasped with recognition. She ran in her elegant wedding gown, veil flying out behind her, down the stage stairs to the double doors. She unlatched them and threw them open.

Dancer stood outside, eyes blazing, front right leg ready to knock again.

"Dancer!" Hilary cried aloud.

The mighty chestnut stallion snorted indignantly. He tossed his majestic head and whinnied imperiously. Rearing up on his powerful haunches, the sleek horse pawed the air and whinnied again. When he felt that he'd sufficiently expressed his displeasure at his exclusion, he dropped down and proudly walked through the doors. He gently nudged Hilary with his nose to ask her to walk along with him, an invitation she gracefully accepted.

Together they arrived at the stage. Hilary ascended the stairs and took her place. Dancer stood regally in the aisle, cooly assessing the wedding party and guests.

Hilary smiled broadly. She squeezed the hand of the astonished Sandy and winked at Joy and Robert, whose eyes had widened in amazement. It was clear to everyone that there was no point in trying to remove him from the theatre.

It was as if he had come to give Hilary away. Hilary's eyes blurred with sudden tears as she thought of her father and how much it would've meant to have him with her on this special day.

Dancer was the most serious creature there. He stood with pride and dignity as everyone around him convulsed with surprised laughter. It came and went in waves. The laughter would subdue, then rise up again, one person's chuckle reinfecting the others.

When the uproar finally subsided, the pastor began the service. People accepted the sight of the large animal in the audience, but when the pastor asked the question, "Does anyone know of any reason why these men and these women should not be joined in holy matrimony? Speak now or forever hold your peace," Dancer snorted. The entire crowd lost control once more.

The pastor threw up his hands in dismay. He slammed his leather book shut and stomped down the stairs.

Rory stopped laughing immediately. His son Sandy would be devastated if this marriage didn't happen. He ran to the pastor, who brushed him off and hastened toward the exit. The friends and family of the two couples suddenly realized that it wasn't funny, and every eye in the house was on the pastor.

Pete Pierson covered a lot of ground for a man with an arthritic hip, and reached the pastor just as he was opening the door. The portly pastor rudely pushed him aside and stepped out of the side entrance door.

There Cody stood, legs braced with astonishment, wondering where this man had come from and whether or not he should run for the hills.

The pastor screamed hoarsely. "A wolf! Help me! Help me!"

"Quick!" yelled Pete, suppressing a grin, "Come back inside before he rips out your throat!"

Rory caught on quickly. He barked, "Close the door or we'll all be mauled!"

The pastor had turned completely white. With Pete on one side of him and Rory on the other, he was walked back up onto the stage.

Pete whispered in his ear, "Get on with the vows, and make it fast."

The pastor nodded obediently, rigid with fear.

"D-d-d-do you, Joy Drake Featherstone, take this man, Robert Wick, as your lawful wedded husband, to have and to hold, through sickness and in health, through richer and poorer, until death do you part?"

"I do." Joy looked lovingly into Robert's shining eyes.

"Do you, Robert Wick, take this woman, Joy Drake Featherstone, as your lawful wedded wife, to have and to hold, through sickness and in health, through richer and poorer, until death do you part?"

"I do." Robert's voice cracked with emotion, and his eyes threatened to overflow.

"Do you, Hilary Marie James, take this man, Sandford Casey, as your lawful wedded husband, to have and to hold, through sickness and in health, through richer and poorer, until death do you part?"

"I do." Hilary's lips trembled as she looked at the man she loved. She felt like she would melt away with happiness.

"Do you, Sandford Casey, take this woman, Hilary Marie James, as your lawful wedded wife, to have and to hold, through sickness and in health, through richer and poorer, until death do you part?"

"I do." Sandy passionately reached for Hilary. He took her in his arms and was about to kiss her on the lips.

"Wait for it!" scolded the pastor harshly. Sandy paused, smiling mischievously at his almost-wife.

"I now pronounce you husbands and wives. You may kiss your brides."

Loud peals of joyful wedding music filled the theatre as Sandy and Hilary kissed, sealing their marriage to each other. The rest of the world was far away. They were alone in their own secret bubble, unaware of the clamorous well-wishers surrounding them.

Dancer stood quietly in the aisle.

Joy and Robert were locked in a romantic embrace, making wishes. To live a long and healthy life together. To never lose the magic of their love. For the strength to support and nurture each other through good times and bad. For the ability to focus on the positives and lighten up on the negatives. To have the common sense to adjust to each other, making compromises when called for. To never forget what they loved about each other.

Abby watched in awe. She saw the bond that tied these couples together. Grandmother and granddaughter, generations apart, both in love and both feeling the same intensity of love.

Maybe the heart didn't have to get old at the same rate as the body, Abby mused. She knew people her age who were already jaded and apathetic. And the Piersons remained young in spirit and in mind even though their bodies were wearing out.

She looked over at them. Pete and Laura were dancing to Joy's wedding selection, arms tightly holding each other, smiles lighting up their faces. Louis Armstrong's "What a Wonderful World" reminded everyone how lucky they were to be alive.

Abby smiled, too. She was happy for everyone. Happy for Hilary and Sandy, starting their life together. Happy for Joy and Robert, who'd found each other after many years apart. Happy for the Piersons, Rory and Christine, her parents, and even Ambrose Brown.

Hilary and Joy turned to the wedding party, ready to throw their bouquets.

"One, two, three," they called in unison. Pulling their arms back, Hilary and her grandmother Joy tossed the flowers with a healthy force, petals floating to the stage floor.

To her extreme delight, Rosalyn Casey caught Hilary's bouquet. "I caught it! I caught it! I'm the next to marry!"

Abby caught Joy's. She clutched it to her chest. She suddenly realized that she didn't want to get married in the foreseeable future. She had too much to do, too much to see. And she would make very sure that she married the right man, or she'd never marry at all. She vowed to fulfill her own dreams in life, and consider marriage only when, or if, it was undeniably the thing she wanted.

Across the stage, Abby waved her thanks to Joy, and grinned at her new friend. Joy smiled back.

Abby felt a paw on her leg.

"Cody!" She looked down into her coyote's intense, imploring grey eyes. "It'll be hard to find a human who loves me as much as you do." She knelt and scratched his ears. He was a hero in the community. Every person at the wedding today would have been injured, or worse, if Cody hadn't disengaged the fuse.

"How did you get in?" she wondered aloud to her pet. "The doors are all shut."

"I let him in, Abby," said Sam with a wink. "He looked so sad when the pastor screamed at him."

He stood in the wings, hands in his suit pockets, head slightly tilted.

Abby stood and faced him.

"Dance?" Sam asked.

Abby nodded. He gently held her hand in his larger one, and

placed his strong arm around her waist. She stepped into his embrace and closed her eyes. They danced on the stage of The Stonewick Playhouse to the music of the wedding quartet.

Cody cocked his head and flicked his tail.

Dancer nickered softly.

SHELLEY PETERSON is the bestselling author of five young adult novels, including *Dancer*, *Abby Malone*, *Sundancer*, and *Mystery at Saddle Creek*. She was born in London, Ontario, and was trained in Theatre Arts at the Banff School of Performing Arts, Dalhousie University, and the University of Western Ontario. She works as a professional actress, and has more than 100 stage, film, and television credits to her name. Peterson has had a lifelong love of animals big and small, with a particular interest in horses. She divides her time between Toronto and Fox Ridge, a horse farm in the Caledon hills, which she shares with her husband, three children and the family dog. *Stagestruck* is her third novel.